The Cafe in Sweet Meadow Park

LIZ DAVIES

Copyright © 2024 Liz Davies
Published by Lilac Tree Books

This book is licensed for your personal enjoyment only. This book may not be re-sold or given away to other people. If you would like to share this book with another person, please purchase an additional copy for each recipient. If you're reading this book and did not purchase it, or it was not purchased for your use only, then please purchase your own copy. Thank you for respecting the hard work of this author.

This story is a work of fiction. All names, characters, places and incidents are invented by the author or have been used fictitiously and are not to be construed as real. Any similarity to actual persons or events is purely coincidental.

The author asserts the moral rights under the Copyright, Design and Patents Act 1988 to be identified as the author of this work.

All rights reserved. No part of this publication may be reproduced, stored in a retrieval system or transmitted, in any form or by any means without the prior consent of the author, nor be otherwise circulated in any form of binding or cover other than that which it is published and without a similar condition being imposed on the subsequent purchaser.

CHAPTER 1

Fiona Tedstone peered through the net curtain out of her bedroom window and scowled. Rapping sharply on the glass, she yelled, 'Scat! Go away,' then muttered, 'I hate that cat,' as she watched the ginger tom saunter down her path, waving its tail in the air and giving her a bird's eye view of its bottom. No doubt it had just done its business in her flower beds.

She glared at it until it had slunk through a hole in the fence and disappeared, her scowl deepening. It looked like she would have to have a word with the cat's owner. *Again.*

It never did any good, but at least she tried. Fiona didn't see why the woman couldn't keep it indoors, or make sure it pooed in its own garden and not Fiona's. At the very least, the animal's owner could clean up after it. Fiona had even offered to supply the poo bags, but the scorn that had been rained down on her had taken her aback. Dog owners were expected to pick up their pet's mess. Why weren't cat owners?

And why did the annoying creature choose *her* garden? What was wrong with its own? Or the park? She wasn't advocating that it left its mess on the paths, but there was the meadow and all that woodland it could use as a litter tray.

She would phone the council and make them aware of her displeasure, and maybe they would do something about it. She wasn't going to hold her breath, though. Look at all the times she'd phoned them about the state of Sweet Meadow Park, and they hadn't lifted a finger. It had taken a slip of a girl (Fiona was allowed to call Molly that because she was more than old enough to be her mother) to tidy it up and breathe life back into it. The council ought to be ashamed of itself.

Mind you, Molly had had some help. Bill Greaves, the grumpy old so-and-so, had surprised Fiona by rousing the townsfolk and rounding up some volunteers. But what had beggared belief as far as Fiona was concerned, was that Molly's fella actually worked for the council – and in the very department responsible for the park's maintenance!

She must have left him a hundred messages, but he hadn't got back to her once. Still, he seemed nice enough when you got to know him, despite his inability to return a phone call. And she supposed he had tried to help with the issue of kids hanging around the park in the evenings and causing havoc, by locking the park gates at night. He had landed himself in hot water with the council over that, although no one mentioned it because he'd saved that boy from drowning in the pond. As far as Fiona was concerned, the silly boy had no business being in the park at that time of night. Where were his parents, she wanted to know. Kids these days have no boundaries and no consequences, she grumbled to herself, although that cheeky little bugger – what was his name? Liam, that was it! – had helped Bill round up some of the local residents and persuaded them to pull their fingers out and help sort out the damned park. That had been a good day. Fiona had been in her element making hot dogs for everyone. It had felt nice to be needed.

Which reminded her… she was supposed to be meeting Molly outside the park's boarded-up cafe this morning. Molly had a mad-cap idea to get it running again, and she wanted Fiona's input. But that wasn't all Molly wanted. Fiona distinctly remembered Molly suggesting that Fiona would be just the person to run it.

Huh! Not on your nelly! She'd had enough of running cafes. After all, she had owned the one in the square for more years than she cared to remember.

She'd sold it so she could have a bit of time for herself to enjoy her remaining years, not to work in a damned cafe in the middle of the town's park. A thankless task that would be. Anyway, the building was in a state, so it was going to take more than wishful thinking on Molly's part to get it up and running again.

As Fiona sat on the bottom stair to put her shoes on, a memory of her mum (God rest her soul) buying Fiona an ice cream from the cafe popped into her mind. It had been homemade, with a sprinkle of hundreds and thousands sticking to the looped swirls of raspberry sauce that had been squirted over the scoop of vanilla ice cream.

Her mouth abruptly watered at the remembered flavours from her childhood, and she could have sworn she could hear a fading echo of the chrome and steel coffee machine with its pipes and spitting steam, that had been the pride of the cafe's owners.

Getting awkwardly to her feet, she smiled as she recalled how scared she had been of it – yet fascinated too. It had been a thing of beauty, not like the coffee machines of today. She seemed to remember that it had been imported from Italy, along with the black wrought iron tables and chairs which used to be set out on the small terrace in the summer. She wondered what had happened to them and guessed that they'd probably been nabbed by the scrap man.

Whatever Molly intended to do with the old cafe, Fiona highly doubted it would be a patch on how it had once looked. And neither would the food and definitely not the coffee.

Fiona hurried out of the house and down the road, heading for one of the park's smaller gates and the path that led past the ramshackle bandstand. She scowled at it in disgust. That was yet another part of the park that needed sorting out. Molly and her fella were doing their best, bless them, but even with help from the locals there was a lot still to be done. The flower beds near the main gates looked pretty though, and the pond was no longer a cesspit of discarded tyres and shopping trolleys.

A newt had been responsible for that, would you believe! It had turned out to be a protected species, so the council hadn't been able to go ahead with their plans to drain the pond and fill it in. Fiona had seen the newt with her own eyes but it hadn't been anything to write home about, being an ugly, slimy little thing. It was fair to say that she hadn't been impressed. But if it meant that the pond looked pretty, she was all for it.

The cafe loomed into view and Fiona was surprised to see that boards covering the door and windows had been removed. But even so, it would take more than the discovery of an endangered newt to lick *that* into shape. It would take a builder and a tonne of money.

But if Molly wanted an expert opinion or some advice, Fiona was more than happy to give it; on the cafe side of things obviously, not the building works. Fiona had never so much as put up a shelf, and she didn't intend to start now.

Molly was standing outside looking up at the old building, but when she noticed Fiona she hurried over to give her a hug. Fiona enjoyed the brief contact, and when Molly released her, she experienced a momentary pang. When was the last time anyone's arms had been around her, aside from David's? Fiona struggled to remember.

'You came!' Molly cried.

'I said I would, didn't I?' She was only here because it was something to do on a Saturday morning.

'Yes, but— Never mind. You're here.' Molly turned her eager gaze to the former cafe. 'What do you think?'

'It needs pulling down, that's what I think.'

'Aw, don't be like that! Imagine it with a fresh coat of paint – a nice bright shade of blue, I had in mind – and the terrace area jet-washed and free of weeds. It would look lovely.'

'Hmph.'

'And you could have chairs and tables outside, and there would be an awning—'

'You?'

'Pardon?'

'You said *you*, as in *me*.'

'That's right, you. I thought we'd agreed that you would run the place.'

'You thought wrong. I didn't agree to any such thing.'

'Oh, I… Hmm.'

'I assumed you wanted my advice, not to work myself to the bone to keep this place going. Running a cafe is hard work, you know. I'm too old for all that nonsense.'

'I bet you still bake a mean lemon drizzle. And you used to do those fairy cakes with the pink icing; I used to love those. Your cafe isn't the same since the new owner took over.'

'You've been there?' Fiona's tone was sharp.

'I had to try it out. If you ask me, it's lost some of its charm since you left. And the new owner changed the name.'

Fiona scowled. It used to be called Clover Cafe, because it was located in Clover Square, but Pamela Edwards, the woman who Fiona had sold it to, had changed it to Best Bites. Fiona thought the name change was unnecessary, and who was to say that Pamela's bites were the best anyway? As far as Fiona could tell, Pamela's food was nothing to shout about.

Sometimes, like today, she regretted selling her cafe, and she especially regretted selling it to the likes of

Pamela Edwards. But it had all been done through an estate agent, the same one Molly worked for, so she didn't get to vet the buyer beforehand. Pamela Edwards wouldn't have been her first choice. Mind you, Fiona suspected that she wouldn't have been happy with whoever had bought her cafe, but she'd not had much choice: running it had become too much for her towards the end.

It was sadly ironic though, that she now had more time on her hands than she knew what to do with. Which was one of the reasons she was in Sweet Meadow Park on a Saturday morning, staring at a building that would be better off being flattened. It would be a shame, but it would take too much money to sort it out and, as everyone knew, the council barely had the funds to fill in a pothole or two, let alone restore a rundown cafe in a park it had washed its hands of years ago.

Boredom wasn't the only reason Fiona was here this morning. She had a lot of respect for Molly. 'If you're trying to butter me up, you're barking up the wrong tree,' she said, but there wasn't any bite to her words.

'I wouldn't dream of it.' Molly gave her arm a squeeze. 'But don't dismiss the idea just yet, please?' She held up a set of keys. 'And I bet you'd like to take a look inside.'

Fiona couldn't deny it. She *was* curious. The building wasn't as big as the cafe in Clover Square, but as far as she could remember the park's cafe used to have about eight tables and a marvellous marble counter.

Fiona sucked in a sharp breath when she caught her first glimpse of the inside and let it out slowly as she stepped over the threshold. 'Goodness gracious me!'

***

Bill Greaves tried to ignore the dilapidated children's play area and concentrated on the revitalised flower beds up ahead instead. Patch seemed just as eager to hurry past the broken swings, and he tugged on his lead, his tail wagging. It wasn't the bright new blooms that the dog was happy about though, it was the possibility that he might see his friend Jet. Jet was Molly and Jack's dog. Formerly a stray, the greyhound-Labrador-cross had made himself at home in the cottage in Sweet Meadow Park when Molly had adopted him, and Patch and Jet had become firm friends despite the size difference. Patch, being a Jack Russell terrier, was a fraction of the size of Jet, but Patch ruled the roost and made sure Jet didn't get so boisterous that he bowled him over.

Patch paused by the little picket fence and gazed hopefully into the garden. Both cars were there, but the cottage door was shut and there was no sign of Jet or his owners.

'You're out of luck today, fella,' Bill said. 'Maybe we'll see him when we come for our evening walk.'

Bill walked Patch twice a day, every day. Sometimes more if he got fed up with his own company and needed to get out of the house. Today might be one of those days, but he'd see how he felt when he went home. He had a few bits and pieces to be getting on with, so it wasn't as though he would be sitting on his backside twiddling his thumbs.

For nine o'clock on a Saturday morning, the park was quieter than he'd expected. He usually encountered a couple of joggers and a handful of dog walkers, but so far this morning all he'd seen was a woman pushing a buggy containing a red-faced bawling toddler and a man in a high-viz jacket who appeared to be on his way to work. Idly Bill wondered what the chap's job was. It was a pity the man wasn't in the park to do something about the kiddie's play area, but being realistic it would take more than one fellow in neon yellow to put it to rights. It would take a few quid, too.

No doubt Molly would get around to it; she had a tendency to get things done – with a bit of help from her friends. Bill would like to think that he fitted into that category.

Rounding a bend in the path, the boarded-up cafe caught his attention. And the reason it did was because the boards had been taken down.

Well, well, well... He increased his pace when he noticed the open door, and the unmistakable figures of Molly and Fiona Tedstone heading inside.

So, Fiona had thrown her cap in with Molly's scheme, had she?

He must admit that he was surprised. He didn't think she had it in her anymore. Maybe providing the food when all those people had turned up to help tidy the park had made her realise what she'd been missing since she handed Clover Cafe's reins to someone else.

He hoped Fiona *was* seriously thinking about resurrecting the cafe. It might cheer her up a bit. He didn't know her very well at all, but as far as he could tell she had become a right miserable so-and-so since she'd retired. A bit like him, he supposed.

He hurried up to the cafe's door and poked his head around it. 'Gotcha!' he cried and sniggered when both women almost jumped out of their skins.

'Bloody hell, Bill! You silly old git. You could have given me a heart attack.' Fiona had a hand on her chest, and an irritated look on her face. She often wore the same expression, but on the rare occasion she didn't, she was an attractive woman. In her late sixties, she was short and plump, with wiry grey hair styled into a neat bob framing a pretty face that looked infinitely better when it smiled.

However, Bill's attention was on the room before him, not on Fiona, although he noticed her bend down to pet Patch, which he thoroughly approved of.

'The roof leaks,' he pointed out, seeing a damp patch on the ceiling.

'Is that all you can say?' Molly asked. 'What about the lovely marble counter and the coffee machine-thingy?' She turned to Fiona. 'Is that the original one, do you think?'

Fiona nodded. 'I believe it is.'

'It'll need a new roof,' Bill persisted. Never mind marble counters if the roof wasn't sound. 'And rewiring.'

Fiona glared at him. 'You're all doom and gloom today, aren't you?'

'You think with a bit of mop around and a flick of a duster it'll be good to go,' he shot back.

'I'm not that daft. I can see that work needs to be done.'

'Who is going to do it, that's what I want to know,' Bill demanded. 'And more to the point, *who* is going to pay for it?' He homed in on Molly. 'If you ask me, it'll take too much money, time and effort, and I bet your chap won't be able to persuade the council to pitch in.'

'No one's asking you,' Fiona muttered.

Bill gave her the side-eye. She was just jealous because he was the one who had rounded up all those people to help when Molly had been in danger of packing in her plans to make Sweet Meadow Park beautiful again.

Molly said, 'I don't expect Jack to help in an official capacity. You know as well as I that the council doesn't have any spare cash. I'll put the word out; there are bound to be a couple of people who'll want to help.'

'There'll be many more that won't,' Bill retorted.

There was no point in having false hope. He was, on the whole, a cup-half-full bloke, but he knew what people were like. They would want the park nice but wouldn't be prepared to put their hands in their pockets to make it that way.

'I'm not expecting the whole town to pitch in,' Molly said.

Bill shrugged. 'That's good, because if you did, you'd be disappointed.'

Fiona shook her head and pursed her lips. 'My, my, who got out of the wrong side of the bed this morning?'

'Mark my words, you're setting yourselves up for a fall, the pair of you.'

'At least we'll have tried, and not sat on our arses grizzling about it,' Fiona retorted.

Bill saw Molly's face light up. 'Does that mean you're on board?' Molly asked her.

Fiona sniffed, her nose in the air. 'I'll think about it. I'm not promising anything at this stage.'

Bill couldn't resist. 'You're not promising anything because you know it'll never get off the ground. It needs too much work.'

'So you keep saying.' Fiona was holding her handbag in a white-knuckled grip, and Bill had a feeling she would like to clobber him over the head with it.

Maybe it was time he beat a hasty retreat. He had given them his opinion and it was up to them whether they took any notice of it. They probably wouldn't. Molly was young and headstrong and believed anything was possible. And although Fiona might be elderly, she could be stubborn.

As Bill made his slow deliberate way home, Patch at his heels, he let out a sigh.

It was an envious one, because if Fiona did involve herself in Molly's mad idea, it would give her something to do. Bill would sell his soul to have a project like that.

CHAPTER 2

As Bill let himself in through the back door, the silence that greeted him when he walked into the kitchen informed him that the washing machine had finished its cycle.

He bent down to unclip Patch's lead from his collar, then pointed to an old towel he had laid out on the floor before they'd left for their morning walk. Patch obediently stood on it. With a grunt, Bill lowered himself into a kneeling position, his knees protesting vigorously, and wiped the dog's paws. It hadn't rained in a while so they weren't muddy, but Patch loved trotting through the dew-damp grass and Bill wasn't taking any chances. Satisfied that the terrier's paws were clean and dry, he heaved himself to his feet, removed his lightweight jacket, then freshened Patch's water bowl.

As the dog lapped eagerly, Bill filled the kettle. By the time he had pegged his washing out it would have boiled, and he'd have a cuppa while he did the crossword.

Opening the washing machine door and removing the damp sheets, his thoughts drifted to his impeccably made bed. He vividly remembered being in the army when he was a young man, and squaring away his bunk for the first time after having been taught (for all of thirty seconds) how to do hospital corners. A subsequent inspection by the drill sergeant hadn't gone well. His sheets and blankets had ended up being dumped on the floor, and he'd been told to make his bed again. And again.

That was what he meant by discipline. Kids today wouldn't be able to cope with it, especially the youffs who hung around the park. Although, to be fair to a couple of them, they had stepped up to the mark not so long ago. And so they should, considering they had been the ones responsible for demolishing Molly and Jack's lovely flower beds. The little gits. It had taken the near drowning and subsequent rescue of one of them by Jack, to shame them into helping make the park a nicer place.

Bill lifted the washing basket and opened the back door. 'Coming?' he asked Patch. His dog liked to supervise Bill's activities in the garden. Patch trotted out ahead, squeezing between the door and Bill's legs.

'Careful!' he admonished. 'You almost knocked me over.'

The dog glanced back at him and wagged his tail. Bill took it to mean that Patch realised he had been a bit careless in his haste to reach the garden and that he would be more considerate next time. A bit fanciful, Bill knew, but he and his dog had an understanding that few non-dog-owners could appreciate. Patch could tell a whole story with one look.

'Hello, Mr Greaves,' a little voice sing-songed from next door's garden.

Bill glanced over the low hedge to see seven-year-old Tamsin beaming at him. Patch, on hearing the child's voice, squeezed through the hedge to greet her.

'Spending the day with Nanny and Grancha?' Bill asked.

Tamsin nodded, squealing as Patch tried to lick her face.

Bill winced. Why were children so *loud?* They couldn't do anything quietly, this one especially. He didn't know how Ray and Mary coped with it. Bill didn't think he could. Mind you, he conceded, he wasn't used to children, having never had any of his own. It was his one big regret: that and Tracey. She had been the love of his life and at one point he believed he would spend eternity with her. Tracey, unfortunately, had had other ideas.

More squealing made him wince for a second time as he placed the basket on the path and gave the washing line a quick once over with a clean damp cloth to remove any dirt before he began to peg out. The kid had a bell on every tooth. A memory popped into his head of getting a clip around the ear for being too noisy, and his grandad telling him that children should be seen and not heard. How times had changed, and in a way he was pleased they had. She was a breath of fresh air, was Tamsin, being a happy, sunny little thing.

'Mr Greaves, would you like a sweetie?'

Bill paused and turned around. Tamsin was holding a lurid, suspiciously fuzzy gummy bear out to him.

'No, thank you,' he said quickly, with a shudder. 'You eat it. I'm too old for gummy bears.'

He turned back to his pegging out, feeling a boop on his calf as Patch let him know he was back on his side of the hedge, and when he looked into his neighbour's garden he saw that Tamsin had gone indoors.

A short time later, when Bill heard Tamsin loudly ask Ray, 'Why is the man next door so sad?' and Ray's reply of, 'I don't know, my lovely,' Bill realised that he probably did come across as miserable. He didn't mean to be, but he was too old to change his ways now.

***

Fiona's head was all over the place. By the time she had left Molly locking up the old cafe, she was thoroughly confused. So much so, that she regretted meeting with her in the first place. If she was honest, she had been flattered when Molly had asked for her thoughts about reopening the cafe, and when Molly had suggested that running it might be something for her to consider, Fiona had been tempted. That was before common sense had kicked in and she remembered that she had retired for a reason: running the cafe had become too much.

She had never minded hard work, but those last couple of years before she had sold the business had been exhausting. What with cooking and baking, the government's ever-changing rules and regulations, employing staff, and dealing with the finances and accounts, she had been run ragged. And working six days a week from seven in the morning until five thirty in the evening had taken its toll.

Putting thoughts of the cafe to the back of her mind, Fiona headed towards the park's main entrance with its tall wrought iron gates.

The path took her past Molly's cottage and she paused to admire it.

The little house looked even better now than she remembered it from when she was a girl. The window frames were freshly painted, the glass sparkled in the morning sun, and the garden was a riot of colour from all the shrubs and flowers Molly had planted. A white picket fence marked the boundary between the cottage and the park, and mature trees provided a backdrop, plus shelter and privacy from the road that ran behind it. The cottage had been transformed from a sad, empty, and unloved house, into a pretty, lived in and cheerful home.

And now Molly wanted to perform the same trick on the cafe in the park.

But Bill was right (even though Fiona hated to admit it). It *was* going to take money and hard work. Hard work wouldn't be a problem for Molly, Fiona thought – Molly was no shirker, and neither was Jack – but funding it could be an issue. She hoped Molly wouldn't be daft enough to use her own money to do up a building owned by the council, because she had a feeling Molly wouldn't be able to convince the council to dip into its pocket. Renovating the cafe would be so far down on its list of priorities, you'd need to dig to Australia to find it. And even though Jack worked for the council, Fiona strongly doubted he'd have any say in the matter.

As she was about to walk out of the gates, Fiona glanced to her right and the children's play area caught her eye. She remembered taking her son there when he was little. It had looked different then of course, and she wasn't just referring to the way the play equipment had changed over the years. Gone was the see-saw and the roundabout, and in its place was a wooden climbing frame. The swings were still there though; however one was wrapped around the top bar, one was missing its seat, and the third was missing entirely. And as for the climbing frame, it was so dilapidated that it was positively dangerous. No wonder there was a padlock on the gate leading to it, despite the fact that no mum or dad in their right mind would let their kids play there. It didn't stop teenagers from getting in and hanging around causing mischief, though.

Which brought her back to Molly's plans for the cafe. Was there any point in going to all that time and effort to reopen it, with the play area in its current state and the bandstand in danger of falling down? People still didn't linger long in the park, except for the teenagers (or *youffs*, as Bill called them). And Bill: he seemed to spend an inordinate amount of time in the park walking that little terrier of his.

Mind you, his garden backed onto the park (as did hers, but her house was on the opposite side) so it was very convenient for him. She just wished he was as friendly as his dog. For an older man, he was quite nice looking, she conceded, and he evidently took pride in his appearance, which she approved of. It was just a pity he was so crabby.

Fiona was happy to amble into town today. It wasn't far to the high street, and she had no reason to hurry, having nothing to dash home for. As she strolled down the road, her thoughts turned to Bill again. He might be right about the cafe, but he needn't have been so peevish about it. She had never met such a crotchety, miserable man in her life. If his mum could see him now, she would be appalled. Fiona remembered Connie Greaves as being a lovely woman. She had been so proud of her son when he went into the army, and just as proud, if somewhat surprised, when he'd come out and joined the merchant navy. Especially since he'd never shown the slightest interest in going to sea – apart from wanting a blow-up dingy when they'd had a caravan in Porthcawl when he had been about eleven. Old Mrs Greaves used to recount the story to anyone who'd listen, especially when she had become a bit doddery and had kept repeating herself.

Despite how proud Connie had been of him, she had always hoped he would marry and settle down on dry land with a wife and a house full of kids. But Bill was still wifeless and childless when he had finally run aground in Sweet Meadow after he'd retired from the national fleet and moved into his mum's old house, and from the day he'd moved in he'd been a miserable sod

Fiona swung between believing he was grumpy because he didn't have a wife, and thinking that he didn't have a wife because he was grumpy. Today, she was convinced it was the second option.

'All right, Fiona? How are you?'

Fiona had only just stepped onto the high street before she was greeted by someone she knew. 'Not so bad. Yourself?'

'Mustn't grumble.' The woman lifted her arm, drawing Fiona's attention to the bag of shopping she was holding. 'Can't stop; got frozen stuff in here. Chips and what not, for the grandkids.'

Another few steps and Fiona was hailed again. She didn't mind, it was nice to have a chat, even if it wasn't for long. And she supposed it was to be expected that she would know so many people considering she had lived in Sweet Meadow all her life, and had run a cafe which had once been everyone's favourite place to stop off for a coffee and a natter.

After picking up the bits and bobs she needed, Fiona found herself sauntering towards the little square with the metal statue of a miner holding a pickaxe and a lamp in the middle of it. It was a nod to the heritage of the town, and to its history as a former coal mining community.

She skirted around it, her feet taking her past Clover Cafe – or Best Bites, as it was now known – and she frowned in displeasure as her attention was caught, as it always was, by the garish highlighter-pen colours of the plastic chairs and plastic tablecloths inside. The chairs, as she knew to her cost from the one and only time she had ventured into the cafe after she'd sold it, were as uncomfortable as sitting on a brick. And the tablecloths might be wipe-clean vinyl, but they had felt sticky to the touch.

Fiona had never gone for tablecloths. She would have liked proper linen ones, but she hadn't been able to face the additional laundry. Instead, she had bought good-quality tables and had given them a squirt and a wipe-over between customers. It had served her well for thirty-odd years.

As far as Fiona was concerned, Pamela had changed things for the sake of it. The woman had changed a lot of things for the sake of it, and absolutely none of them for the better in Fiona's opinion.

The cafe was busy though, she had to give Pamela that. Mind you, she thought to herself, Best Bites was the only cafe in town, so it wasn't as though Sweet Meadow's residents had any other option. It was either that, or the pub.

The lack of competition was one of the reasons the cafe had been such a success, and why it still was, despite the lurid tablecloths and fake friendliness of its new owner. Fiona never had to pretend to be friendly. It had come naturally to her. It was only since she'd given up the cafe that she had grown surly. She didn't enjoy being cranky, but recently it had become her default setting.

Her eyes widened and she let out a small gasp as a realisation hit her. Good gracious! She was almost as curmudgeonly as Bill!

'Yes, I know,' Glenys Sidwall said at Fiona's elbow, making her jump, and for a moment Fiona feared she'd said it aloud. But Glenys's eyes were on Best Bites and her mouth was pressed into a thin line of disapproval.

'That Pamela Edwards can't keep staff for love nor money,' Glenys said, and Fiona realised the woman was staring at a 'Help Wanted' sign in the cafe's window. 'I heard that Madeleine left because Pamela wouldn't let her have the afternoon off to go to her eldest's leaving ceremony.' She turned to Fiona. 'They do that in schools these days, have leaving ceremonies when a kiddie goes from primary up to the big school. We never had anything like that, did we? Nobody made a fuss when we were that age. We were just expected to get on with it.'

'I think it's quite nice,' Fiona said. 'It's a huge step for a child to move to secondary school.'

'Oh, I agree. Which is why I think Pamela should have let her go. It's not as though Madeleine expected to be paid for the time she had off. Anyway, there was some shouting, a few choice words and Madeleine walked out, leaving Pamela shorthanded. Serves her right.'

Fiona's blood began to boil. She had employed Madeleine several years ago after Nathan, her youngest child, had started school full time. The woman was a good worker, and a damned good baker, and often used to step in to cover Fiona when she had the occasional day off.

Glenys snorted. 'And don't get me started on her poached eggs on toast.'

Fiona resisted the urge to ask what was wrong with them: she didn't want any part in rubbishing Best Bites. She would keep her opinions to herself and hope that Pamela didn't wreck the cafe's reputation – a reputation which Fiona had worked hard to achieve.

'Ooh, I wish you were still behind that counter,' Glenys said. 'You're sorely missed, you know.'

'It's been eighteen months,' Fiona pointed out. Not that she was counting.

'That long?' Glenys looked surprised. 'I could have sworn it was only about six. Gosh, doesn't time fly!'

Personally, Fiona thought it had dragged. She had gone from not having enough of it, to having more than she knew what to do with.

'I don't know about you,' Glenys carried on, 'But I have no idea how I managed to work as well as fit everything in now that I'm retired. There aren't enough hours in the day.'

Fiona experienced a flash of irritation: there was no need to rub it in. 'Do you miss it?' she blurted.

'Nursing? Sometimes. I miss the job – caring for patients, and the like – but not the hours.' She leant in and chortled, 'I tell you what I *do* miss though – all those fit young doctors.' She gave Fiona a nudge that nearly knocked her sideways.

'Are there any?' Fiona asked, after she had recovered her balance. None of the doctors she had come into contact with had ever made her want to look at them twice. Saying that though, since she'd lost Bradley all those years ago, she hadn't looked at *any* man twice.

'Oh yes, the young ones definitely, although some of the consultants were rather hot.'

Hot? Did Glenys just say *hot?* Good grief. Anyone would think she was in her twenties, not her sixties, and late sixties, at that. Fiona narrowed her eyes. Glenys had always enjoyed a reputation as somewhat of a man-eater. And Fiona really did mean *enjoyed,* because Glenys revelled in it. The woman had never made any secret that she liked male company, or that she wouldn't be averse to marrying husband number three if the opportunity arose. Leopards don't change their spots, Fiona mused, so why had she assumed retirement would see Glenys calm down?

Glenys said, 'Is there no one on the horizon for you, now that you're no longer tied to the cafe?'

Fiona snorted. 'Not blimmin' likely! No one can ever replace my Bradley.'

With a sympathetic head tilt and a pitying smile, both of which set Fiona's teeth on edge, Glenys said, 'It was terrible what happened and of course you'll never replace him, but don't you wish you had a companion to keep you warm at night?'

Crumbs, that was a personal question. 'A hot water bottle will do me fine. And if that doesn't work, I could always get a dog.' Her reply was sharp.

Glenys didn't appear to notice. 'You could borrow Bill's.'

Fiona narrowed her eyes. 'Why would I want to borrow Bill's dog?'

'To see if it suited you to have a pet. There's no point in going into dog ownership with your eyes shut.'

'What do you know about it? You've never had a dog.'

'No, but I went out with a man last year who had three. Yappy little things they were, and don't get me started on all the hair. Ugh.' She shuddered theatrically.

Fiona made a note that there seemed to be a lot of things she shouldn't get Glenys started on.

'Ask Bill if you can borrow his,' Glenys persisted. 'You and him get on all right, don't you?'

'Not particularly.'

'Oh? I thought you did. I could have sworn I saw the two of you in the park earlier.' Glenys gave her a keen look. 'Why were you in the old cafe, anyway? Are you thinking of doing it up?'

'Not me. Molly's got plans for it.' Fiona had enough of the conversation. 'You'll have to excuse me, I've got errands to run.'

'Me, too. I can't stand here gabbing all day. Nice to see you, my lovely.'

And with that Glenys hurried off, leaving Fiona to stare after her with a vague sense of disgruntlement and more than a little envy, as she'd guessed that Glenys genuinely *was* busy – whereas the rest of Fiona's Saturday would be even more disheartening.

CHAPTER 3

Bill sank the garden fork into the soil, being as careful as he could not to spear a spud with the tines, and wiggled it back and forth to loosen both the earth and the potato plant alike. Gently, he angled the fork and put a bit of weight behind it, then grunted in satisfaction as several dirt-speckled ovals appeared. There was nothing better than homegrown potatoes fresh from the ground, boiled and eaten with a slather of salted butter. He would have them for his tea with bacon and runner beans, which he had also picked from the garden this morning.

After placing the new potatoes into a frayed and dusty trug, he was about to go indoors when a flurry of activity on the field below the meadow caught his eye. A group of boys were playing football, and he stopped for a moment to watch. He couldn't see the whole field from his garden, but he could see enough of it to make him smile. He used to play footie and rugby on that very same field when he was a boy. He also used to spend hours in the meadow, searching for ladybirds, caterpillars and grasshoppers, and far too much time fishing in the pond. As far as he could recall he'd never had as much as a nibble, let alone caught anything, even though he and his friends had been desperate to hook the giant catfish that was rumoured to lurk in its depths.

With the benefit of age and hindsight, Bill highly doubted whether there were any fish in the pond at all, and he was almost positive that there hadn't been a catfish. However, there were frogs, newts, insect larvae and pond skaters, and dragonflies swooped over the surface of the water during the day, with bats taking the night shift. Rabbits lived in the swathe of woodland, and sometimes he managed to spot a fox. There were birds and squirrels in abundance, as well as bees and butterflies.

Although Bill lamented the state the park had fallen into over the years he had been at sea, he suspected the wildlife had been more than happy with its gradual disuse – the wilder areas, at least, but perhaps not so much around the bandstand and the children's play area, where teenagers preferred to hang around. Very few people ventured into the meadow though, fewer still went as far as the pond, and only one or two made it into the overgrown woodland, the snagging vicious thorns of the blackberry bushes made sure of that. Reuben, one of the volunteers, the one who had found the species of endangered newt in the pond, had recently cleared a path through the woodland, and Bill had to admit that it was a pleasure to walk through it. Patch certainly loved darting through the undergrowth and chasing squirrels up trees.

Realising he would be late for his Saturday afternoon game of bowls if he didn't get his skates on, Bill called Patch and went inside. The spuds could wait. They would be fine on the draining board until he came back, as would the green beans.

He washed, got changed out of his gardening clothes and into something more suitable to wear to bowls, then after a quick check to make sure he had his wallet, he grabbed his keys, clipped Patch's lead onto his collar, and headed out.

Never in a million years would Bill have thought he would enjoy bowls. But there was something about the genteel game that appealed to him; whether it was the flat expanse of perfectly manicured lawn, or the unmistakable clunk as a bowl hit the jack, or whether it was the slow but determined nature of the game, Bill couldn't say. All he knew was that it filled an afternoon or two during the warm summer months. He had also been surprised to discover that the sport wasn't solely the province of Sweet Meadow's retired contingent. A fair number of younger men, and even some boys, were members of the bowls club, and several were in evidence today.

'All right, Bill?'

'Charlie.' Bill nodded to the man who'd spoken.

'Nice day for it,' Charlie said.

'It is.' The afternoon was warm but not too hot, with barely a breath of breeze; perfect for a game or two, followed by a pint in the clubhouse. He would only have the one, then he'd be off to have his tea.

The members of Sweet Meadow Bowls Club were serious about the game and played in the league, but although Bill was a decent enough player, he played for fun and not competitively, and had a relaxed approach. Some blokes were very competitive though, so it wasn't a surprise to Bill when one of them, a chap by the name of Morris (Bill had never been able to work out whether Morris was his first name or his surname), frowned when he spied Patch.

'That—' Morris jerked his chin at the dog '— shouldn't be here. Dogs aren't allowed on the green.'

'He won't be on the green. He'll be on the terrace.'

The terrace was a grandiose name describing the strip of concrete immediately in front of the clubhouse. On it sat an assortment of white plastic chairs. Patch, Bill knew, would happily lie under the shade of one until it was time to go.

Morris wasn't convinced. 'Dogs aren't allowed,' he persisted.

'I always bring him.'

'You shouldn't, that's all I'm saying. Nasty creatures, are dogs.'

'Not as nasty as some people I could mention,' Bill shot back, irate.

Morris drew himself up to his full height of five foot two, and bristled like an annoyed porcupine. 'I hope you're not referring to anyone here.'

'Just the one.' Bill gave Morris a pointed look and Morris gasped, indignation on his florid face.

'Well, I never!' He bristled some more. 'As stand-in chairman of this club, I order you to remove that dog.'

Bill became aware that everyone was watching and listening, and he couldn't decide whether the shaking heads and the mutters were because the other chaps agreed with Morris, or because they thought the man was out of line.

Deciding not to find out in case he didn't like the answer, Bill thought it best to leave. He had forgotten that the chairman was recovering from a hernia operation and that Morris had elected himself to the position, otherwise he wouldn't have come today.

'My dog is a damned sight nicer than you,' he growled as a parting shot, then with Patch at his heels, he stalked off.

It would remain to be seen whether he would ever return. As far as Bill was concerned, if Patch wasn't welcome, neither was he.

Hoping that the terrier hadn't understood that he was being ejected, Bill consoled him by taking him for a sniff through the park.

As it had yesterday, some unusual activity around the decrepit cafe caught his eye.

Molly and Jack appeared to be clearing it out, evidenced by the several chairs and a couple of tables that had been put outside. They were an old-fashioned bistro style, with black wrought iron backs, seats, and legs in intricate designs. They were in need of a good clean and a cushion, because those seats were as uncomfortable as hell if you sat on them. Bill remembered them from his childhood, when the cafe had been the hub of the park and everyone used to gather there in the summer months for Italian ice creams and cups of coffee. He'd often suspected that the design would be imprinted on your bottom if you sat in them for too long.

Molly was staring up at the building, frowning, and Jack was scratching his head.

Bill said, 'You're going ahead with it, then?'

Jack pulled a face. 'It looks like it.'

'I'm surprised the council wants anything to do with it.'

'They don't.' Jack sighed. 'It's complicated, but what it boils down to is that Molly has been granted a lease to operate a not-for-profit cafe.'

'What's the point in that?' Bill was perplexed.

'Any profits will be used towards the upkeep of the park.'

He was still confused. 'But how can Molly run a cafe for free? And what about her job? Will she give it up?' As soon as he'd asked them, Bill realised that the questions were rather personal. It was none of his business what she did.

'I wish I *could* afford to give it up,' Molly laughed, and Bill was relieved that she hadn't taken offence. 'The cafe will be run by volunteers, although there will probably need to be a salaried manager. Not me,' she added quickly.

Bill didn't say anything, but he had a feeling Fiona might be in line for the job. 'It needs a bit of work,' he observed. 'I take it the council won't be footing the bill for it?'

'No, it won't,' Jack confirmed. 'It'll have to rely on volunteers. Would you like to help?'

'Not with my knees.' He wasn't making an excuse either – he truthfully did have crock knees. If he used them too much, by God did he know about it, although walking on the flat at a nice gentle pace didn't cause them to play up too badly.

'Pity. We need all the help we can get,' Jack replied.

Bill had no doubt of that. It was going to take more than a couple of locals armed with a paintbrush and a mop to knock it into shape, and even more time and effort to run the damned thing. And who would bother frequenting it, that's what he wanted to know. No one would, not with the kiddie's play area in such a mess.

Molly had worked wonders with the park's landscaping, but Bill had the feeling she had bitten off more than she could chew when it came to giving the park its cafe back.

***

Another week had gone by, and Fiona had nothing to show for it. When she tried to recall how she had filled the intervening days between last Saturday and this, she couldn't remember a single thing of note. Washing, ironing, cleaning, cooking and shopping. That was it. She remembered phoning the council about next door's cat, but as usual she hadn't had any joy. The woman in reception had done what she always did, which was to make a note of Fiona's complaint and promise to pass it on. And Fiona, as always, refused to divulge her name, her email address, or any other piece of private information to the nosy madam. Why the woman couldn't just put her through to someone there and then, Fiona didn't know.

It had been the same when she'd phoned all those times to complain about the state of the park. Did it matter *who* was calling? The litter was a fact, and knowing who had reported it wasn't going to make it disappear. There was considerably less of it now though, and that was mostly down to Molly. And Bill, too, Fiona grudgingly admitted. Molly because she had taken it upon herself to litter pick every morning when she took her dog for a walk, and Bill because he had rounded up people from the local community to help knock the park into shape.

It was nice to see that people were finally starting to take pride in the place. And, rather surprisingly, one of those was a youngster who used to run riot in the park with his group of loutish friends. They still did, to a certain extent and were usually to be found hanging around the bandstand, swearing, smoking and drinking, all of it done at the tops of their voices. Why were kids so *loud?*

There was a distinct lack of them on this Saturday morning, and she guessed they were probably still in bed. That was another thing that irritated her when it came to young people, their ability to sleep for hours on end. It was pure envy on her part, of course. The days when she could sleep for longer than three hours at a stretch were long gone.

However, there was *something* going on in the park, and her tummy swooped with unexpected excitement when she saw an electrician's van parked outside the old cafe, and that the door to the cafe itself was wide open. She could see Molly and a woman who was wearing overalls inside.

Fiona couldn't resist, and as she sauntered casually (so she wouldn't look too eager) up to the door, she realised that Molly and the woman were discussing rewiring the place.

The woman said, 'I can do it at cost, as a favour, and as the company's contribution to the park's renovation.'

'That's very kind of you, Harper, but how much is cost?'

'I'll have to get back to you once I've worked out how much I'll need in the way of materials.'

'Can you give me a ballpark figure?' Molly asked.

The electrician moved deeper into the building, Molly following, so Fiona didn't hear what she said. But as she crept nearer, she caught Molly's worried response.

'Raising funds to cover the cost of that, plus repairing the roof and the other things that need doing, isn't going to be easy. I can't ask people to put their hands in their pockets and chip in financially, even if it is for the benefit of the community. Everyone is so strapped for cash these days.'

'Let me know if and when you want me to go ahead. The job will have to be done in the evenings and on weekends, so it might take longer than usual.'

'Understood. I'm just grateful that you're willing to do it at all. Thanks, Harper.'

Fiona edged away from the door and stood to one side as the electrician left.

Molly looked pleased to see her as Fiona explained, 'I saw the electrician's van. This place looks a lot bigger without all the tables and chairs. Where have they gone? I hope you haven't thrown them out.'

'Good grief, no! They're in my dad's garage for the time being. Leaving them in here whilst the renovations take place wasn't an option.'

'Good.' Fiona's gaze roamed around the room, taking in the ancient machine that used to spit out scalding clouds of steam as well as hot water and milk, the chrome soda fountain, and the Carrara marble counter.

When she was a little girl, the cafe had been owned by an Italian family (not the council), which probably explained the Italian counter and the marble-topped tables. Guessing they would be very easy to wipe down and keep clean, she smiled wryly, thinking you could take the woman out of the cafe but you couldn't take the cafe out of the woman. It was in her blood. Actually, she mused, that may very well be true, because she was certain that somewhere in her ancestry there was Italian blood. From the late 1890s, Italian immigrants were responsible for opening a range of cafes and ice cream parlours in the region. If she did have an Italian cafe-owner ancestor, it would explain a lot.

'You'll have to do some fundraising,' Fiona said absently, as she continued to gaze around the space, memories of the way it had once looked superimposing themselves on the dingy room. It would be marvellous to see it brought back to life.

'Hmm, you're right. Maybe a Fundscape campaign?'

'I have no idea what that is. I was thinking more along the lines of a jumble sale. I'm happy to make cupcakes to sell on the day, and a celebration cake to raffle off.'

'A jumble sale is a marvellous idea, and it's so kind of you to offer to make cakes. I'll pay you for the ingredients, of course.'

'No, you won't!' Fiona was adamant. 'Consider it my contribution to the cause.'

Molly gave her a look and raised her eyebrows, which Fiona interpreted to mean that Molly was anticipating more of a contribution from her once the cafe was open for business. Much more. Like, running it, for instance…

Despite having told Molly that she was off her rocker to even ask, the more Fiona thought about it, the more she was coming around to the idea. Not *running it* obviously, but she wouldn't be averse to doing a spot of baking, and maybe even helping out in the cafe itself now and again.

The rumble of an engine disturbed the peace, and Fiona was surprised to see another van trundle into view and come to a halt outside the cafe. Gosh, the park had more traffic than the local supermarket this morning.

Fiona decided to hang around for a while longer and, as she watched, a rather nice-looking man climbed out of the van. The vehicle had the words *Gavin Mitchell, General Builder* written on the side, and she assumed that the man must be Gavin himself. He looked quite young to have his own business, though. But then, everyone under forty looked young to her these days.

Molly hurried to greet him. 'Thanks so much for coming. You've just missed the electrician.' She pulled a face. 'It needs a complete rewire.'

'I'm not surprised. How long has it been empty?' Gavin was staring up at the roof.

'At least forty years. Possibly longer.'

'Hmm.'

Molly bit her lip and said, 'It's never good news when a builder says *hmm*.'

He turned to look at her. 'To be honest, the roof doesn't look too bad from here. I can't tell for sure until I get up there and take a proper look, but I'm fairly confident it won't need to be replaced. I might have a problem sourcing Welsh slates for the repairs, though. They're not easy to get hold of and they're expensive.'

Molly gave a small smile. 'Oh dear, but at least it doesn't need a whole new roof, so that's good news.'

'I can use other slates, but you might have to make do with whatever the builder's merchant has in his yard.' he told her, and her face brightened. However, it quickly fell again when the builder told her the inside of the cafe needed to be replastered.

'Darn it, I was hoping it wouldn't.'

Gavin tapped his knuckles along the nearest wall. It sounded hollow in places. 'Hear that? The plaster has blown. It's come away from the brick underneath.'

Molly sighed. 'If it has to be replastered, then so be it.' She looked so dejected that Fiona felt for her.

Why the girl had set her heart on reopening the cafe was a mystery, but Fiona had to admit that it would be lovely to see it selling teas and coffees once again.

However, the cost of getting it up to standard would be considerably more than the amount a couple of jumble sales could generate. Raising that kind of money wouldn't be easy.

Molly needed help.

And Fiona knew just the person who could give her that help – Bill Greaves.

CHAPTER 4

Fiona had never seen the inside of Bill's house, and she was surprised at how tidy it was. But not half as surprised as Bill was when he opened his door to see her standing there.

He had invited her in with obvious reluctance when she said, 'I need to talk to you about something,' and Fiona concluded it was only because he preferred to hold the conversation in his living room rather than on his doorstep and not because he was being friendly. Nosey neighbours were a given in a small town like Sweet Meadow.

'Tea?' he offered.

'That would be lovely.' She waited in the living room as he went into the kitchen and she heard him fill the kettle. Patch, who had barked vociferously when she'd rung the bell, now greeted her with tail-wagging enthusiasm, and she bent down to stroke his ears.

'Don't stand on ceremony,' Bill said, poking his head into the room. 'Sit down. Milk? Sugar?'

'Just milk please, and not too strong.' Fiona perched on one side of the sofa and glanced around curiously. My, but it was old-fashioned. The room looked like a relic from the middle of the last century, and she suspected that little had changed since Bill's mother had been alive. He kept it neat and tidy, though. There wasn't a speck of dust, and he plainly vacuumed often, judging by the absence of dog hairs.

Bill returned to the living room with a cup and saucer in one hand and a plate of biscuits in the other. He gave the tea to Fiona and balanced the plate on the arm of the sofa.

'Help yourself,' he said, going back into the kitchen to fetch his own cup. 'Right, then,' he began, sitting down in the armchair which was angled towards the telly. 'What do you want to talk about?'

'Molly and the cafe. I've just come from there, and she's had an electrician and a builder in to take a look at it.'

'And?'

'It's going to cost.'

'I could have told her that. In fact, I think I did.'

'*She* can't be expected to pay for it, and I know the council won't.'

'Are you suggesting she has a whip round?'

Fiona tutted. 'Don't be daft. She needs to do some fundraising, but I don't think she knows where to start. That's why I'm here.'

'You want *me* to fundraise for the cafe?'

Fiona didn't appreciate the way he was looking at her, like she'd lost the plot. 'Well, yes.'

'I think I've done my bit when it comes to the park. If you recall, I rounded up half the town to help clean it up.'

'It was hardly half,' she scoffed. 'Twenty people wasn't even a street's worth. OK, maybe there had been thirty, but that was it.'

'It was twenty more than before. I don't recall *you* offering to get your hands dirty when Molly and Jack called that meeting at the bandstand. You were only there because you thought there was going to be live music.'

Fiona glared at him. 'Anyone can make a mistake. And *you* were only there to see how many turned up.'

'I made up for it, didn't I?'

'So did I! Enjoyed the hot dog, did you? You ate two, if I remember rightly.'

Stalemate ensued as they glowered at each other. Then Fiona decided to be the bigger person (because

Bill certainly wasn't) and she subsided. 'Let's not argue over who did what. Can't we put our heads together and come up with a way to raise the money needed to re-open the cafe?'

Bill slumped back in his chair. 'I reckon it's a waste of time and money. No one will use it. That's why it closed in the first place.'

'How do you know? You weren't here.'

'My mother kept me in the loop,' Bill said. 'She used to love telling me all about the goings on in Sweet Meadow.'

Fiona said slyly, 'I bet your mum would have liked to see it brought back to life.'

'Keep her out of it.'

'*You* were the one who brought her into it, not me.'

They glowered at each other again, then Fiona got to her feet. 'Sorry to have disturbed you. I can see myself out.'

Bill rose, hard on her heels as she stalked to the door; probably to make sure she left.

She didn't bother saying goodbye, because she was too upset. And the reason she was upset was because she feared he was right. When she was a girl, the park had been a busy place – people out for a Sunday stroll, kids playing ball on the field, nippers on the swings and hurtling down the slide. There was always someone there she knew and who she could play with, and when she was older she used to sit in the long grass in the meadow and make daisy chains with her friends.

She had met Bradley in the park. He had been a couple of years above her in school, so she knew *of* him, but he hadn't noticed her until she was about sixteen and had started wearing cheesecloth shirts and flared jeans. She also remembered the Salvation Army brass band playing their trumpets and trombones on the bandstand, and someone shaking a tambourine. You never saw tambourines these days, and she wondered when they had gone out of fashion. Probably around the same time she stopped wearing flares.

Were her fond memories of the park clouding her judgement, and was her longing to have something purposeful to do screening her from the reality that the cafe was unlikely to open again anytime soon, no matter how much Molly wanted it to?

And even if it did reopen, Fiona was too old to even consider managing it. She'd left all that behind when she'd sold the cafe, and the reason she'd done that was because it had become too much for her. She must have been daft to even entertain the idea. Did she honestly want the commitment? Or the hassle?

But there had been that frisson of excitement this morning when she'd seen the electrician's van…

Frisson or not, she had put her cafe days behind her.

Feeling rather down, she hurried through the gate and made her way to Molly and Jack's cottage. She may as well make it clear to them that even if, by a miracle, Molly managed to open the place, Fiona wasn't the one who would be running it.

Molly beamed when she saw her, and Fiona felt awful that she was about to wipe the smile off the girl's face.

'I've been thinking about the cafe,' she began solemnly. 'It's lovely of you to think of me and even nicer of you to ask, but I'm afraid I'm going to have to refuse your kind offer. Managing the cafe is beyond me now. I'm too old and too past it.'

'You definitely aren't!' Molly cried, but Fiona shook her head.

'To be honest, I'm not sure I want to be involved at all, but I wish you all the best with it.' A sudden prickling at the back of her eyes made her blink and she swallowed hard. Tears? How silly. She really must be getting old.

'Please don't dismiss it out of hand,' Molly urged. 'See how you feel when it's open.'

But that was the problem, wasn't it? Bill was right. The odds of it being open anytime soon were non-existent. Not only that, it had been silly of her to get her hopes up just because she was bored. She needed to find something else to do to occupy herself, rather than dream of having a cafe again. But the fact was, all she knew was how to feed people. She simply wasn't good for anything else.

***

A second ring of his doorbell took Bill by surprise. It appeared to be a day for callers. He could go weeks, months even, without anyone knocking on his door (apart from during the local elections, when every person and their dog wanted to speak to him), and now he had two callers in one day.

Seeing Fiona earlier had been a surprise. Seeing Molly was even more of one, and he wondered what she wanted.

After inviting her in, he made a second cup of tea for a visitor in as many hours, then sat in his favourite chair and gazed at her expectantly.

Molly took a sip of her drink, then dived straight in. 'I'm worried about Fiona.'

Bill kept his expression blank, but he felt a flicker of concern.

The young woman continued, 'I believe you're aware that I asked her to manage the cafe once it's up and running, and I honestly thought she was going to do it; she seemed to be all for it this morning. But she came to see me just now and told me she feels that she's too old. Fiona's not old!' Molly's expression was worried. 'Didn't you tell me not so long ago that she's bored? And as she used to own a cafe, I'd say that this would be ideal for her. I thought she was coming out of her shell, but she's gone back into it.'

'You shouldn't have got her hopes up.'

'What do you mean?' Molly's brow creased into another frown.

Bill snorted. 'It won't work. It's not cost-effective; not enough people spend time in the park, and I don't blame them.'

'But they *will*, 'Molly insisted. 'It's looking tonnes better already, and people are going there for a stroll or a game of ball with the kids, whereas they only used it as a cut-through in the past. And when the children's play area is repaired, it will be even nicer.'

'Sweet Meadow has already got a cafe,' Bill pointed out, unwilling to concede defeat in the face of Molly's logic, enthusiasm, and vision.

'It won't be in competition with Best Bites,' Molly argued. 'If people are in town, they'll call into Best Bites for a coffee. The customers for this cafe – *our* cafe – will be those people who are already in the park.'

She had a point.

Suddenly Bill felt guilty for poo-pooing the idea and refusing to help. Was it his fault that Fiona had changed her mind about managing the cafe? He didn't know her particularly well, but even he could see that she'd gone downhill since she'd sold her business, yet as soon as the spark had returned, he had thrown a bucket of cold water on it.

Maybe he had been too harsh. And did his opinion matter anyway? He knew nothing about how a cafe operated, but one thing he did know was that Molly was a very focused and determined young lady. If anyone could pull this off, it was her. Look at what she had achieved already: the cottage was a credit to her (despite Bill thinking that she had been a mug for buying it), she had managed to get the council on board with regular litter-picks and new bins, the pond was now a thing of beauty, and everything about the park felt more hopeful.

Molly was passionate, committed, and enthusiastic. If he had been lucky enough to have had a daughter, he hoped she would have been like her.

When she put her mind to something Molly moved heaven and earth to achieve it, and Bill felt a twinge of nostalgia as he remembered being like that once.

He guessed Fiona might have been like it, too.

Were the advancing years responsible for the passion fading and the enthusiasm dimming? Or was it that you *allowed* yourself to become jaded and more embittered, he wondered.

Bill didn't have the answer, but he knew that since he'd retired the lights in his proverbial house were dimming one by one. If it wasn't for Patch, he doubted whether he would be bothered to get out of bed in the morning, and he suspected that Fiona might be feeling the same way.

There was something else he suspected, and that was Fiona might come to regret turning down the opportunity. The thought of *her* lights dimming made his chest ache.

'Would you like me to have a word with her?' he asked, feeling awful.

'Would you? I'd very much appreciate it. You saw what she was like during the clean-up, when she cooked all those hot dogs for everyone. She was in her element. There was a glimpse of the old Fiona. But when I spoke to her earlier…' Molly shook her head, her worry apparent.

'Leave it with me,' Bill said, feeling even worse.

He had made this mess, it was up to him to sort it out, and if that meant telling Fiona that she shouldn't listen to an old codger like him and that he was envious that the cafe would give her a new lease of life, then that's what he would do.

The thing was, it might be true. Bill sensed that his own feet were on the same slippery slope as Fiona's. Not all that long ago he had captained a commercial cargo ship, with all the responsibilities and challenges that went with being a master in the Merchant Navy. Now look at him… He *was* envious.

But Fiona had come to him for help, so help was what he would give her. And if he became less of a misery-guts in the process, then he would call that a win.

***

Fiona's hand hovered over the phone. She desperately wanted to have a chat with David but she knew that she would end up moaning, which would only make her son worry. The last thing she wanted was to alarm him or to be a burden, and it peeved her to think that he might view her as such. She had raised him singlehanded after Bradley died, and in her mind's eye *she* was the rock, the one he could always depend on.

But Fiona had sensed a seismic shift since she'd sold the business. It was as though *he* was *her* parent, not the other way around. It was subtle, but evident in the way he spoke to her and the way he took over sometimes. She knew he only wanted to help, but she was perfectly capable of changing a plug! And how did he think she managed when he wasn't around?

Fiona let her arm drop to her side. She would phone him later in the week; no doubt she would have perked up a bit by then. She hoped. Because at the moment she felt rather blue. It was normal to feel down now and again – everyone did – but lately the blue had darkened to black.

Once upon a time, when her little family was a threesome, her world had been a sunny yellow. Then Bradley had been killed in an accident at work, and Fiona's world had been plunged into darkness. The only thing that had kept her going was David. Her son had needed her more than ever.

Gradually, light had returned, and although she still had her down days, she had found a degree of contentment, and keeping busy had also helped. But now that she was no longer busy, she felt as though she had lost her purpose, that she was fading away, becoming less of herself and more of an invisible old person shuffling inexorably towards the grave.

Gosh, how morbid! She needed to buck her ideas up, and she was just wishing she could summon some enthusiasm for something *(anything)* when she had a visitor.

When she saw Bill standing on her doorstep, she was able to appreciate how he must have felt this morning, when she had turned up on his. She was so shocked that all she could do was step aside for him to enter.

There was an odd expression on his face, and it wasn't until he spoke that she realised what it was. He was sheepish.

'I'm sorry about earlier,' he said. 'You caught me in a bad mood.'

'Hmph. You're always in a bad mood, Bill Greaves. Anyway, you're right. Molly *is* flogging a dead horse.'

'Not necessarily.'

Fiona blinked. 'You've changed your tune.'

'I've had a chance to think, and I believe I was wrong.'

'I'd better sit down.'

Fiona led him into the kitchen, Patch on his heels, and flicked the switch on the kettle before she took a seat at the little table that was only big enough for two.

Bill sat on the opposite chair and the dog immediately settled at his feet. 'Let me explain, and maybe you'll forgive me for being so negative. I still think it's going to take money and hard graft to bring the cafe up to snuff. But I once thought the same thing about Molly's cottage, which is twice as big – and look what she's done with it.'

Fiona nodded. She couldn't argue with that.

He continued, 'And what a difference she has made in the park. I know she had help, but if it wasn't for her, everyone would have continued to complain about the place but nothing would have got done.'

Was Bill referring to *her?* Fiona pursed her lips, wondering whether he was having a dig. She had complained weekly to the council for over a year, to no avail. Had Bill expected *her* to pick up the litter herself? Did he think that *she* should have told the loutish teenagers to have more respect? Then she realised that Molly had done exactly that. But Molly was half Fiona's age, and Fiona was too old and too tired to pick up litter and confront youths.

She hadn't noticed Bill do anything, either. All he had done was grizzle. It was Molly who had been the catalyst for change. Without her, the park would still be an eyesore.

When she tuned back into the conversation Bill was saying, 'At least, give it a go. If it doesn't work out, all you'll have lost is a bit of time.'

'I haven't got much time left. I'm an old woman, in case you hadn't noticed.'

'You're not that old! Anyway, what else do you do with your time? Nothing, as far as I can tell.'

'What about you?' she retorted. 'What do *you* do with *yours*?' How dare he tell her what to do. If she wanted to sit on her backside all day, staring at the four walls, that was up to her. Anyway, he was no better. All he did was walk his dog and play the odd game of lawn bowls. Hardly riveting, was it?

However, what he said next surprised her. 'I'm going to help knock that cafe into shape. I want to see it open again.'

Fiona stared at him, confusion flowing through her. Just a couple of hours ago, he had dismissed the cafe out of hand – he had been quite scornful, in fact – yet here he was, declaring his desire to see it open and vowing to help.

Was it something she'd said? Had *she* changed his mind?

A spark ignited in her chest. Could it be hope, or was it excitement? If *Bill* was convinced that the cafe's reopening was a real possibility, then maybe she should be, too. And if anyone could make it happen, it was Molly.

Fiona felt the dark cloud lift as a ray of sunlight broke through. 'I'll make us some tea,' she said, realising that the kettle had boiled a while ago. 'And I might be able to dig out a couple of slices of orange and almond cake, because we could be here for a while. We've got a fundraiser to organise!'

CHAPTER 5

'I suggested a jumble sale,' Fiona began, as Bill tucked into a generous slice of cake.

His eyes almost rolled back in his head in delight – damn, this woman knew how to bake.

'We could hold a raffle as well,' she continued.

'What would we raffle?' he asked, his mind still on the cake as he chewed.

'I'll bake a cake, for a start, and I thought we could ask local businesses for donations.'

'What sort of donations?'

'A hairdresser might offer a cut and blow dry, for instance. Or a beautician could offer a facial.'

'We'll need several things to make it worthwhile,' Bill said, forking another mouthful of delicious cake into his mouth.

'Let's make a list of who we can ask,' she suggested, getting up to fetch a notepad and a pen.

Patch, who was sprawled at Bill's feet, raised his head and then dropped it down again with a sigh. The dog was bored.

'One of the pubs might offer a meal,' Bill mused, as he reached down to scratch the terrier's ears. 'And we could ask the supermarket if they'd like to donate a bottle of wine or a box of chocolates.'

'A bouquet from the florist, and a fruit basket from the grocers?' Fiona suggested.

'A leg of lamb from the butcher?' Bill added.

There was a pause as Fiona stared at him.

Bill stared back.

Then they burst out laughing.

'Maybe not a leg of lamb,' Bill conceded with a chuckle, imagining a hunk of meat sitting on a table next to a tin of shortbread. 'Perhaps a voucher instead.'

'That's a better idea.' Fiona's eyes widened. 'I think we might be getting ahead of ourselves. Where would we hold it? Not in the park – if it rained it would be a washout.'

'St Hilda's church has got a nice big hall,' Bill said. 'I believe they hold mother and toddler sessions in it.' He squinted as he thought. 'The Bowls Club has a decent function room, too.' But after this morning's debacle, he wouldn't ask Morris to throw a bucket of water over him if he was on fire. 'The church hall is the better option. Do you want to speak to the vicar, or shall I?'

'I'll do it. He's partial to my scones. I'll take him half a dozen.'

Bill experienced a twinge of envy. No one had ever baked *him* scones. He took a gulp of tea and told himself off for being silly. The scones were hardly a declaration of friendship: they were more akin to a bribe.

After agreeing that they should sort out the venue first, Fiona pushed the notepad and pen across the table and got to her feet.

For a second, Bill thought that their impromptu meeting was over and disappointment nipped at him. He had been enjoying himself.

'I may as well make them now,' she said. 'You can carry on taking notes.'

Ah. Good. So that's what she was doing. She wasn't kicking him out after all. And he might get to taste one of the scones, if he was lucky.

He watched her retrieve a mixing bowl from a cupboard, along with flour and baking powder, before she took butter and milk out of the fridge. Patch was watching her too, and Bill guessed that the terrier was hopeful of being offered a morsel of whatever Fiona was making.

'I'll pop to the vicarage in the morning,' she said. 'In the meantime, do we have any other ideas?'

The thought of scones with jam and clotted cream reminded him of something, and a fleeting memory of women in nice dresses and men in suits dancing on a rainy afternoon in Baltimore fluttered at the edge of his consciousness. Why was he thinking about—?

'A tea dance!' he cried, making Fiona jump.

The bag of self raising flour she had been holding plonked onto the counter, releasing a cloud of fine white powder.

Patch whined.

'We could hold a tea dance,' Bill continued in a more normal tone. 'Not only would it raise money for the repairs, you could also showcase your cakes and so on. It would be a kind of free advertising for the cafe.'

'That's brilliant,' she said, wiping away the fine layer of flour that coated the workshop, before measuring the correct amount into the bowl. 'Do you think we could hold that in the church hall as well?'

'I don't see why not, if the vicar is willing.' Bill chuckled. 'You might want to take him some jam and cream when you give him the scones, to sweeten the deal.'

'I'll pick up some cream in the morning on the way.' She smiled happily. 'I love that idea. I don't think I've ever been to a tea dance. What made you think of it?'

'Scones.'

She gave him a quizzical look, but he didn't explain. The tea dance itself wasn't the issue. The woman who he had attended the dance with, *was*.

To change the subject, he said, 'Do you think we should have something for the kids? I don't think a jumble sale will enthuse them much, and I can't see anyone under forty attending a tea dance.'

'What do you suggest?' She poured some milk into a glass jug and popped it into the microwave.

While she waited for it to ping, Bill wracked his brains for an idea.

Fiona asked, 'Has the newt that Reuben found got a name?'

'It's a great crested newt, I believe.'

'I know, but that doesn't trip off the tongue, does it? It needs a name.'

'Fred?' Bill suggested. 'Or Warty?'

Fiona took the milk out of the microwave, checked its temperature, then added a few drops of something out of a small brown bottle, and squeezed in the juice of half a lemon. 'Do you think we could run a competition to name it?'

'Name That Newt?' Bill chortled. 'I don't see why not. We could charge 50p a go, and Reuben could choose the winner. Shall I ask him what he thinks?'

'It can't hurt.'

'I'll do it now.' Bill took his battered mobile out of his pocket and peered at the screen. Even with his reading glasses on, he struggled to see it properly sometimes. Finding Reuben's number, he dialled it, and after explaining, he ended the call with a smile. 'He thinks it's a great idea. He's looking at it from the conservation side of things, of course. Says it'll highlight the plight of the newt, and so on. He also suggested that the winning name could be put on a plaque by the pond, and so the pond would be known as Warty Pond, for instance.'

'I'm sure the kids will come up with a better name than Warty,' Fiona laughed. She had just put the scones in the oven. 'Another cup of tea?'

'Go on then, if you insist.' He tapped the notepad with the pen. 'Is that enough to be going on with, do you think?'

She said, 'I've got another idea, one that I hope will encourage people to continue to take pride in the park – and that's to have a plant-a-thon.'

'A what?'

'A plant-a-thon.'

'Is that where people plant as many plants as possible in the shortest amount of time?'

'Hmm, it does sound like that's what it should be, but I was thinking more in terms of teams being responsible for planting up one of the flower beds that

Molly and Jack haven't managed to get around to yet. There are quite a few of them. This way, the beds would look pretty and the event would raise a bit of money.'

'How?' Bill asked. 'Plants aren't cheap.'

'I was hoping to tap up the garden centre for a few freebies. Then there's the allotment behind Lavender Lane. I'm sure they'll have a plant or two to spare, and I know Molly's mum has got loads of seedlings that will be ready to go in the ground soon.'

Bill wasn't sure it would work as a fund-raising activity. 'It sounds like we should be paying people to plant them, not the other way around,' he said.

Fiona deflated. 'You're right; we can't expect people to pay to stick a plant in the ground.'

'It's still a good idea, though. The area around the cafe could do with prettying up. Perhaps we could ask people to help with the planting and call it 'Adopt a Bed'?'

Fiona giggled. 'That sounds a bit risqué. How about Strictly Come Planting?'

Bill slapped his thigh and let out a bark of laughter. 'That's great! What a name! I don't think anyone will be able to resist Strictly Come Planting,' he chortled.

He was still chuckling as he and Patch strolled through the park on their way home, Bill having been sent on his way with two scones in a bag, and a piece of paper with a to-do list on it, in Fiona's neat handwriting. The next few weeks promised to be interesting.

***

As Fiona was walking back from the church the following morning, she wondered whether she should have invited Bill for Sunday lunch today. She had put a small chicken in the oven to roast before she'd gone to speak to the vicar this morning, but there would have been plenty for Bill, and Patch. Was it too late to phone and ask?

She checked her watch: it was just gone eleven, so she decided to ring him.

'Bill? It's Fiona,' she began.

'Have you spoken to the vicar? Is there a problem?'

'No, no problem. I just wondered whether you would like to come to lunch? Or have you got plans? Don't worry if you have, it was only a suggestion.'

Bill was silent for so long that she wondered whether they'd been disconnected. She was walking home from the church, so it was quite likely that she'd lost signal.

'I'd love to,' he said, just as she was about to hang up and try again. 'Can I bring some new potatoes from the garden? I've got some runner beans as well.'

'Lovely! Shall we say twelve o'clock?'

'Can Patch come with me? I hate leaving him at home.'

'I fully expected him to.' Never once had Fiona seen Bill without his dog. With Bill, it was very much a case of love me, love my dog, and she had a feeling that Bill would give short shrift to anyone who didn't accept the little terrier.

Luckily, she liked dogs, and Patch was gentle and well-behaved. Unlike next door's cat, who had hissed and spat at her this morning when she'd clapped her hands at it because she'd discovered it doing its business in her dahlias. Maybe Patch's scent in the garden would prove to be a deterrent? She could live in hope.

As soon as she got home, Fiona checked on the chicken then set about making an apple tart for pudding. She had just put the pastry in the fridge for thirty minutes when her doorbell rang.

Smiling, Fiona wiped her hands on a towel and hurried into the hall. 'Come in, come in,' she urged. It felt good to have someone to cook a meal for: David didn't visit nearly often enough.

'This is for you,' Bill said, handing her a bag.

Expecting to see new potatoes and runner beans, she was surprised to discover that there was also a bottle of wine. 'I thought we could have a glass with lunch, or you could have one later, if you don't want to open it now,' he said.

She passed him the bottle. 'You can do the honours. The glasses are in there.' She put the potatoes and beans on the draining board.

Feeling quite decadent, although she was a little concerned that Bill might make a habit of drinking during the day, which she didn't approve of, Fiona placed a pan of salted water on the hob, then turned her attention to cleaning the potatoes.

He said, 'I was going to have them for my tea last night, with the beans and a couple of rashers of bacon, but I didn't think I could manage a big meal plus a scone, so I just had a bacon sarnie. The scone was delicious, by the way.'

Fiona inclined her head. She expected nothing less, considering she had been making scones since she was a teenager. If she hadn't got it right by now, there was no hope for her.

'Did you grow these yourself?' she asked, scraping the delicate skin off one of the potatoes.

'I did. Most of my garden is given over to vegetables, with only a little bit of lawn for Patch. I'll bring you some tomatoes next time.'

Fiona lowered her head, concentrating on her task. Did he mean next time he came to lunch? If so, that was rather presumptuous of him.

'Reuben dropped these off earlier,' Bill was saying, and Fiona only realised he had brought a kind of satchel with him when he tapped the bag and put it on the countertop. He eased a sheaf of paper out of it.

Fiona popped the newly cleaned potato into the pan and dried her hands. Picking the top piece of paper off the pile, she read it whilst Bill opened the wine, and a grin spread across her face.

It was a leaflet with the words *Name the Newt* written across the top, followed by a photo of a great crested newt (maybe Bill's suggestion of Warty wasn't too far off the mark), and a bit of info about the newt in the park and how its discovery had saved the pond from being filled in. At the bottom of the leaflet were spaces for the entrant's details and their suggestion for a name.

'This is brilliant!' she exclaimed.

Bill wasn't finished. 'That's not all. When we know the date and venue of the tea dance, Reuben said he will do the posters for that too. And for the jumble sale.'

'That's so kind of him.' Fiona beamed. 'I've got a provisional date for both, but I wanted to run it past you, Molly and Jack before I confirmed it. The vicar was most accommodating.' She grinned again as an image of the pleasure on the face of Reverend Jenkins popped into her head when she had presented him with the scones. He used to love her scones, and when she owned the cafe he often used to call in for one for his breakfast.

Whilst she carved the chicken and dished up, Bill spoke to Molly on the phone and brought her up to speed with their fund-raising progress so far. Fiona was relieved that Molly was happy with the dates, so Bill sent a quick message to Reuben.

As he took a seat at the table, a steaming plate of food in front of him, he said, 'I've just spoken to Reuben, and he is going to print out some posters. He's promised to have them ready for this evening, so we can ask people to put them up tomorrow at the same time as we give the *Name the Newt* leaflets out.'

Fiona picked up her knife and fork, butterflies fluttering in her tummy. 'This is really happening, isn't it?'

'You bet it is.'

She put her cutlery down without taking a bite, having abruptly realised that the butterflies weren't caused by excitement: they were caused by worry. The fundraising didn't bother her – delivering a few leaflets and making some sandwiches for a group of foxtrotting pensioners was neither here nor there. What bothered her was the thought of being in charge of a business again. Because, regardless of whether the cafe was a not-for-profit organisation, it would have the same issues of managing staff rotas (albeit volunteers), keeping meticulous accounting records, ordering stock, and ensuring that food hygiene standards were met.

And that was just for starters.

Managing a cafe wasn't as simple as popping a pinny on and shoving some cakes in the oven. There was so much more to consider, and she didn't know whether she was up to it. Not a second time. Both Molly and Bill seemed to believe that her involvement meant that she was. It was only fair that she shouldered some of the blame for that, because she had been swept away by the wonderful feeling of being needed, of being involved. Besides, she could honestly say that she was no longer bored.

'I'm worried,' she began, her eyes downcast as she studied her plate.

'Don't be. People will turn up. Everyone loves a jumble sale, especially with money being tight, and I'm sure the tea dance will be a big hit. And it's not as though we have to raise thousands, is it? Both the electrician and the builder said they'd do the work for free, so we only have to raise enough money to cover the cost of the materials.'

'It's not that. It's the cafe itself. I'm not as young as I was and I'm worried that it'll be too much for me.'

Bill stopped chewing. Reaching across the table, he put his hand on hers and gave it a squeeze. 'You won't be doing it alone. There's me, Molly, and Jack, to name three, and I'm positive Molly will rope other people in to help. Not only is she very persuasive, but she's also a very determined young woman. You'll have lots of help.'

Fiona let his words sink in, then nodded. He was right, the responsibility for this cafe wouldn't be on her shoulders alone: Molly simply wouldn't allow it.

Feeling better again (what a rollercoaster this was turning out to be), Fiona picked up her knife and fork once more.

This lovely lunch that she had prepared wasn't going to eat itself, and she'd be damned if she was going to let it go cold.

CHAPTER 6

On the outside, Sweet Meadow Primary School had changed little since Bill first set foot inside its walls all those years ago. A Victorian building, it was constructed out of the same hewn stone that many of the town's houses were built out of, and Bill vividly remembered the school's high ceilings, big windows, and ancient (mostly ineffectual) radiators.

He was surprised that it hadn't been knocked down and replaced with something newer and easier to maintain, but he was pleased it hadn't. It held so many childhood memories, most of them good: playing tag and kick-the-can, stodgy but filling school dinners, sitting on the parquet floor in the hall and singing the Welsh national anthem on St David's Day whilst dressed like an absolute plonker.

There were also the not-so-good memories, of course: the toilets that had been located outside the building, so if you needed a wee you often got drenched and cold; the spelling tests he had been hopeless at; being sent to stand outside the headmistress's door because he'd cheeked his teacher…

He hadn't given the school a second thought for years, walking or driving past it without a glance, yet here he was at the opposite end of his life, about to go inside and wondering how the intervening years had flown by so fast.

Pushing the slightly depressing thought aside, he gave his attention to the task at hand, and eyed the locked gate leading onto the playground doubtfully. 'Are you sure about this?'

Fiona patted his arm. 'Don't worry, the children don't bite. We probably won't get to see any of them anyway, because they'll be in their classrooms. You'll be perfectly safe.'

Bill scowled at her. 'Very funny. What I meant is, will they go for it?'

'The children or the teachers?'

'Both.'

Fiona gave him a wry smile. 'They'll jump at the chance not to have to do sums or spelling, and I'm talking about the teachers as well as the pupils.'

He supposed she was right. Thinking up names for a newt would be much more fun than algebra. Did primary school children learn algebra? Or was that a secondary school subject? He couldn't remember.

'We should have phoned first,' he muttered. What was it about schools and children that made him so uncomfortable? Was it because he'd never had kids of his own, so he hadn't learned how to behave around them? His job hadn't given rise to any contact with them either; you didn't get any kids on a container ship, or in a busy dockyard.

A wave of sadness washed over him. His mum, bless her, would have loved to have been a granny. At one point he had thought it might have been a possibility, but that was water under the bridge now.

Fiona said, 'I *did* phone, so stop grizzling.'

Bill picked Patch up and tucked him under his arm, fretting that he would be told off for bringing a dog onto the premises. For some reason, he felt that carrying the dog didn't count. Which was daft, when he thought about it.

They were buzzed into the schoolyard, and from there into the building itself, where they were met by a receptionist sitting behind a screen.

'Bloody hell, it's like Fort Knox in here,' he muttered, earning himself an elbow in the ribs and a '*Shh*' from Fiona.

'You said you've got a poster and some leaflets for us?' the receptionist asked.

'We have.' Fiona took them out of her bag. She unrolled the poster and held it up.

The woman scanned it quickly. 'There's going to be a cafe in the park again? How lovely! I remember having a Coke float there when I was little.'

Fiona beamed. 'Ah, yes… A glass of fizzy cold Cola with a scoop of vanilla ice cream dropped into it. It was a taste of heaven.'

Bill had never heard of a Coke float, and he wondered what had been missing.

'Is this your new venture?' the receptionist asked Fiona.

'It's Molly Brown's idea,' Fiona said. 'I'm just along for the ride.'

'But you will be working there, right? I miss your lemon drizzle cake.'

'That's sweet of you. I'm sure I can bake one or two, just for you. But before that happens, we need to raise some funds so we can get the repairs done.'

We, Bill thought, the word rolling around in his head. It felt good to know he was part of something again, and he realised just how adrift he'd been feeling since he'd retired. This mightn't be anything like what he had been used to, but then again it was hardly going to be, was it? The South Wales Valleys weren't famed for their cargo ships.

Fiona edged the leaflets closer. 'Can you ask the headteacher if she will put up the poster, and can these be handed out to each child, please?'

'*Name the Newt Competition*,' the receptionist read as she scanned the leaflet. '*The Park's very own newt saved the pond from being drained, and now he needs a name.*' She looked up. 'Can I have a go? How about Newty McNewtface?'

'Write your name and suggestion on the form underneath, and donate 50p, and you can most definitely have a go,' Fiona laughed.

'When's the closing date?'

Fiona pointed it out to her, and added, 'The winning name will be announced at the end of the jumble sale.'

The woman turned her attention back to the poster. 'Oh, you're holding a jumble sale? I love a good rummage. And you're also having a tea dance. It sounds lovely. I've never been to one before. Do you have to dress up?'

'You can if you want,' Fiona said. She had quizzed Bill about it yesterday over lunch, then they had looked tea dances up on the internet to get some ideas.

'My partner and I will definitely be there,' the receptionist said. 'Good luck with the cafe.'

Bill and Fiona thanked her, then left.

'That wasn't so hard, was it?' Fiona teased. 'Now for the secondary school.'

Bill sighed. He had a feeling this was going to be a long morning.

***

'Why don't you take one side of the street and I'll take the other?' Fiona suggested as they stood at the top end of the high street a short while later. 'Then we can meet back here when we're done. I'll do this side and the square,' she added. The reason she wanted to do the square was because she didn't want Pamela in Best Bites to be given a poster. Fiona couldn't say why exactly, but it didn't feel right to ask Pamela to advertise the very thing that might make the cafe in the park come to life.

'Good idea. Divide and conquer,' he agreed. 'This way we'll be done in half the time. I don't know about you, but I'm gasping for a cuppa.' He gave her a teasing smile. 'It's a pity the cafe in the park isn't open, otherwise we could have stopped off on the way home.'

Fiona bumped him with her shoulder and rolled her eyes. Then she marvelled at how far the two of them had come in a couple of days. This time last week she would never have dreamt she would feel so at ease in Bill's company. She had gone from thinking he was a grumpy old bugger, to hoping they were now friends.

She had enjoyed cooking lunch for him yesterday, and they'd made a good team as they'd bounced ideas off one another. Bill had a sensible head on his shoulders, and she couldn't believe how supportive he'd been, considering he had dismissed the cafe in the beginning. Maybe he was one of those people who took a while to warm up to an idea.

She supposed that he needed to be cautious, considering the job he used to do and the huge responsibility that went with it. She didn't know anything about boats or the sea, but she guessed that rushing into something without thinking it through could lead to a ship running aground or smashing onto rocks. Better to be cautious and considered, than flighty and impetuous, she thought.

As she set off down her chosen side of the street, it occurred to her that having Bill sitting at her kitchen table hadn't seemed as strange as she'd thought it might, considering no other man had sat there (apart from David) since Bradley died. What would her husband have made of all this, she wondered as she entered the first shop, with a poster in her hand and a smile on her face. It saddened her that she would never know. But then, there were so many other things that he hadn't lived to see – his son reaching adulthood being one of them.

By the time she'd walked out of the dentist, she had managed to put the melancholy thoughts behind her (for the time being at least – they never went away for long), and she was pleased with her reception so far. Every shop and business she'd asked, had been more than happy to put up a poster. Some had even given her a raffle prize, and the foldaway shopping bag she kept in her handbag was bursting at the seams. But now that she had reached the square, her confidence ebbed away.

She had a gut feeling that Pamela Edwards wouldn't be happy when she knew about the cafe, so Fiona scurried into the pharmacy next door and hoped the cafe owner didn't spot her dishing out posters.

Oh lord, there was Glenys, waiting for a prescription. The last thing Fiona wanted was to be drawn into a Pamela-bashing conversation, especially when there was a captive audience of customers and staff.

Thankfully Glenys seemed to be in a hurry, because just as she noticed Fiona, her name was called and she was handed the prescription she had been waiting for. 'Hello, Fiona, can't stop. Mrs Pemberton is waiting for her tablets. She's having trouble doing a number two, and the poor dear is in agony.'

Mrs Pemberton lived a few doors up from Fiona, and Fiona winced, thinking that the old lady probably wouldn't be happy if she realised that half of Sweet Meadow was aware of her constipation. For an ex-medical professional, Glenys had a mouth on her – 'indiscreet' must be her middle name, and Fiona was relieved that she had never been on the receiving end of Glenys's ministrations.

However, the woman's heart was in the right place; she would do anyone a favour and would go out of her way to help if she could. It wasn't only Mrs Pemberton who Glenys ran errands for, so maybe her tendency to speak before she thought was a small price to pay.

Glenys hurried outside, Fiona marvelling at her energy. They were roughly the same age, give or take a couple of years, yet Glenys acted like a woman twenty years younger, and Fiona wished she knew her secret.

Fiona was about to turn back to the counter and the pharmacist's assistant who was waiting to serve her, when she caught sight of Bill and Patch on the opposite side of the square. He was coming out of the barbers, his arms full of what Fiona assumed to be raffle prizes (or maybe he had done his shopping at the same time as handing out posters) and who should spot him too, but Glenys.

Fiona watched as the woman made a beeline for him, and she continued to watch as Glenys simpered and flirted.

Gah! Even from this distance she could see Glenys batting her eyelids as she fished a reusable shopping bag out of her pocket and gave it to him. And Fiona positively glowered when Glenys placed a hand on his arm as Bill showed her one of the posters. She moved closer to him to read it, then gazed up at him, her eyelashes fluttering again.

Give it a rest, love, Fiona thought. The woman was so obvious, it was embarrassing. But what was even more galling, was that Bill seemed to be lapping up the attention.

Cross with herself because it was none of her business who Glenys flirted with, Fiona turned her attention back to her task. Having received assurances that the poster would be displayed in the window, Fiona left the pharmacy, her eyes scanning the square, but Bill was nowhere in sight. And neither was Glenys.

When she arrived at their agreed meeting place, Fiona was relieved to find him alone. For some reason she'd got it into her head that Glenys might have wormed her way into their little fund-raising gang, and during the short walk to the end of the street she had decided that if Glenys was in, she was out. Though why she felt that way was a mystery. Surely the more hands, the better?

Feeling fractious, she joined Bill outside the flower shop.

'Did it go all right?' he asked. 'Did someone give you grief?'

'No, why do you ask?'

'You seem annoyed.'

'I'm not annoyed. Not in the slightest. I'm perfectly happy, thank you.' He looked startled at the vehemence of her reply, and she realised she had been a bit sharp. 'I'm fine,' she said, softer this time.

'Thank goodness for that. I thought I'd have to have a stiff word with someone.'

While Fiona appreciated the sentiment, she didn't need anyone to fight her battles for her. 'If there are any stiff words to be said, I can say them myself,' she retorted.

'Right. Yes. I wasn't— Never mind.'

Now look what she'd done. She had upset him. What on earth had got into her? Maybe her blood sugar was low? Or perhaps she was tired from the unaccustomed excitement.

'I could do with a coffee,' she said. 'And a sandwich.'

His face cleared. 'I used to know someone who got hangry.'

'Eh?'

'You know, getting angry because you're hungry: *hangry*. It's a shame Best Bites doesn't allow dogs, otherwise we could have had something to eat in there.'

Fiona was pleased that Pamela didn't. She had only set foot in the cafe once since she'd sold it, and she had no desire to do so again.

'We could pop into the Farmer's Arms,' Bill suggested. 'Unless you want to get off home?'

Home wasn't particularly appealing, but having a spot of lunch in the pub with Bill was. 'Let's go to the pub,' she agreed. 'We can ask if they'll put up a poster and make a donation to the raffle while we're there.'

Bill showed her his borrowed bag. 'I've been given a few, and some people have put their posters up already.' He gestured to the window behind him, and when Fiona glanced at it she was delighted to see the poster on display.

In the end, Fiona didn't order a sandwich or any of the other 'lite bites' on the menu. Instead she opted for scampi and chips, reasoning that it would save her cooking a main meal for herself later. No wine today, though. However, she might have a glass this evening, as the bottle that Bill had brought over yesterday was still half full and the wine wouldn't keep for long now that it had been opened. It would be a shame to waste it.

She briefly considered asking Bill if he would like to help her polish it off, but decided not to. They had more or less been in each other's pockets since Saturday, so they could probably do with a break.

Still, having lunch out was a real treat and she gazed around with interest, not having visited a pub or restaurant in ages. And she hadn't been inside the Farmer's Arms since it had been taken over by new people and refurbished, which must have been eight or nine years ago.

'It's nice in here,' she observed, surprised at how tastefully it had been done out. Under its previous management it had sported dark-coloured walls, horse brasses and hideously patterned carpets. 'Is this your regular?'

Bill shrugged. 'I don't have a regular, as such. I don't go to the pub often, if I'm honest. This is a treat for me.'

'Me, too!' She beamed at him, then thinking she might be coming across as a bit odd, she turned the wattage down and sipped her lemonade. Bill, she noted, also had a soft drink. 'Do you like rum?' she blurted.

Bill's lips quirked. 'Not much.'

'Oh, I just thought...' She trailed off.

'That I used to be a pirate?' Now he was laughing at her.

She snapped, 'Don't be silly. You look nothing like a pirate.'

'What are pirates supposed to look like? Eye patches and parrots? Wooden legs and beards?'

'You're making fun of me.'

His smile was warm. 'Yes, I am. But there's no malice intended.'

Fiona didn't assume there had been, but she wasn't going to let him off the hook that easily. 'Isn't there a tradition of rum rations in the Navy?'

'You're thinking of the Royal Navy. I was in the *Merchant* Navy. The tradition was abolished around 1970, although a company called Lambs do have a brand of rum named Navy Rum, but I've no idea how it differs from any other rum. My old dad always kept a bottle of it in the house. He used to say that a tot a day kept a cold at bay.'

Fiona glanced up to see a waitress approaching with their meals, and she reached for her napkin. Assuring the woman that she didn't require any sauces and after sprinkling salt and vinegar on her chips, Fiona asked, 'What is the Merchant Navy exactly?' She hadn't considered it before, but now she was curious.

'It's a term used to describe commercial shipping, and the vessels and crew who transport goods around the world. It has nothing to do with the military. The ships are privately owned, and the crews are civilian. That's not to say that there isn't some migration between the two, as the Royal Navy often recruits people who have worked for private companies, and vice versa.'

Fiona had carried on eating as Bill answered the question, but she had also been observing him. She noticed that he appeared to gain in stature as he spoke, and she caught a glimpse of the man he had once been.

Abruptly, she realised that he was still that man: the only thing that had changed was people's perception of him, hers included. In fairness, she hadn't known him in his previous life, but she was as guilty as the next person of only looking at the outside and not the inside. Then she wondered whether the people she had known for years, the ones who she had served for decades, now saw a doddery old woman instead of the competent, capable cafe owner she had once been. It was a sobering thought.

'You must have had a great deal of responsibility,' she guessed.

He nodded. 'Thousands of tons of shipping, millions of dollars in cargo, and not to mention the crew's lives in my hands.'

He wasn't boasting, Fiona realised. He was saying it like it was. 'I bet you've seen some wonderful places.'

'And some not-so-wonderful ones. Sometimes the turnaround meant that we didn't get much time on shore, or if we did, it wasn't advisable to leave the dock area. Occasionally, we didn't want to because it was nicer onboard – and that's saying something!'

'How many countries have you been to?' Fiona was fascinated.

He swallowed the morsel in his mouth before answering. 'I've lost count, but it's safe to say that the only continent I haven't been to is Antarctica.'

'What's your favourite place?'

'That's a hard one. I suppose it depends on what you mean by favourite. Some are beautiful for a holiday, but I wouldn't want to live there. Some are lively and exciting, like Hong Kong, but I wouldn't want to live there, either.' He hesitated, pulling a face. 'This might sound corny, but my favourite place is here, in Sweet Meadow.'

'It's not corny at all. It's where you grew up.'

'*Hiraeth*,' he said solemnly.

Fiona utterly agreed with the sentiment. Although the Welsh word was difficult to translate into English, she could well imagine the yearning homesickness he must have felt when he was away. She too, used to have a longing for home whenever she left it, and she'd never been away from her little Welsh town for more than a couple of weeks. It was lovely to go on holiday, but there was nothing quite like home, was there?

'Have you never been tempted to settle down in any of those far-flung places?' she asked.

A cloud passed over his face but was gone so quickly that Fiona thought she must have imagined it.

'Once or twice.' His voice was light, but she sensed something off about it. However, he carried on, 'My home was whichever ship I was on at the time.'

'Why cargo ships? Why not cruise ships?' With every answered question, a dozen more popped into her mind.

'That's easy – passengers. Too many people, and I would have been expected to be nice to them. Give me a sea can any day.'

'Sea can?'

'Shipping container; those big metal boxes that are used to transport goods.'

'What goods did you transport?'

His lips quirked. 'All kinds. You name it, I've shipped it. Oil, grain, car parts, wood, chemicals, plastic ducks… Whatever needs to be moved from one location to another by sea. The list is endless.'

'Do you miss it?' As she asked the question, she recalled asking Glenys the exact same thing a few days ago, and wondered whether she was asking people that because she missed her time at the cafe.

'Now and again. The good bits, mostly. The bad bits tend to fade over time, or they don't seem as horrible as they were. I believe it's called nostalgia'

'True…' Although Fiona distinctly remembered the reasons she had decided to sell up and retire, lately she had begun to question them. Bill had hit the nail on the head – *nostalgia*.

'Should we be naughty and have pudding?' Bill asked, and when Fiona glanced down at her plate she was surprised to see that she had cleared it.

'Why not? I'll have a coffee too, if you don't mind.'

'Not at all. I'll join you.'

Fiona uttered a sigh of satisfaction: she couldn't remember the last time she had enjoyed lunch as much. Actually, yes, she could – yesterday's lunch had been equally as lovely. And the common denominator had been *Bill*.

Now, that was food for thought.

CHAPTER 7

Was there anything he needed to do with regards to either the jumble sale, or the tea dance, Bill wondered. Fiona had booked the venue (the church hall), Molly and Jack had said they would set up for both events, the vicar was supplying the music for the tea dance (although Bill did worry that the music in question might be hymns and therefore not at all suitable), the posters had been distributed, and Fiona was in charge of the refreshments. So there was little left to be done, and even less to be done by *him*. And now that the excitement of the weekend (planning) and yesterday (delivering leaflets and posters) was out of the way, Bill was at a loose end.

He could run the vacuum cleaner around – with Patch there were always dog hairs that needed hoovering up – and he could put a load of washing on, but he wasn't in the mood for housework.

Feeling restless, he found himself upstairs, standing in front of his mum's large walnut wardrobe. *His* wardrobe now, he supposed, but he couldn't help continuing to think of this bedroom as his mother's, despite her having passed away some years ago. He had returned home as soon as he'd been notified of her stroke, and he had remained in Sweet Meadow until she died a couple of weeks later. After the funeral, he had gone back to sea for another three years before retiring and returning to Sweet Meadow for good. But no matter how long he lived in this house, he would always think of it as Mum's.

After her death, when he was at sea and Sweet Meadow had seemed a lifetime away, he had debated whether he should sell up, but he had never got around to it. It was too late now, as he was far too comfortable with his living arrangements, even if a three-bed house was too big for him. A face-lift wouldn't go amiss, and he wondered what Fiona had made of it when she'd popped in the other day.

Thinking of Fiona reminded him why he was peering into the wardrobe's open door.

He had been flattered that she had shown such an interest in his days in the Merchant Navy, but when she had asked him whether he had ever thought about settling down the question had brought long-buried memories to the surface and he had nearly blurted out the truth. Luckily he'd caught himself in time, and had batted the question away with some nonsense about home being whatever ship he had been on. And once upon a time, that had been more or less true – until Tracey.

Bill lowered himself to the floor, his knees popping loudly and earning himself a concerned boop from Patch as he let out a grunt. Getting up was going to be a cow, but his back wouldn't have taken much bending if he was going to rummage around in the bottom of the wardrobe. He had turned it into a kind of storage area for all those things he wanted to hang onto but didn't know what to do with. He could have shoved them up the attic, but getting up there was a precarious business as he didn't have a proper loft ladder. So into the wardrobe they'd gone.

Moving a small artificial Christmas tree to one side, he lifted out a cardboard box of baubles and tinsel, most of which dated from his childhood. Underneath, at the very back and hidden by a stack of old ledgers from before the days of computerisation, was a carved wooden box, no larger than a shoe box. Swallowing hard, he took it out and placed it on the carpet in front of him.

He hadn't touched this box since he'd put it in the wardrobe not long after his mother had died. Why he felt the need to look inside it now was a question he couldn't answer, but talking to Fiona yesterday had stirred up memories.

With trembling fingers, he opened the lid and put a hand to his chest.

He felt his heart thud alarmingly, because staring back at him was Tracey, the woman he had loved with every fibre of his being. The woman who had jilted him three days before their wedding.

***

Feeling restless was getting to be a habit, Fiona thought, as she lifted her lightweight jacket off the hook under the stairs. She probably wouldn't need it, as the morning was a warm one, but she reasoned that it was better to have it and not to need it, than to need it and not have it. It was the same reasoning which made her keep a folding umbrella in her bag, no matter what the season. Summer in Sweet Meadow didn't mean that it wouldn't rain.

Shopping held no appeal, so she set her feet on the road towards the park instead. A bit of fresh air would do her good. The exercise would stop her from stiffening up after all the walking she had done yesterday traipsing around town delivering leaflets and posters, and she wanted another look at the cafe. It had been boarded up for so long, that it was a novelty to see it without.

Half-expecting to bump into Bill as he took Patch for his morning walk, Fiona was dawdling past the bandstand and doing her best not to look at it because the state it was in got her goat and might prompt yet another phone call to the council, when the sound of hammering caught her attention. It was coming from the cafe, and as she drew closer she spotted the open door.

Of course she had to go see what was going on. How could she not?

Sticking her head inside, she began to cough. The air was clouded with swirling dust and the floor was strewn with lumps of grey plaster.

'Goodness gracious!' she exclaimed. 'Someone's been busy.'

That someone was Jack. He was in the middle of chipping off the ancient plaster, exposing the bare brick underneath. He had nearly finished one wall, and she wondered how long he had been at it.

He turned at the sound of her voice, his face almost completely obscured by a pair of goggles and a mask. Putting the hammer and chisel down, he reached for a bottle of water, and gestured for her to go outside. When he removed his safety equipment, Fiona was amused to see the echoes they had left on his otherwise filthy face.

'Getting on with it, I see,' she observed.

'I thought I may as well, considering I've got the day off.'

'On a Tuesday?'

'That's the beauty of flexitime. I can build up my hours and take time off when I want.'

'And you wanted to do *this?*' She pointed to the cafe.

Jack lifted a shoulder. 'It needs doing, and I wasn't sure how long it would take.'

'Can't you rope in some help?'

'Probably, but with Molly sorting out the tradespeople and all the admin, and you and Bill in charge of the fundraising, I thought I'd better do my bit.'

Fiona gave him a shrewd look. When Jack had originally moved into Molly's cottage – before he and Molly had got together – it had been on the understanding that he wouldn't have to pay rent as long as he helped her renovate it. Gradually he had also been drawn into her scheme of restoring the park.

Now that they were a couple, it seemed that Jack was no longer working in the park out of obligation, but out of love – love for Molly and the park he now lived in. And of course he'd do anything for Molly: that was as obvious as the nose on his face. A nose that was currently covered in dust and dirt.

Even so, he was still a handsome chap. In some ways he reminded her of Bradley when he'd been a young man. Jack had the same kind eyes and easy smile, the same breadth to his shoulders and upright stance. Bill's stance was the same, despite his more advanced years. And if you cared to look beyond the grumpy exterior, you'd see the kindness in his eyes too, Fiona thought. Although he didn't smile very often, it simply made it more special when he did.

She glanced around the park but he was nowhere in sight, and her gaze came to rest on Jack once more. 'I should let you get on,' she said. 'You don't need me holding you up.'

He unscrewed the cap on his bottle of water and took a gulp. 'I'm glad of the break, to be honest. It's hard work, not to mention hot and dusty. How did yesterday go? Reuben said he'd dropped the posters off, and that you and Bill were going to hand them out.'

'We did, and I must say that we had a good reception. People seemed quite enthused about a tea dance. But saying they like the idea, and actually turning up, is a different matter.'

Jack swiped the back of his hand across his mouth, smearing the dirt, and grinned at her. 'We've sold thirty-four tickets already,' he said, and Fiona clapped her hands.

'That's marvellous! You'll keep me updated?'

'Absolutely.'

'I need to know how many to cater for,' she fretted, worrying that she wouldn't prepare enough food. Or that there would be loads left over.

She couldn't believe how nervous she felt, and as she continued her walk, she gave herself a silent talking to. Throughout the course of a normal day in the cafe, she used to serve a couple of hundred people, and she would do that day in, day out, week after week, month after month. Surely she could manage a hundred or so people for one afternoon, and Jack had promised to keep her abreast of how the ticket sales were going. She would have plenty of notice as to how many she would be catering for.

Although bubbling with excitement and wanting to share the news of the early ticket sales with Bill, she refrained from taking a walk up his street and knocking on his door, guessing that he might have had enough of her over the past couple of days. Just because she had enjoyed his company, didn't mean he felt the same way. Although, to be fair, he hadn't seemed desperate to get off home yesterday. If he had been, he wouldn't have suggested lunch.

However, their friendship was in the early stages and although they appeared to get on well, she didn't want to derail that. Knowing how cantankerous and how short-tempered he could be at times, she had no intention of rubbing him up the wrong way. Her news could wait. For now, she had plenty to keep her occupied by deciding what food she was going to serve at the tea dance, because as far as she was concerned, the dance would remind people why they used to visit Clover Cafe and hopefully put the cafe in Sweet Meadow Park firmly in their minds.

***

The idea must have come to Bill in the middle of the night because he awoke the following morning knowing exactly what he could do to help.

After taking Patch for an early walk, Bill changed into a shirt and a pair of slacks, and wrestled the dog into the harness that he wore whenever he was in the car, which wasn't very often as Bill didn't drive much these days. Today though, he would have to if he wanted to put his plan into action.

The nearest branch of the building society he banked with was a thirty-minute drive away. It did make him incredibly cross that the branch in Sweet Meadow had closed a year or so ago, and the inconvenience irked him. It was lucky that he'd mastered online banking, wasn't it? Otherwise, he would be an incredibly annoyed customer. But what he wanted to do today couldn't be done online, and he doubted whether it could be done over the phone, either. Therefore, a trip to the building society was needed in order to make his request in person.

The traffic wasn't too bad but Bill took his time anyway, trying not to think about how he used to navigate ships weighing thousands of tonnes, yet he was now overly cautious about driving a fifteen-mile journey in a medium-sized hatchback. Because thinking about it brought home to him how small his world had become. He could sense that he was closing in on himself, and he didn't like it.

When they arrived at their destination, Patch was ecstatic to be released from the car and he bounced around Bill's legs as he patted his pocket, checking yet again that he had his wallet.

'No need to get so worked up,' he told his dog. 'We're not going anywhere exciting.'

Patch took no notice, trotting happily at Bill's side, his tail wagging, pulling on his lead now and again if he caught an interesting scent. Although what could be interesting in a pedestrianised precinct filled with shoppers, Bill could only guess.

It didn't take long to get to the building society, and as he approached the door he scooped Patch up into his arms. He had brought his dog here a couple of times previously, so he knew the staff probably wouldn't object.

'I'd like a banker's draft for five hundred pounds, please,' he said to the cashier, pushing his bank card through the little slot.

'Certainly, sir. I can order one for you today and it will be ready for you tomorrow. I must inform you that there is a charge for this service.'

Bill frowned. He didn't object to the charge, but he did object to having to come back tomorrow. 'Why can't you give it to me now? I only want five hundred pounds.'

'It's not the amount, it's the process,' she explained.

His frown deepened. He knew he was being awkward when he said, 'In that case, I'll order a banker's draft for the full amount in my account, plus any interest. I know it's not your fault that my local branch has closed, but it's not mine either and I'm simply not prepared to come back tomorrow. Therefore, I wish to close my account.'

The cashier gave him a look, then began tapping away at her keyboard. Suddenly her eyes widened, and he guessed she must have checked his balance. It was a substantial sum.

'Would you mind waiting a moment?' she asked. 'I'd like to have a quick word with the branch manager.' And with that she slipped out of her seat and walked away.

Bill hoped they weren't going to be awkward; he had every right to remove his money and close his account.

In less than a minute a lady in a smart navy suit appeared in the foyer and asked him to follow her. Showing him into a small side room, she invited him to take a seat. And less than another minute later, she had informed him that a banker's draft for five hundred pounds would be available to him in about an hour, if he cared to wait.

'There is one more thing,' he said, chancing his arm. 'Could you write a brief note on headed paper to the recipient of the cheque, telling them what the money is to be used for?'

And when he explained, she was more than happy to oblige.

***

Sweet Meadow Park at night was a different kettle of fish to the daytime. There were fewer people around for one thing, and for another those people tended to be of the teenage variety. They were usually gone by around half past ten or eleven though, and Bill occasionally took a stroll at that time, knowing he would have the park to himself.

Despite having Patch with him, he would see a fox now and again, a rabbit or two, and maybe a hedgehog, and in the warmer months he would catch sight of bats, and even an owl if he was lucky.

This evening he had a purpose other than taking the dog out for a final wee before bedtime. Bill had a letter to deliver.

He had contemplated posting it, but he was worried that it might go astray, so popping it through Molly and Jack's letterbox was the only option. He would have to be quick though, because he fully expected Jet to sound the alarm that there was an intruder on his property, and Bill didn't want to be spotted. The whole purpose of obtaining a banker's draft was that it was anonymous, with the recipient having no idea who the money was from, and Bill intended to keep it that way.

This donation was his way of helping bring the cafe back to life. It meant a lot to Molly, but it meant even more to Fiona. Over the past few days he had seen her grow and flourish in front of his very eyes, and where he had not very long ago thought her a dotty old bat, he now realised she was anything but. She had merely needed a purpose, that was all, and the cafe was it.

Five hundred pounds would hopefully go some way to have the roof repaired, because that was the most important job, as the building needed to be watertight before any other renovations could be embarked on. If more money was required after their fundraising efforts, he would pay the building society another visit. He could certainly afford it, and after his monthly bills were settled, he didn't have anything else to spend his money on.

But perhaps he would phone first next time, rather than throw his toys out of his pram.

He was slightly ashamed of his behaviour in threatening to close his account, but it had worked; he had got his cheque, and he and Patch had enjoyed a sandwich and a coffee while they'd waited for it to be processed.

As he approached Molly's cottage, Bill kept to one side of the path, using the bushes and trees to hide his approach. But before he arrived at the gate in the middle of the little picket fence, he put Patch back on the lead and tied him to a tree, reasoning that if Molly or Jack happened to glance out of the window, seeing Patch would give him away, whereas a shadowy figure dressed in dark clothing slipping out of the gate could be anyone.

Bill was as stealthy as he could possibly be, but the letterbox rattled when he pushed the envelope through, which alerted Jet, who started barking, so Bill didn't get away completely unscathed.

However, he was fairly confident that he hadn't been seen, so it was with a spring in his step and a lightness in his heart that he made his way home, inordinately pleased with the day's work.

CHAPTER 8

Having received a mysterious summons to the cottage in Sweet Meadow Park, Fiona was intrigued. She'd had a phone call from Molly earlier today asking her if she wouldn't mind popping in this evening at around six o'clock for a bite to eat – which was lovely – but Fiona had a feeling there was more to the invitation than a bit of supper.

There was something going on, she felt it in her water, and when Molly told her that Bill and Reuben had also been invited, she was sure of it.

Whatever the reason, Fiona was delighted to be asked. She never went out in the evening, and she felt a thrill of anticipation as she got ready.

'What's the occasion?' she'd asked Molly, but Molly hadn't said, and now that Fiona was walking through the park, she hoped it wasn't someone's birthday because she would feel awful turning up without a card.

She had a bottle of wine with her, so that was better than nothing, she supposed.

Molly met her at the door and took her jacket. The evening was a warm one, but Fiona guessed that the temperature would drop once the sun went down and she'd get chilly on the way home. She wasn't looking forward to walking through the park in the dark, and she hoped the meal wouldn't go on too long. She didn't like being out at night, and now that she no longer had a cafe to see to, there was no reason for her to be. She used to hate locking up in the depths of winter, when it was dark by four p.m. And it had been even worse when it was cold and lashing it down.

Realising she was still clutching the wine, she handed it to Molly.

Molly asked, 'What's this for?'

'I couldn't come empty-handed.'

'You shouldn't have! But thank you anyway.' Molly led her through to the lounge. 'Bill is already here, but Reuben couldn't make it. He had to shoot off to the Peak District; something about pine martens, but don't ask me what.'

Molly passed the wine to Jack, who was hovering in the doorway to the kitchen. The heady smell of garlic and onions wafted out of it, making Fiona's mouth water.

'We've got a bottle of red on the go, if you'd like a glass,' Molly offered, 'Or we could open the one you brought.'

'Red is fine, thank you.'

Fiona was invited to take a seat, and as she lowered herself into an armchair, she smiled and said hello to Bill. He looked rather relaxed, his legs out in front and crossed at the ankles, a glass in his hand.

Jack disappeared into the kitchen, Molly with him, so Fiona took the opportunity to hiss, 'Any idea what this is about? It's not someone's birthday, is it? Or...' Her eyes lit up as the thought occurred to her. 'I wonder if they've got engaged.'

'Not that I know of. I think it's just a meal to say thanks, maybe?'

'Ah, right.' Feeling silly because she had read too much into it, she was glad when Molly returned with her wine, Jack accompanying her.

'Jack's making a lasagne,' Molly said. 'It'll be twenty minutes yet, so while we're waiting, would you like to hear our news?' Molly was beaming and Jack also had a smile on his face, so it must be good.

Fiona shot an I-told-you-so look at Bill, then glanced at Molly's left hand, hoping to see a ring. Her finger was disappointingly bare. Fiona loved a wedding. Then she dropped her gaze to Molly's tummy and speculated whether the former park keeper's cottage would soon be ringing to the sound of a baby's cry.

Molly sank onto the sofa, Jack perching on the arm next to her, and waved an envelope in the air. It was long and white, the kind that official letters came in, not birthday cards.

She said, 'Someone popped this through our letterbox on Wednesday evening.'

'What is it?' Fiona asked.

'A cheque for five hundred pounds.'

'That's nice.' It certainly was, but Fiona couldn't for the life of her think why Molly felt the need to share the information with her and Bill.

'Who is it from?' Bill asked.

'No idea.' Jack's expression was puzzled. 'But it's made out to Molly, and there was a note with it saying that the money is to go towards repairing the cafe's roof.'

Fiona clapped her hands together. 'How wonderful! An anonymous donation.'

'Are you sure you don't know who it's from?' Bill had sat up and was leaning forward slightly.

Molly said, 'Not a clue. We were hoping you might.' Her gaze flickered between Fiona and Bill.

'Why would we know?' Fiona asked. She had been nowhere near the park on Wednesday evening. Come to think of it, Bill may have been… She turned to him. 'Bill?'

He shook his head and shrugged.

Jack continued, 'We wondered whether anyone had mentioned giving a donation.' He looked hopeful.

Fiona stared at Bill. Bill stared back at her. She spoke for both of them, certain that Bill would have mentioned it over lunch on Monday if that was the case. 'No, no one.'

Bill shook his head again.

'That's a shame. I would like to thank them.' Molly pulled a face.

Fiona thought for a minute. 'Might there be a clue in the note? The handwriting perhaps?'

'Take a look.'

Molly passed it to her, but Fiona was none the wiser when she read it. It was from a building society, presumably the same one who had issued the cheque, and all it said was that the 'donor would like the money to be put towards repairing the roof on the cafe in Sweet Meadow Park'.

She passed it across to Bill, who barely glanced at it. Fiona moved on to more practical matters. 'Will it be enough, do you think?'

Molly grinned. 'Yes, it will. Gavin is only going to charge us for the materials, so this should more than cover it, as long as he doesn't come across anything unexpected such as a joist needing to be replaced. He won't know until he removes the damaged slates.'

'Fingers crossed he won't.' Fiona held up her crossed fingers.

'I'd better check on the lasagne,' Jack said, getting up and going into the kitchen.

'When can the builder start?' Bill asked.

'Tomorrow, he says. Because it's only a single-storey structure, he says there won't be any need for scaffolding.'

'A couple more minutes yet,' Jack announced, coming back into the living room with the wine bottle in his hand. 'Who's for a top up? Then I think we should drink a toast to our generous benefactor, whoever he or she may be.'

Fiona raised her glass with enthusiasm, but noticed that Bill only took the smallest of sips out of his and she hoped he was feeling OK. He managed to put away a hefty portion of lasagne though, and was lively enough throughout the meal, so she promptly forgot about it.

***

With the jumble sale only a week away and David popping by later this afternoon to help her transport her contributions to the church hall in readiness, Fiona decided she had better get her skates on and have a good sort out to see what she could find. She hadn't had one in years, and she knew there were loads of things that would benefit from a new home, rather than remain lurking in the back of her cupboards.

She dug out a few sturdy bags and got to work, starting with David's old room. It was a spare room now, she supposed, because he hadn't slept in it for around twenty years. The silly thing was, it hadn't changed a great deal in all that time; it even had some of her son's old clothes and books (which were dry recommended reading from his university days), along with oddments such as a globe that was so old several countries had since been renamed.

As she idly turned it on its axis, her fingers trailed across continents and oceans alike, and she wondered which routes Bill had taken during his time on the high seas. No doubt he'd sailed the Atlantic and through the Suez Canal, and possibly the South China Sea if he'd travelled to Hong Kong. There would have been loads of others, she assumed.

Placing the globe in one of the bags (surely someone would want it?) she thought how nice it was of Bill to offer to walk her home yesterday evening. She had been fretting about it on and off throughout the meal, but hadn't said anything. How could she confess that she was worried about walking through the park on her own, when it wasn't even nine o'clock yet and still light. Everyone would think she was a pathetic old woman, scared of her own shadow.

But she couldn't help it. The teenagers who hung around the bandstand intimidated her, even though she didn't think they meant to. They were just so loud, and their movements were quick and unpredictable. The other day she had spied three of them on their way home from school, swinging each other around by the straps of their school bags, heedless of who they might cannon into. A pensioner like her could easily be knocked over, and she shuddered at the thought of breaking a hip.

Yesterday evening it hadn't surprised her to see at least a dozen of them loitering by the bandstand and getting up to all sorts, no doubt. If she had been on her own, she wouldn't have had the courage to walk past them. Instead, she would have retraced her steps and exited the park by the main gates, walked into town, and then trundled back up the hill. It would have made her journey four times as long, but she would have felt safer.

With Bill by her side last night, she hadn't been fearful at all, even when he'd greeted the group of youngsters (youffs, as he called them), and he had referred to a couple of them by name, Liam being one and Connor another. They were names she recognised.

'Wasn't Connor the boy who almost drowned in the pond?' she had whispered, when they were out of earshot. 'The one Jack had to jump in to save?'

'It was.'

'And wasn't Liam the one who egged him on, the ringleader?'

Bill had offered her his arm, the path under their feet being somewhat uneven, and she had taken it gratefully.

'I don't know about Liam being the ringleader,' he'd said, 'but he's undoubtedly the mouthiest. I don't think he's a bad boy, though.'

'Hmm.'

'You don't sound convinced.'

'It was him and his gang who vandalised the flower beds earlier in the year,' she reminded him. 'Molly and Jack had worked hard on those. And what about all the litter they leave around? And the shouting and swearing.'

'You've forgotten the smoking and drinking.'

Fiona released his arm now that they had negotiated the rough path, and shot him an aggrieved look. 'I haven't forgotten at all,' she retorted. 'You've changed your tune – you used to complain about them all the time.'

'Oh, I think they've redeemed themselves, don't you? Liam, in particular, did his part in rounding up people to help tidy up the park.'

'Hmm,' Fiona repeated.

'And kids will be kids,' he added.

She didn't want to argue with him, but her David hadn't behaved like that when he was a teenager.

Changing the subject, she had tried to talk to Bill about the mystery donor, but he had been reticent and she'd worried that she might have offended him. The thought had vexed her, and she had been debating whether to apologise when they'd arrived at her house and he'd shocked her by leaning forward and pecking her on the cheek. Surprised, she had bidden him goodnight and hurried inside, pleased that she hadn't upset him.

While she'd been mulling over the events of last night, Fiona had worked her way methodically around the room and had managed to fill half of the bags. At this rate her stuff would need a table all by itself. Finishing up, she moved on to the next room. There wouldn't be anything in the bathroom that she could get rid of, but her bedroom was chock full of things she had been meaning to throw out, starting with her clothes.

Some of the blouses and jumpers she'd had for years and years, and although she didn't profess to be a fashionista (was that what they were called?) neither did she want to be viewed as an utter frump. She would be ruthless, she vowed, because she was fairly sure it would be years before she had another sort out.

By the time Fiona had finished with her wardrobe, the pile of clothes she intended to give away was bigger than the pile she intended to keep and she felt quite cleansed. De-cluttering and getting rid of those things she no longer wore or liked (and in some instances, didn't fit or no longer suited her) was quite therapeutic and made her feel lighter. She could certainly see her remaining clothes better now, as they were no longer crammed together.

The tallboy was the next in line, and she opened the top drawer. Full of underwear, none of which she had any intention of allowing anyone else to set eyes on, let alone paw through, she closed it and skipped down to the fourth drawer. This one was what she termed an odds-and-sods drawer. Here she found scarves, a floaty wrap to go over a swimsuit that had never been worn and still had the tag on, a poncho (when, and more importantly *why* had she bought that?), a single sheepskin mitten (if she kept searching, she might find the other one), and a pair of leg warmers.

Something at the back of the drawer made her pause, and sadness washed over her as she took out a plaid woollen scarf. Lifting it to her nose, she inhaled deeply. All she could smell was a faint mustiness. Bradley's scent had faded long ago. She had worn it constantly in the months after he'd died: it had been the closest thing she could get to feeling his arms around her. How many times had he stood behind her and draped himself around her neck whilst she had been washing up, or sorting the laundry?

Despite knowing she would never wear it again, she couldn't bring herself to part with it, so she returned it to the drawer and carried on with her task, her heart a little heavier than when she'd begun.

However, by the time David was due to arrive, she'd perked up, and when the doorbell rang and she heard his key in the lock, she greeted him with a pile of bags and a satisfied smile.

'Woah, Mum, you can't give *everything* away,' he laughed when he saw them, bending down to give her a hug.

David was tall, like his father had been, with the same mop of unruly brown hair and pleasant face. He also had his dad's brains, and her determination, and he'd made the most of the combination by becoming a quantity surveyor. Whilst she wasn't entirely sure what that entailed (something to do with construction) she was aware it was a responsible and sometimes stressful job. She was also immensely proud of him.

David stepped back, his hands on her shoulders. 'I'm glad to see you're looking more like your old self.'

'What do you mean?' She gave his cheek a pinch, then bustled off to the kitchen.

Her son followed. 'You were starting to look rather down. To be honest, I was getting worried about you. This cafe project seems to have perked you up no end.'

'It has,' she agreed. She had told him all about it when she'd spoken to him earlier in the week to ask him whether he had anything for the jumble sale. 'Did you find much?'

'Loads. The kids were a bit reluctant to part with some of their stuff, though. I would have brought them with me, but Kirsty's got a swimming competition and Ben's got football, then he's off into town with his mates. Gone are the days when they want to hang out with their old dad.'

By 'town', David meant Cardiff. He and his family lived on the outskirts of the city, and although it wasn't particularly far from Sweet Meadow, it meant that Fiona couldn't just pop in on the off chance for a cup of tea.

Although she was disappointed at not seeing her grandchildren today, she understood. David had been the same when he was their age, and she dared say that she had probably been the same too. It was only natural that they'd want to do something more exciting than help their dad ferry bric-a-brac around.

'They're good kids; they'll come back to you when they've had a chance to grow up a bit,' she assured him.

It didn't stop her worrying about them though, and occasionally she wondered what they got up to when their parents weren't keeping an eye on them. Did they hang out in their local park? Did old ladies feel intimidated when they encountered them? Surely not... Her grandchildren were nothing like those teenagers in Sweet Meadow Park. They wouldn't dream of littering, for a start!

'Can I make you a cup of coffee?' she asked.

David checked the time and Fiona's heart gave a squeeze when she saw that he still wore his father's watch. Though it gave her a little pang to see it on his wrist, she was comforted too, knowing that her son wasn't forgetting his dad.

'Um, not today. I'm playing golf later.'

'Then straight to the clubhouse afterwards?' Fiona teased.

David chuckled. 'It would be rude not to. Let's get this lot into the car.' He eyed the bags full of neatly folded clothes. 'I hope you've left yourself something to wear.'

It didn't take David long to load the car (thank goodness he had an estate), then they were off to the church.

Reverend Jenkins showed David where to put them, and Fiona was pleased to find that donations had already started to trickle in.

'This is the last of it,' David said, placing a large cardboard box next to a pile of others.

Back at the house, he gave her another hug. 'See you soon,' he promised, kissing her cheek, and she waved him off with a smile.

She was just about to close the door when a glint of glass on the pavement made her pause, and she took a step towards it for a closer look.

'Oh, no…' The words lodged in her throat as she realised that the object was David's watch.

She picked it up, her eyes welling with tears. The strap had broken and the glass was cracked, and it made her unbearably sad to see it. Giving into the tears that had threatened earlier, Fiona took Bradley's scarf out of the drawer and sobbed into it. Thirty-one years seemed like yesterday, and whoever said that time heals was a great big liar.

***

Bill couldn't resist taking a look, although he managed to hold fire until midday. There had been no sign of the builder when Bill had patrolled the park with Patch this morning, but maybe seven forty-five was a bit early considering the chap probably didn't make a habit of working on Saturdays and he was doing this out of the goodness of his heart.

Rounding the bend, Bill was satisfied to see a white van outside the cafe when he ventured into the park for the second time today. A ladder was propped against the cafe's wall, and a man was standing on the top of it.

Bill came to a halt just beyond the bollards surrounding the ladder and stared upwards. 'Found any issues?' he called.

Gavin glanced down. 'Not yet.'

'Is it a long job?'

'Should be finished by the end of the day, all being well.'

That was good news. Pleased that his donation was moving the work along, Bill stayed to watch for a while. A short time later, Jack and Jet joined him, the dogs greeting each other in a paroxysm of wagging tails.

Jack was carrying a tray containing three mugs and a plate of Jammie Dodgers.

He said, 'I've been keeping Gavin supplied with tea and I saw you from the window. Milk, no sugar, isn't it?'

'I don't mind if I do. Thanks.' Bill took a mug. He helped himself to a biscuit as well, Patch gazing at him with pleading eyes.

The builder joined them, and all three slurped their tea and stared up at the roof.

'Nice day for it,' Bill said. He turned to Jack. 'Your chap says he'll be done by the end of the day.'

Jack nodded. 'Hopefully. As soon as the roof repairs are done, we can arrange for the electrician to come in and do her bit.'

'Her?' Gavin asked.

'Harper Blake.'

'You're using *Bright Sparks*?'

'That's right. Is there a problem?'

'Not at all. She's a damned good sparky. I've worked on a couple of jobs with her dad.' Gavin drank the last of his tea. 'Back to it. Thanks for the tea.'

Bill watched him climb the ladder to the platform.

Jack squinted up at it. 'I offered to help, but he seems to be managing on his own.'

Not to be outdone, Bill said, 'I'd offer, but I can't climb a ladder. Not with my knees.' Constant up and down ship's ladders was what had buggered them up in the first place. He conveniently forgot about his advanced years and how unwise it would be to venture up a ladder when he was the wrong side of seventy.

Jack said, 'It's lucky Molly is at work, otherwise she'd be up there like a shot.'

'Not scared of getting her hands dirty, is that one.' Bill smiled fondly. 'I remember when I first saw her. She had just bought the cottage and I thought she was mad.'

'Oh, she's definitely mad, all right,' Jack smiled. 'I wouldn't want her any other way.'

Bill pressed his lips together, then gestured to the cafe and said, 'Do you think she'll make a go of it?'

'I *know* she will. Molly is one determined lady.'

'So I noticed.' Bill hesitated. 'It's just... Fiona seems to have set her heart on it, and I'd hate to see her disappointed.'

'She won't be.' Jack sounded confident.

Bill continued to stare at the roof, but his mind was elsewhere. 'I used to think she was a daft old biddy. I feel bad about that.'

Jack chuckled. 'I used to think Molly was a pain in the butt. Now, I think she's the most wonderful person in the world. How you feel about someone can change as you get to know them.'

How very true, Bill thought as he made his way home. His opinion of Fiona had certainly been flipped on its head this past week!

CHAPTER 9

Friday morning saw Fiona going to call for Bill. She had arranged for them to collect the *Name the Newt* entries, then pop into town to speak with Reverend Jenkins and ensure everything was tickety-boo for tomorrow. 'Tickety-boo' was a term Bradley used to use and it always made her chuckle, but she supposed that with Bill being a sea-faring man, she should say 'ship-shape' instead.

She was quite looking forward to seeing him. Although they had spoken on the phone when he'd rung on Sunday evening to tell her that the repairs to the roof had been completed, and she had phoned him to sort out the details for this morning, she hadn't seen him since the meal at Molly and Jack's house last Friday.

Strangely, she'd found she'd missed him, and she wondered whether they would have a bite to eat together today. She hoped so; she had thoroughly enjoyed lunch in the pub the other week, although it had occurred to her that she might have enjoyed the company more than the food.

It had been interesting getting to know him better, although she suspected she had only scratched the surface. Bill was a much more complex man than she'd first thought.

He was sitting on the low wall outside his house when she arrived, Patch lying at his feet, and she smiled a greeting, following it up with, 'How are you today?'

'Keen to get a look at these *Name the Newt* suggestions,' he said. 'I bet there are some right corkers.'

Fiona certainly hoped so, because all she had been able to come up with was Paul Newman. It wasn't particularly clever, and she had a feeling that most young people wouldn't have a clue who Paul Newman was.

The same woman was manning the primary school's reception desk as last time, and when she handed over several bags of money sorted into various denominations, Fiona's eyebrows shot up.

'How much is here?' she asked. 'Have you counted it?'

'We have, mainly because I need you to sign for it. I must say, this little competition of yours has proved to be very popular, and not just with the pupils. Most of the staff had a go, and we had to photocopy more leaflets because their parents had a go, too. Some of them had us laughing our heads off. There are quite a few duplicates, though.'

'I suppose there are only so many names for a newt,' Fiona said.

The secondary school was less productive, and Fiona assumed that newt naming might be beneath the older children. Still, she was impressed by the amount of money raised, and very grateful. All she hoped was that the jumble sale wouldn't be a total wash-out.

'Cor blimey, look at all that stuff!' Bill exclaimed when the vicar showed them into the hall.

Fiona's eyes widened. How were they going to sell all that?

Boxes and bags were piled high, and amongst them were toy pedal cars, pushchairs, a lawn mower and even a length of rolled-up carpet. People had patently brought what they could, and Fiona was very grateful; but would they *buy*?

She turned a worried gaze to Bill. 'Are we going to have time to sort this lot out in the morning? There's so much of it. I think we may need a few more people to set it all out, and before that we've got to price it.'

Reverend Jenkins came to their rescue. 'The hall is free for the rest of the day, so you can start now, if you want. I can give you a hand for an hour, which should be enough time to put the tables out, at least – if you're up for it, Bill? The trestle tables are kept in a room off the vestry. They're not heavy, just awkward.'

Bill drew himself up. 'I'm sure I can carry a table.'

The vicar rubbed his hands together. 'Great! That's settled. If Bill and I bring the first one out, perhaps you could begin sorting, Fiona?'

'Right you are.' Fiona tried to sound upbeat, but she was faintly alarmed by the size of the task in front of them. They would be here all day!

However, it soon became apparent that there were several categories of items, and when she came up with the idea of popping all the books on one table, all the ornaments on another, and so on, the job became that much easier. She wasn't looking forward to pricing it all up though, especially since they hadn't even thought about what they should be charging for things.

At some point after the vicar left, Bill insisted they stop for a break and Fiona realised she was starving. Breakfast seemed an awfully long time ago, and as she wasn't used to quite this level of busyness anymore, her stomach was now demanding to be fed.

'If you don't mind looking after Patch for a couple of minutes, I can pop out and get us something,' Bill suggested.

There was a bakery up the road which sold sandwiches and pasties, and she assumed that was where he was going, but he returned with something far more interesting – fish and chips, wrapped in paper and smelling so delicious she almost drooled.

'Couldn't resist,' he told her. 'I put salt and vinegar on yours. I hope that's OK. I noticed you putting some on your chips when we had that meal in the pub last week, so…'

'Perfect!'

'And I got us a can of lemonade each.'

'You are a lifesaver,' she declared, clearing a space on the nearest table, and dragging a couple of chairs towards it.

When Patch whined, Bill said, 'Don't worry, boy, I haven't forgotten you. I bought you a sausage.'

He started to unwrap their lunch and Fiona delved into her bag, bringing out a small bottle of antibacterial gel and offering him a splodge.

Hands now clean, she devoured the first chip, then flapped a hand in front of her mouth. Was there anything better than hot fluffy chips and succulent cod in batter?

'Hot,' she tried to say, and Bill chuckled.

As they ate, Fiona took stock of what they'd achieved so far. About a third of the bags and boxes were left, and Bill offered to see to those whilst she sorted through the tables to check whether any of the items could be set aside for the raffle. She had already added vouchers from the hairdresser and the pub, a bottle of champagne from the off-licence, a gift card from the beautician, and a pair of silver earrings that the jeweller had donated, when Fiona had taken Bradley's old watch in to be repaired.

She suddenly remembered that she still had a cake to bake, as well as cupcakes. Reverend Jenkins had kindly offered them the use of his urn, so Fiona was hoping to provide teas and coffees on the day, as well.

'Damn and blast,' she muttered, as she also remembered that she was supposed to be collecting a fruit basket from the grocers on the corner. There was still so much to do!

'Everything all right?' Bill asked, lifting a carriage clock out of a box.

Fiona pulled a face and told him, ending with, 'And we haven't put prices on anything yet.' She could feel herself beginning to get panicky.

Bill set the clock down and put his hands on his hips as he surveyed the hall. 'We need reinforcements. The vicar should be back soon – I'm sure he won't mind pitching in again. And Glenys has offered to lend a hand if we need it.'

I bet she has, Fiona thought, wondering how she could back-pedal. She could do without Glenys's help, thank you very much!

'I'll see what Molly and Jack are doing this evening,' she replied, and was relieved when Molly turned up ten minutes later in response to her phone call.

'Oh, my days! You've done a marvellous job!' Molly cried when she saw the hall. 'You get off home, Fiona. You too, Bill. I've taken an early finish, and Jack will be home from work soon. We'll do the rest. You must be exhausted.'

Fiona had to admit to feeling tired. She could do with a sit down, and a nap wasn't out of the question, either. She said as much to Bill as they made their way home, him insisting on walking her to her door, which she thought was rather sweet of him until he told her that Patch needed some off-lead time in the park. Then he redeemed himself by offering to help her with the baking.

'Thank you, that's very kind, but I can manage.' It wouldn't take her long to whip up a few dozen cupcakes, and now that Molly had taken over at the church hall, Fiona no longer felt as stressed. Baking was her comfort zone – jumble sales weren't.

When Fiona had first suggested it, she had no inkling that she and Bill would end up doing most of the organisation and the preparation. It had been her own choice, of course: she couldn't blame Molly. And it was fun, just hard work, which she wasn't used to anymore, that was all. And when Bill offered to drive her and her assorted baked goods to the church tomorrow, her forgiveness had turned into gratitude and a warm glow at his thoughtfulness.

Under that gruff exterior, Bill was a nice man. A very nice man indeed!

***

Fiona was in her element. She was manning the refreshment table and thoroughly enjoying herself, despite the growing ache in her feet and the knowledge that her back would undoubtedly complain about it later. As soon as the vicar had unlocked the church hall at two o'clock on the dot, there had been a steady trickle of people through its doors, the temptation of grabbing a bargain proving irresistible. And it only took one or two of the younger customers to notice the brightly iced cupcakes and to nag their parents for one, for sales of teas and coffees to gather momentum.

After a nap yesterday afternoon, Fiona had been keen to start baking, and she had ended up making more than she'd planned. As well as cupcakes decorated in varying shades of swirly buttercream icing and an assortment of sweets from Smarties to Jelly

Tots, Fiona had made Welsh cakes and flapjacks, finishing up with an iced red velvet cake for the raffle.

True to his word, Bill had loaded everything into his car this morning and had driven her to the venue, where Molly, Jack, and Reuben had been waiting to carry everything inside.

'How's it going?' Fiona asked Molly, who had been fizzing around for the past couple of hours, tidying the stalls and helping out where needed, whether it was taking the money, or refilling the urn with water.

'Busy.'

Fiona handed a mug of builder's tea to a man with a large bag of Lego under his arm. 'Help yourself to sugar,' she told him, indicating a plastic tub.

She was fast running out of clean teaspoons, and she glanced around at Bill, who was taking the money for the tea. 'Teaspoons,' she said.

Nodding, he gathered up the used ones and went out the back to the little kitchen, taking a couple of dirty mugs with him. Thank goodness there was a stack of them in the cupboard above the sink, otherwise she would have been forced to send someone out for more disposable ones, as the supply she had brought with her had quickly run out. As it was, she owed the vicar a box of tea bags because she had used the last of hers over half an hour ago, and still more people were arriving.

Whilst Bill was out the back rinsing off the teaspoons, Molly took over his cake-selling duties.

'I think I'd better buy a couple of these before they all go,' she said, putting two cupcakes to one side. 'They're going like *hot cakes*, he he he,' she added with a snigger.

Fiona rolled her eyes indulgently. Molly was a breath of fresh air, so full of life and enthusiasm. Fiona wished she had half her energy!

Bill returned to the table and Molly dashed off to sell more raffle tickets to the next influx of customers, leaving Fiona to deal with Madeleine, her next customer.

Fiona beamed at her. 'Hello!' she cried, hurrying around the table to give her a hug. Then she sobered. 'Sorry to hear you resigned.'

Madeleine's eyes narrowed. 'That damned woman. It's not as though I was leaving Pamela in the lurch or expecting to be paid for the time off. I'd arranged for someone to come in and cover for me. And it was hardly going to happen every week, was it? Kids only have a leaving ceremony once in primary school. By the way, both of mine have entered the *Name the Newt* competition.'

'Ooh, good luck. The winner will be announced at the end of the jumble sale, but don't worry if you can't hang around for it.'

'We only popped in on the way to the hairdresser. I'm desperate for a trim and so is Susie.'

Fiona glanced at Madeleine's eldest. 'Gosh, hasn't she grown!'

'They have a habit of doing that, don't they! I no sooner buy her a pair of school shoes, than she's grown out of them. Costs me a fortune, they do.'

'Have you got anything else lined up?' Fiona asked. 'Jobwise, I mean.'

Madeleine shook her head. 'Not yet. Pamela has kind of put me off.'

'I'm sure you'll find something suitable,' Fiona assured her as Madeleine said goodbye.

Fiona's gaze followed her, only snapping back when she realised someone was waiting to be served.

It was Glenys. Her eyes were on Bill. He was dealing with Ray and Mary Withers's little granddaughter, Tamsin, who couldn't decide whether to have a pink-iced cupcake or a purple one.

'What can I get you?' Fiona asked.

'He's so good with kiddies, isn't he?' Glenys crooned, her gaze remaining on Bill. 'It's a pity he never had any of his own, he would have made a lovely dad and grandad.' She tinkled out a laugh. 'He could borrow mine, if he fancies. I've got six grandkids, as you know.'

'Tea? Coffee?'

'Cappuccino, please.'

'We've only got instant. Sorry.'

Glenys grimaced. 'I suppose it'll have to do.'

Fiona bit her lip to keep a sarcastic retort in. She had never been rude to a customer, and she didn't intend to start now.

Glenys raised an eyebrow at the sight of the utilitarian white mug which had seen better days, and when she took a sip of the hot liquid, she grimaced again.

'Cake?' Fiona asked through gritted teeth. What did the woman expect? This was a jumble sale, for Pete's sake, not a blimmin' cafe.

Then her heart sank as an awful thought popped into her head. Would people assume that the standard of liquid refreshment here would reflect the standard of catering in Sweet Meadow Park's cafe? She flippin' hoped not!

Her thoughts flew to the tea dance next weekend, and she realised she would be using the same urn and the same scruffy white mugs, and serving the same instant coffee out of a jar.

Fiona tugged at Bill's arm. 'Bill? Bill! I need to find Molly. Can you manage on your own for five minutes?' She was aware that Glenys was staring at her, but she didn't care.

'Is everything all right?' he asked, concern etched across his face.

'I'm not sure.' Fiona glanced around the hall, searching for her. 'There she is! I'm just going to have a quick word. I won't be long.' As she hurried off, she heard Glenys call after her, 'Would you like me to step in for you? It's no bother,' but she didn't respond.

It made no difference what Fiona said; if Glenys wanted to help, then help Glenys would, no matter whether they wanted it or not.

Fiona reached Molly, who was about to announce the winners of the raffle, Reuben by her side. Hurriedly, she explained the coffee crisis and the mug disaster, then stood there worrying at her lip.

'I see the problem,' Molly said, looking equally concerned. Then her expression lifted. 'Why don't you have a look online this evening, and see if you can find some suitable china, cutlery, and so on. You'll have a much better idea of what's needed than me. We'll use some of the proceeds from the jumble sale to pay for it. We'll have to buy this stuff eventually, so we might as well do it now.'

'But what about the coffee itself? People will be expecting lattes and cappuccinos made with proper beans.'

'You can borrow my coffee machine,' Reuben said. 'It's got a milk frother, and it also grinds the beans.'

Fiona could have kissed him. 'You're a lifesaver!' she cried, then dashed back to Bill to share the news.

Delighted to discover that Glenys had wandered off in her absence, Fiona waited until the hubbub in the hall had quietened down as Molly announced the winners of the raffle, before she told Bill about the coffee machine, whispering in his ear.

'You'll have to teach me how to use it,' he whispered back. 'I've always wondered how they worked.'

'It's easy, as long as you make sure— Oh, hello again, Glenys. Are you after another cup of coffee?'

Glenys shuddered. 'Not likely! I've come to show you what I won in the raffle. Ta-dah!' She held up the bottle of bubbly. 'This is *so* me. I love champers. All I need is someone to drink it with.'

Fiona clenched her teeth as Glenys fluttered her mascara coated eyelashes. The flutter was blatantly aimed at Bill, but Bill didn't answer as Reuben chose that moment to call for quiet, leaving Fiona wondering whether he might have taken Glenys up on the offer.

'Now for the bit you've all been waiting for,' Reuben called. 'The *Name the Newt* competition.'

He was greeted by applause and whistles, plus more than a few froggy croaks from the back of the hall, made by people who didn't know the difference between a frog and a newt.

'We had some absolutely fantastic names,' he continued when the noise subsided, 'which made it very difficult to pick a winner. Quite a few of you suggested Sir Isaac Newton.' This was met with laughter and groans. 'Or Olivia Newton-John. What about Abbot – short for Newton Abbot?'

More groans followed that one.

'And to the child who thought Stinkybutt was a good idea, I'm not sure I want to tell people I need to catch Stinkybutt for his annual check-up. Molly particularly liked Newty McNewtface and I also liked Macbeth – eye of newt, double, double, toil and trouble? Geddit?'

Fiona noticed a couple of puzzled looks, and guessed that the Shakespeare allusion had passed them by.

'But the winner is...' He paused, letting the silence and the anticipation stretch. Then with a flourish, he announced, 'Tiny! And if any of you are wondering why we are calling a great crested newt, the largest species of newt in the UK, *Tiny,* it's because it's a play on words – my newt... mi-nute... *minute*? Get it?'

Clever, Fiona thought, as the groans were only just exceeded by the laughter.

'Several people came up with this idea, so I've put everyone's names in a hat. Molly, do you want to draw the winner's name out? They don't win anything, you understand, apart from the honour of putting the plaque up.'

Reuben produced a bobble hat out of his pocket which contained several folded pieces of paper. Molly stepped forward and dipped her hand in. She pulled one out and gave it to Reuben.

He cleared his throat. 'The winner is... Liam Evans!'

Fiona was astounded. Who'd have thought that the boy would even participate in the competition? She would have assumed he'd think it deeply uncool and beneath him. Mind you, she would never have thought that Liam would be a lynchpin in the park's clean-up operation, but he had. So maybe he wasn't the yob she had assumed.

And if someone like Liam, who'd had scant respect for Sweet Meadow Park previously, was getting involved in it, then maybe there *was* hope for the cafe yet.

CHAPTER 10

'This is a nice surprise,' Fiona said, for probably the third time since Bill had picked her up in his car this morning, and he smiled. It warmed his heart to think how happy a little trip out made her. He hadn't seen her for a couple of days, not since the jumble sale, because having been in each other's pockets all day Friday and most of Saturday, he'd assumed she could do with a break from him.

He had also felt quite tired Sunday and hadn't been up for doing more than walking Patch or slumping in front of the telly. He had felt livelier yesterday, but had spent the day catching up on chores, of which there had been several, and working in his garden.

Today, however, he had woken up full of beans and wanting to make the most of the day and do something different, so when he took Patch for an early walk to stretch his legs, he debated what he could do for a change. As usual, he was tempted to head to the coast, but the thought of exploring somewhere like Abergavenny or Hay-on-Wye also appealed. Both were market towns, set in glorious countryside. Then he remembered something he'd read, and he knew where he wanted to go – Brecon. Like the other two, it was a small town near the border with England, and like the others it was nestled in the bottom of a lush valley which was surrounded by mountains. But Brecon had something the others didn't – boat trips along the canal.

In the past Bill had found that going places on one's own (even with Patch) hadn't been as much fun as he'd anticipated, and although he had enjoyed himself, it wasn't quite the same as sharing it with someone, whether it was a lovely view or a nice meal.

As he'd strolled through the meadow, he wondered whether Fiona would like to join him, so as soon as he got back from his walk he had given her a call. She had seemed rather taken aback when he'd said he was off to Brecon and wanted to know whether she would like to come with him, but she readily agreed.

'I haven't been to Brecon for years,' she repeated now, having said the same thing on the phone. She was sitting in the passenger seat of his car, gazing at the scenery with a smile on her face. They were currently pootling along the A470, which was the main trunk road from Cardiff in the south, to the pretty market town of Brecon on the other side of the famous mountain range where the SAS trained.

Bill smiled to himself as he thought of the surprise in store for her. First though, there was some stunning scenery to enjoy as the road wound its way through the mountain pass.

'Ooh! Look at all those people,' Fiona cried, pointing to the right, and Bill risked a glance to see a line of people hiking up a mountain track. From the road they looked tiny, putting the size of the mountain into perspective. He didn't envy them the trek.

'They're going up to the summit of Pen Y Fan,' he said. 'Have you ever been to the top?'

'Not on your life! It's too steep and too far for me. David hiked up there when he did his Duke of Edinburgh Award in school. He said the view from the top was awesome, but I've never been tempted. Have you?'

'I've been to the top once or twice when I was younger. Not up for it now, obviously.' His knees wouldn't thank him for it.

Fiona laughed. It was a light, carefree sound, and he chuckled in response. They hadn't arrived at Brecon yet and he was already having more fun than he'd had since— Ah, best not go there. Those memories were better off not being aired, especially not today.

As they dropped down into the wide valley where Brecon nestled, Fiona's thoughts moved away from hiking up the third highest peak in Wales. 'I still can't believe how much the jumble sale raised. We did a good job, didn't we?'

'We certainly did.'

'I hope the tea dance is as successful.'

'It will be.' He noticed her nibbling her bottom lip out of the corner of his eye. 'Almost all the tickets have been sold,' he reminded her, in case she was worried about the turnout.

'It's not that, it's...' She trailed off.

'The catering?' he guessed, knowing how important it was to her to make an impression. The future of the cafe in the park might depend on it. He didn't know what she was so concerned about, she was a brilliant baker and a fantastic cook.

She nodded. 'I'm out of practice.'

Bill snorted. 'You could have fooled me! Look at all those cakes you baked for the jumble sale.'

'That was different.'

'In what way? Because it was just a jumble sale and not a *tea dance*?' He emphasised the last two words. 'It'll probably be many of the same people there, Fi. Half of Sweet Meadow must have turned up on Saturday.'

Fi... he had called her *Fi*, not Fiona. He hoped she didn't mind the familiarity.

'I suppose you're right,' she conceded.

'And you know most of them. Heck, you probably know *all* of them. And they know you. You've been serving them for decades.'

Fiona harrumphed. 'Stop it with the decades.' But there was a smirk on her lips.

Dropping down out of the mountains, the road levelled off as they entered the outskirts of the pretty market town, and Bill fell silent as he concentrated on negotiating the traffic, arriving at the car park with a sigh of relief. He'd never been much of a driver – having spent most of his life onboard ship – and navigating unfamiliar streets was stressful, but he'd got them there in one piece and now he could relax.

'Oh, how pretty!' Fiona exclaimed as she spotted the start of the canal with its small boats and barges moored up. The Monmouthshire and Brecon Canal originated at this point, meandering through thirty-five miles of verdant countryside, and the Brecon stretch was particularly popular. Bill had chosen this car park for that very reason.

After finding a space and unclipping Patch from his seatbelt harness, Bill suggested a quick look around the town, then lunch in one of the many cafes.

'Or we could go to the Castle Hotel? I've been told it's very good.' They had outside tables, so hopefully

Patch would be welcome. He kicked himself for not checking beforehand.

'A cafe will be fine.' Fiona took his arm as they walked down the side street from the parking area to the main part of the town.

It was years since Bill had been here (not since he was a schoolboy) and he was relieved to find that it hadn't changed much. It still sported quirky independent shops and had a bustling atmosphere, although he hadn't appreciated it at the time.

Fiona paused to stare through the window of an art gallery. 'I like that one,' she said, pointing to an oil painting of a coastline. 'And that.'

They must all be by the same artist, Bill thought, noticing the similarities in style and composition. They were very good; expensive though, and he had nowhere to hang one, as all of them were quite large. Anyway, they would look out of place in his old-fashioned house.

They moved on, strolling along the street, happily window shopping. Bill didn't need anything, but it was a nice change being somewhere different. And it was even nicer being there with Fiona.

Her pleasure was lovely to see. She kept pointing things out, chattering away, her face shining. He was very aware of the arm which she had threaded through his and having her by his side gave him a warm feeling.

After a nice wander around the stalls in the market hall, plus a nose in an antique shop (with Patch safety tucked under Bill's arm, in case the dog happened to bump into something), they were ready for lunch.

A cafe with planters outside which were filled with colourful flowers drew them in, especially since a sign in the window proclaimed that dogs were welcome. After finding a vacant table and perusing the menu, Bill went up to the counter to place their order.

'What can I get you?' a smiling lady asked, looking up as she slid a delicious-looking scone onto a plate.

'One smoked salmon on a brioche roll, and a fried chicken burger, please.'

'Can I get you any drinks to go with it?'

'Tea, for me, please.'

'And for your wife?'

Taken by surprise, Bill blurted, 'Oh, Fiona isn't my wife. She's just a friend.'

But there was no *just* about it. It occurred to him that he was beginning to think of her as a very dear friend, and as he turned around to ask her what she would like to drink, his heart skipped a beat.

Patch was perched on Fiona's lap, and they were nose to nose as the terrier stared into her eyes. Her lips were moving and although Bill couldn't hear what she was saying, Patch seemed to like it. His tail was wagging, and his ears were pricked.

Seeing the pair of them together like that, no one could be blamed for thinking that Fiona was Patch's person. The dog adored her, and she seemed quite smitten with Patch. Far from feeling put out or usurped, Bill was gladdened, and it warmed his heart. Patch was a good judge of character and he clearly thought the world of Fiona. Ever since she and Bill had decided to work together on the reopening of the cafe, the dog always greeted Fiona with excited whimpers and lots of ecstatic tail wagging.

Whilst Bill waited for their drinks (the food would be delivered to their table when it was ready), his attention kept straying to his companion. Once more he thought what an attractive woman she was. She must have been quite a catch in her day. Heck, she still was! Any man would be proud to have her on his arm.

He returned to their table, carefully balancing the tray with their drinks on it, and set it down. She popped Patch back on the floor, but not before she had bestowed a kiss on the dog's furry little head. Patch's happy smile seemed to echo Fiona's beaming grin.

'This is getting to be a habit,' she said, pouring the tea.

'A good one, I hope?'

'Definitely. Let's continue to have a meal out now and again, after we're done with fundraising.'

'Yes, let's. Although, you might be sick of food once the cafe is up and running.'

'Don't you believe it! I'll be too busy making and serving the sandwiches and cakes, to be able to eat them. Besides, I'll want to be waited on for a change.'

Bill stirred his tea, thinking. 'I suggest we combine it with a day out somewhere. There are so many lovely places within an hour's drive from Sweet Meadow.'

'That would be marvellous.'

Just then their food arrived and conversation halted for a while as they tucked in, and as he ate Bill discovered that he was very much looking forward to continuing their friendship, and another day out would be smashing. Hopefully today's outing would be the first of many.

'There's more tea in the pot,' Fiona said. 'Fancy a top-up? And maybe a slice of cake for afters?'

Bill scrambled to think of a reason to refuse. 'Not for me thanks,' he replied, hoping she wouldn't have one if he didn't, and adding for good measure, 'They looked a bit stale to me.' He whispered this last bit, worried that someone might overhear. The cakes actually looked delicious, but having one now would scupper his plans.

Her face fell. 'That's a shame.'

When they retraced their steps to the car park, Bill sensed a vague disappointment emanating from her, and he guessed she wasn't ready to go home just yet but didn't like to say anything.

On reaching the area where the Brecon Canal began, Bill suggested a quick stop to admire the boats that were moored up. With pretty cottages on the one side of the water, and a building that housed a theatre and a cafe on the other which also had outdoor seating, the area was busy with people enjoying the view.

Checking his watch, Bill led Fiona nearer to the boats. A couple of barges were tied up, their long narrow shapes reminiscent of a bygone age, alongside some smaller vessels.

'This must be small fry to you,' she joked, eyeing the boats. 'Oh, look, they hire them out.'

'They also do trips,' he said, reaching for her hand. 'Come on, let's go on one.'

Fiona hung back. 'Don't you have to book?'

His smile was wide. 'I already have. We're going on a two-hour punt along the canal, with drinks and cakes included.'

She halted, pulling free and putting her hands on her hips. Narrowing her eyes, she said, 'There wasn't anything wrong with those cakes, was there?'

'No.'

'That was sneaky!'

He made a face and began to turn away. 'If you don't want to go—'

'I do!' she cried, digging him in the ribs with her elbow.

Laughing, he grabbed her hand again. Today was proving to be even more fun than he'd hoped, and he was enjoying himself immensely. That the enjoyment had a great deal to do with the woman whose hand he was clasping so tightly, wasn't something he wanted to think about too deeply right now…

CHAPTER 11

The narrowboats were rather quaint, but Bill led her towards one of the smaller vessels. Unlike the barge which had seating for at least sixty people, this one would just be him, Fiona and the skipper. Bill had considered the barge, but with the inside being enclosed, (although there were windows running the full length on both sides) he wanted Fiona to have more of a view.

The boat he had chosen certainly had that, he thought, as he settled her into a seat at the prow and sat next to her with Patch in between them.

It was only when the skipper was handed a coolbox and had given him a nod, that Bill realised how intimate this trip was going to be, and he wondered whether he had done the right thing in hiring a private charter. It was considerably more romantic than being in a barge along with loads of other people, which wasn't his intention at all. Bill didn't do romance. He hadn't done romance since…

He gave himself a mental shake. Best not to think about that.

Fretting that Fiona might think this was more than a couple of friends enjoying a day out, he lied gruffly, 'I tried to get us on the barge, but it was fully booked.'

Fiona replied, 'I'm glad. This is so much nicer. I wouldn't want to be packed in like a sardine. And we get to sit at the front.' Her face was alight with pleasure, and he was so pleased he'd thought of it this morning.

'Next time we'll go to the seaside,' he said.

'More boats?' she guessed.

'Or just a stroll along the front with an ice cream.' Boats weren't everyone's cup of tea. Fiona may be happy being on a canal's slow still waters, but a choppy sea ride was an altogether different prospect.

Just being at the beach with the smell of the sea in his nostrils, the sound of the waves and the gulls, and the taste of salt on his lips, would be enough. He didn't need to feel the rise and fall of the ocean under his feet.

'And fish and chips,' he added.

'Ooh, yes! There's nothing nicer than fish and chips at the seaside.'

'Except for coffee and cake on the canal?' he teased.

'Except for that,' she agreed as the boat chugged away from its mooring, gliding under the first of what

Bill assumed would be several bridges. It was a beautiful stone arch and he wondered how old it was. Last century, certainly.

Once they had cleared the canal basin and were on the canal proper, it felt like they were in a different world. Gone was the lively bustle of the cafe with its outdoor seating, and in its place were leafy trees bordering the one bank, and open fields on the other. Walkers strolled along the towpath, stepping aside for the occasional cyclist, and now and again another boat passed them going in the opposite direction.

Suddenly Fiona gasped and gripped his arm as a tunnel appeared up ahead. As tunnels went, it wasn't a particularly long one and Bill could see through to the other end. However, it was narrow, with room for only one vessel at a time, and on the right-hand side was a raised walkway with a steel railing to prevent pedestrians from toppling into the water.

'I don't think I would like to walk through that!' she exclaimed.

Their skipper said, 'It's not so bad. Only takes a few minutes.' His voice bounced off the walls of the tunnel as he steered the boat through it, and Bill could hear the faint rumble of traffic from the road overhead. They were soon out the other side and into the sunshine once more.

Going through a lock was fascinating, and although he had navigated a ship through the IJmuiden marine lock, which served the Port of Amsterdam and was the largest sea lock in the world, this little lock seemed more real somehow. Barges and other canal craft had used this lock for over two hundred years, and Bill felt strangely humbled to think that in another two hundred years a couple just like him and Fiona could be sitting in a little boat and doing the exact same thing.

No sooner were they out of the lock with its steep sides, than the boat was high in the air as it travelled across the Brynich Aqueduct, a length of the canal that traversed the River Usk. The canal narrowed considerably at this point, and it almost felt like they were floating, with the chasm and the rushing river beneath. Bill wasn't too bothered, but he sensed Fiona's relief when the boat exited the aqueduct and there was firm ground on both sides once more.

After steering the boat towards the bank, the skipper cut the engine and jumped out. He was holding a rope which he tied around a mooring point. Then he hopped back on board, opened the coolbox and produced a bottle.

'It isn't wine,' Bill hastened to inform Fiona, in case she might think he was wooing her. 'It's sparkling juice. It was either that, or a can of pop. The boat doesn't have the facility to make hot drinks.'

'This one is apple and white grape,' the skipper said, 'or we have passion fruit and mango.' He held a second bottle aloft, the glass beaded with condensation.

They both opted for the apple and white grape, Bill because it seemed the most like a white wine. Whilst they sipped their drinks and nibbled on a selection of bite-sized cakes, (Bill had brought a bowl, water and some dog treats for Patch) they gazed at the view. Right now, their boat was the only one in sight, and apart from a jogger running along the towpath, they had this little stretch of the canal all to themselves.

'It's so tranquil,' Fiona sighed. She looked the happiest Bill had ever seen her. 'I can't believe you planned all this. It's so lovely of you.'

'I thought we could both do with a treat after our hard work over the past couple of weeks. You, especially.'

'And it's not over yet,' she reminded him, selecting a morsel of cake and popping it into her mouth. 'I've got so much baking to do.'

'I suppose this,' he gestured to the almost empty plate, 'must be like a busman's holiday to you.'

Fiona giggled. 'In the same way that being on a boat on a canal is a busman's holiday for *you?*'

'You've got me there,' he laughed. 'Do you need any help with the baking? Or sandwich making? I can butter bread with the best of them, and I still need to learn how to use the coffee machine.'

'That would be wonderful, thank you. I must admit to feeling a little overwhelmed.'

'You'll be fine.'

She straightened her shoulders. 'I know I will, but it's going to take me a while to get into the swing of things again.'

'Molly is sorting out volunteers to help man the cafe, isn't she?'

'Apparently so, but I'm not sure how reliable volunteers will be. At least if someone is being paid, there's more of a commitment. I just wish the cafe could support more than one paid position.'

'Maybe it will in time.'

'I hope so.'

'In the meantime, you can count on me – if Patch is welcome, of course.'

'I'm sure he will be. Plenty of eateries have resident dogs. As long as he stays away from the food prep area, it should be fine.'

They finished off the remainder of their sparkling juice as the boat glided serenely back to its mooring in Brecon, Bill musing on what a lovely time he'd had. He should definitely do this kind of thing more often. Although nothing had prevented him from going on day trips like this by himself, it wasn't the same doing it on his own, which was why he rarely bothered. It was far nicer when you have someone to enjoy it with, he thought. It was just a shame that he and Fiona hadn't become friends sooner – look at how much fun he'd missed out on. Fiona too, he suspected.

Neither of them spoke much on the drive back, but the lack of conversation didn't feel awkward. If truth be told, it felt perfectly natural, and it was rather peaceful to be with someone who didn't feel the need to fill every second with chatter.

Pulling up outside Fiona's front door, Bill did the gentlemanly thing and switched off the engine, getting out of the car before she had managed to gather up her bag and cardigan. But on opening the passenger door, he noticed her eyes widen and she seemed flustered.

Stuttering, she said, 'I... er, oh, didn't expect you would, um, want to come in.'

Bill was confused. Whatever had given her that idea? 'I wasn't planning on it,' he said. 'I've got to water my garden. Thanks for the offer, though.'

She sagged a little and her face cleared. 'I see! Oh, my, I thought... Oh, dear, never mind.'

'Do you *want* me to come in?' By now Bill was thoroughly perplexed. He was happy to pop in for a cuppa if she wanted him to, but he couldn't stay for long. He had his tea to cook and his veggie patch to see to.

'If you like.'

Bill had only intended to drop her off, but she didn't appear to want the day to end. Or – a thought struck him – perhaps she felt obliged to invite him in out of politeness. Was this what friends did these days? Was this an accepted practice that had passed him by? He sometimes wondered whether he had spent too long at sea: maybe this confirmed it?

Fiona was looking at him expectantly, and he realised she was waiting for an answer.

'I can't stop long,' he warned. 'I've got Patch to think about. He'll need to stretch his paws.' That was a euphemism for Patch needing a wee.

'He can have a run around my garden.'

Patch was thrilled. He leapt out, his tail wagging, a happy smile on his face as Fiona unlocked her front door. Without the slightest regard for manners, the terrier pushed past her legs and shot off down the hall.

'He can smell my beef hotpot,' Fiona said, turning to Bill with a smile.

He gave a rueful grin in return. 'That dog's got no manners.'

Bill followed Fiona into the kitchen and saw Patch sitting in front of the kitchen cupboard, on top of which sat a slow cooker. He was staring up at it intently, one paw raised.

'I think he's saying please,' Fiona said.

'He can say please as much as he likes, the cheeky little blighter. I've got some leftover chicken that needs using up,' Bill said. 'He can have some of that.'

'He's welcome to have some hotpot, and so are you. It should be cooked by now. I put it on this morning, just after you phoned. I didn't know how long we'd be out, and I thought it would be nice to come home to a meal that was already cooked.'

It sure would be, Bill thought, sniffing the air appreciatively and wishing he had thought of that. Mind you, he didn't own a slow cooker, so it was a moot point.

He said, 'I was going to have chicken. I'll add it to a jar of curry and do myself some oven chips.' It didn't sound nearly as appealing now that he'd caught a sniff of beef hotpot.

'Leftover chicken?'

He nodded.

'Sit yourself down,' Fiona instructed. 'You're having tea with me. It's the least I can do after such a lovely day out.'

'What about my veggies? They need watering.'

'Will they mind if you're an hour late?'

'I doubt it.' He felt a smile creep across his face.

'Well, then. Say no more.'

Bill didn't. Leftover chicken couldn't compete with the mouthwatering aroma filling the kitchen. So he stayed for tea and thoroughly enjoyed every morsel.

It was as he was helping Fiona clear the table after they'd eaten, that she said, 'Do you think we'll ever do something together that doesn't involve food?'

Bill had no idea where his next thought came from, or why he'd thought it in the first place, but out of the blue he imagined the two of them cuddling up on the sofa, with not as much as a Custard Cream or a Bourbon biscuit in sight.

Blinking it away, he said, 'The cinema?'

'Popcorn. You've got to have popcorn at the cinema.'

'A nice long walk?'

'Tea and cake at the end of it. It's the law.'

'Shopping?'

She giggled. 'Coffee and cake, because you need a break halfway through.'

'A visit to a museum,' he began, then halted. 'Don't tell me, there will be a cafe on site.'

'Of course!'

'A stroll around the park?'

'There'll be a cafe in it soon. You do see my point though, don't you? Everything involves food at some point.'

'Which bodes well for the cafe,' he pointed out.

'I suppose it does.'

'And I suppose I'd better get off home.' He called Patch to him.

The dog was sprawled in the living room, availing himself of the comfort of the rug in front of the mantelpiece, but he leapt to his feet at the sound of his name and trotted into the hall.

'Thank you so much for a lovely, lovely day,' Fiona said, seeing him to the door. 'I've had a wonderful time.'

'Thank you for accompanying me,' Bill replied.

Fiona's face had been wreathed in smiles, but her expression became more solemn. 'Would you have still gone if I hadn't come with you?'

'Probably not.'

'I thought as much. You can call on me anytime, Bill. I hope you know that. And not just for days out.'

He nodded slowly but couldn't think of anything to say in response.

So, for a second time, he kissed her cheek.

The brief contact made his lips tingle, and a shaft of longing went through him. She looked surprised. Bill was surprised, as well. He had never been one for displays of affection. Not since…

Bill stiffened. He didn't want to think about his ex-fiancée, not after such a lovely day. And certainly not when he was in Fiona's presence.

It didn't seem right somehow, but he couldn't think why.

CHAPTER 12

Fiona had just slid another tray of scones into the oven when the doorbell rang. Wiping her hands on a towel, she hurried to answer it.

Bill saluted her. 'Reporting for duty, ma'am!' he joked, as Patch darted inside.

'Why don't you come in, Patch?' she called to the dog, rolling her eyes and chuckling.

Bill stepped across the threshold, hesitated, then pecked her on the cheek.

'How have you been?' she asked. She hadn't seen him or spoken to him since Tuesday and their trip to Brecon, and she wondered what he had been doing with himself.

'Grand. And you?'

'Busy. Reuben dropped his coffee machine off yesterday, so I spent an hour working out how to use it and making loads of cups of coffee. I was buzzing by the end of it. And then I went shopping for all the ingredients.'

Bill slapped a hand to his forehead. 'I hope you didn't carry it up from town. I'm sorry, I should have offered to come with you. I didn't think of it.'

'No need to worry, I got a taxi back.'

He continued to look mortified, so she thought the best thing to do was to set him to work. Being useful would make him feel better, so she handed him a pinny to pop over his head and tie around his waist.

After washing their hands and popping on some catering gloves, the two of them stood side-by-side at the worktop and set about buttering bread. Molly had informed Fiona that all the tickets had now been sold, so she knew she had to cater for around one hundred and forty people altogether. Calculating how much food she would need to prepare was second nature, and she could guess almost to the slice just how many loaves of bread she would need, and how many cakes and pastries she would have to bake.

Making the fillings for the dainty sandwiches, such as smoked salmon, coronation chicken, and cream cheese and cucumber for the vegetarians, was the first thing she did. Then she made caramelised onion & thyme sausage rolls, mini quiches, and pea and mint fritters, and she did all that before eight o'clock this morning.

She had just started on the sweet offerings when Bill turned up to make the sandwiches.

As he buttered slice after slice of bread, Fiona saw him glancing around her kitchen. Every available surface was covered with cooling savoury bites.

'Did you make this lot, or buy it?' he asked, his eyes like saucers.

Pretending to take offence, she said, 'How dare you! I made them, of course. There'll be no shop-bought muck at my tea dance.'

She saw him wince, then he realised she was teasing him and he chuckled, laughing aloud when she showed him a printed card that she had persuaded Reuben to make. It said, *A selection of the home-made sandwiches, cakes and savouries which will be available from the cafe in Sweet Meadow Park. Opening soon.*

'You can't beat some free advertising,' she said.

She'd thought of it when Reuben had phoned to tell her he was bringing the coffee machine over, and she'd asked him if he wouldn't mind creating a card for her to display on the buffet table. He had made two, bless him, one for each end, and had brought a couple of wooden stands to prop them up on. He really was a sweetie.

Bill was also proving to be a godsend as he made sandwich after sandwich, cutting them neatly into perfect triangles and placing them carefully into

Tupperware boxes. She would arrange them nicely on serving platters at the venue.

In between supervising the sandwich making, Fiona baked batches of cakes, and soon there was a conveyor belt of them in and out of the oven. When she took the last batch out, she breathed a sigh of relief, wiping the back of a floury hand across her brow as Bill asked, 'Are we done?'

'Just about.' She checked the time. The tea dance was due to start at three o'clock. It was now twelve-thirty. There was plenty of time for the cakes to cool (she needed to add frosting or glaze to a couple of them, and a filling to others), and to transfer all the food to the church hall, as well as to have a bit of lunch. She also wanted to change into something more appropriate than jeans and a top, although she would be wearing a fresh apron over her dress.

'What's next?' Bill asked.

She was about to tell him that a break for a cuppa and some food was in order, when she became aware that he was peering at her intently.

He stepped towards her, his eyes on her face, and although they had worked together side-by-side in the relatively small confines of her galley kitchen for the past couple of hours, she became abruptly aware of his presence. He seemed to fill the space, and suddenly she couldn't breathe. It was as though the air had been sucked out of the room.

He was now so close that she could smell the soap he used, and she swallowed hard. Oh, God, was he going to kiss her?

He raised a hand to her face, and she steeled herself for his touch. She wasn't ready for this. She—

'Got it!' he announced.

He showed her his finger: it had a blob of buttercream on the end.

Fiona stared at it.

'You might want to give your face a wipe,' he added, as he swilled his hands under the tap.

Drawing in a shaky breath, Fiona willed her pulse to slow down. It was going like the clappers and was making her feel rather lightheaded.

Goodness, what had she been thinking? Bill would no more dream of kissing her, than *she* would dream of kissing *him*. The fact that she had thought (even briefly) that he might, unsettled her, and it took her a few moments to gather her wits.

She hurried off to the loo to wash her face, her heart continuing to beat faster than usual. And the reason for that was even more concerning – because she was horrified to discover that she was *disappointed* that he hadn't! Not having thought about another man in that way since Bradley died, Fiona couldn't understand how she could feel like this.

Flustered, she walked back into the kitchen and hoped that Bill wouldn't notice her discomfort.

Without meeting his eye, she said, 'Shall I make us an omelette? We had better have lunch before the dance.'

'How about a sandwich?' he asked deadpan, and it took her a second to realise he was joking. Whether he meant it to or not, it dispelled the awkwardness she felt, and lunch ended up being quite a calm affair after the frantic activity of earlier.

And now, with the kitchen being more or less clean and tidy, it was time to show Bill how to operate the coffee machine, before they loaded everything into his car.

'Will the machine in the cafe be similar to this?' he asked, as Fiona watched him make a second latte, this time on his own without her showing him what to do.

'I'm hoping to be able to use the one already there. It's a bit of a museum piece, but once the rewiring is done, I'll get someone out to service it and with any luck they'll be able to get it going. It's such a lovely old thing and part of the history of the place, so I'd hate to have to replace it.'

'I wondered why the electrician hadn't removed it. She was there this morning, when I took Patch for a walk.'

'How long before she's done?'

'Another couple of days, I think. I stopped to have a quick chat, and she said she was squeezing in an hour before she had to go see someone about connecting up a cooker.'

'It's so good of her to do the work for cost,' Fiona said. 'I can't believe how generous people have been. Everyone seems to be looking forward to having a cafe in the park again. I just hope I don't let them down.'

'Never!' Bill glared at her. 'If anyone can make a go of the cafe, it's you. There's no better person to run it.' He sounded so adamant, that Fiona had to smile, despite her nerves.

Maybe she would feel more confident when the tea dance was done and dusted.

***

Fiona paused to watch a lively foxtrot as she ferried a plate of savouries from the compact kitchen out the back and into the hall.

Mrs Sykes from Rock Street was teaching Jack to dance. Or should Fiona say *trying to*, because Jack seemed to have two left feet and he appeared to have no control over either. The pair of them were laughing fit to burst, so if they were having a good time, it honestly didn't matter. Molly was filming it on her phone but was hardly able to hold the mobile steady because she was giggling so much.

Molly's mum and dad had also come along, as had Molly's gran, Evelyn. Evelyn Brown used to call into Clover Cafe every Monday, Wednesday and Friday morning after she'd done her shopping, but Fiona hadn't seen her for a long time and she was pleased to see how well the old lady looked. She was a bit too doddery to dance, which wasn't surprising since she was nearly ninety, but she was tapping her foot in time to the music and swaying from side to side as though she was up there in the thick of it.

She also noticed Bill's neighbours, Ray and Mary Withers, twirling around the dance floor in perfect synchronisation. They had evidently danced a few jigs together!

Bill appeared at Fiona's elbow. 'Everyone seems to be having a whale of a time, even Patch.' The dog was lying under a chair, well away from the buffet table in case anyone complained. So far, no one had, and the terrier had enjoyed plenty of pats and fussing.

The hall was filled with music and chatter, and as far as she could tell most people had got up for a dance or two. Fiona thought she might have a spin around the room herself later, once the food was eaten and if she could find someone who wanted to dance with her.

She placed the serving platter on the table with the others and stood back to admire the buffet. It looked pretty good, she thought, checking her watch. She caught Molly's eye and nodded to signify that the buffet was set up if Molly wanted to call a break for refreshments.

The dance came to an end and as the music faded Molly made the announcement. With Bill on tea-making duty, Fiona on the coffee machine, and Molly and Jack on the cold drinks, the next ten minutes were busy, but when the rush subsided and Fiona was able to take stock, she was gratified to see that great inroads had been made into the buffet. And when she glanced at the people sitting at the tables dotted around the room, they all appeared to be enjoying the food.

All except one. Pamela Edwards had a look of disgust on her face as she glared at the contents of her plate, and as Fiona watched, the woman prised open a sandwich and poked at the filling with a bony finger.

Bill was also watching her. 'What's the saying – never trust a thin chef?'

Fiona glanced at him. 'I hope you trust *me*.'

'Of course I do!'

'So, are you saying I'm plump?' She was, and she didn't care, but the opportunity to tease him was too good to pass up.

'I would never—!' he began, then stopped when he saw her smirk and any further discussion was halted by Ralph Curtis, who wanted to know whether he could have seconds.

Fiona said, 'I don't see why not, and I'd hate for any of it to go to waste.'

'Stunning spread, Fiona,' he said, helping himself to another sandwich. 'Me and the missus were saying how lush it looked, and it tastes even better than it looks. I'd forgotten how moreish your scones are.'

'Those sausage rolls are to die for,' someone else said, eyeing them hopefully. 'Can I have another?'

'Help yourself.' Fiona picked up the platter and held it out.

The chap said, 'Will you be making full-sized versions?'

'Absolutely. Everything you see here will be available in the cafe.'

A woman approached carrying a cup and saucer. 'Any chance of a refill?'

Bill took it from her. 'Tea, wasn't it?'

'That's right, love. Lady Gray.' As he found the right tea bag, the woman said, 'I'm glad the cafe in the park is reopening. No one can make a pasty like you can. I used to call in every Friday, if you remember.'

Fiona did, but she couldn't put a name to the face. 'Lovely to see you again,' she replied diplomatically.

'What times will it be open, do you know?' This was from the sausage roll man. 'And will you be open in the winter as well, or will it just be a summer thing?'

Fiona felt herself getting panicky again.

Luckily for her, Bill noticed and stepped in. 'Let's get the repairs done and the place up and running, then we can look at opening times.'

'*We?*' Pamela Edwards snapped.

Fiona's heart sank. 'Hello, Pamela. I hadn't expected to see you here. I didn't think this was your kind of thing.'

'It isn't.' Pamela glared at her. 'But with half my customers buying a ticket, I thought I'd better see what all the fuss was about. It's something of nothing, if you ask me.'

It was hard not to snap that no one *had* asked her, but Fiona bit down on the comment.

Pamela continued, 'I'm surprised the council is letting you go ahead with opening the cafe again.' She glowered at the card Reuben had made. 'There was a reason it shut down in the first place.'

'It's not my doing,' Fiona said. 'It's Molly's.'

'I might have known. She's got the council's ear, and a lot more besides.' Another glare, this time directed at Jack.

Fiona bristled. 'It's all above board.'

'I bet.' Sarcasm dripped from Pamela's lips. 'It isn't what you know, it's *who* you know. Oh well, I dare say it'll only be open on those days when the weather is nice, and even then it won't get much trade. That park is hardly Kew Gardens. If you ask me, it's a bloody eyesore.'

Once again Fiona had to bite her tongue, but Pamela hadn't finished.

'I'm surprised you want to get involved in it, at your age.' She began to walk away, then stopped. 'Good luck. I reckon you're going to need it.' And with that, she stalked off. She didn't return to her table. Instead, she marched to the door, yanked it open and let it slam shut behind her.

Bill came to stand beside Fiona. Putting his arm around her shoulder, he gave her a swift one-armed hug before releasing her. 'Sour grapes, Fi?'

'Possibly, but there's no reason for it. The cafe in the park is no threat to her. Best Bites is in the centre of town.'

'I'm sure she'll come around.'

Fiona hoped so. The last thing she wanted was bad blood between the two establishments.

She was still fretting about it when the music grew louder, signalling the end of the break. It was time to clear up, and Fiona had just started stacking the empty plates, when Bill took them from her and put them on the table.

'I think we deserve to have a dance after all our hard work,' he told her, reaching for her hand. 'Come on, they're doing a waltz.'

'Can I take my apron off first?' she asked, laughing.

'Keep it on: it looks quite fetching.'

Fiona undid the ties. 'If you think I'm going to dance with a pinny on, you can think again.' She lifted it over her head, dropped it on the table, then smoothed her dress over her ample hips.

'Ready now?' he asked, holding his hand out again.

She took it. 'I haven't danced for years,' she warned him. 'I hope you've got steel toecaps on.'

'I'm more likely to tread on *your* toes,' he replied, putting a hand on her waist as she placed her left hand on his shoulder.

With their right hands intertwined, they were off, spinning and turning, Bill taking the lead and steering her through the other dancers. Soon Fiona found herself lost in the music and the joy of being twirled around until she was breathless and giddy. But it was only when the tempo changed to a slower dance and she realised that she was still giddy, that she began to speculate that it mightn't be the dance responsible for her happy state of mind – it might be Bill himself.

***

Bill didn't like to admit it, but when Fiona went to powder her nose he was pleased because it gave him a chance to catch his breath. He wasn't getting any younger and all this dancing was taking its toll. He also wanted to make sure Patch was OK. He had left the dog sitting under a chair, and had been keeping an eye on him, but he thought the poor lad could probably do with a chance to stretch his legs and have a sniff.

'I'll take him out for you,' Jack offered, as Bill headed for the door with Patch in tow. 'You go enjoy yourself.'

'What about you?'

Jack chuckled. 'You may have noticed that I can't dance for toffee. I think I've trod on everyone's feet, and I'm now banned from the dance floor. I'll take Patch out for a few minutes and keep an eye on him while you take Fiona for another spin. She looked like she was enjoying herself. So did you.'

Bill thanked him and gave him Patch's lead, thinking that Jack was right – he *was* enjoying himself, far more than he thought he would. Fiona, despite her protestations, was a good dancer, light on her feet and nimble. He was a bit of a plodder compared to her, but it had felt natural to hold her in his arms, as though they had been dancing together for years.

Without being aware he was doing so, he scanned the room looking for her, then flinched when his gaze landed on Glenys. She was skirting the dancers, heading towards him with a smile on her lips and determination in her eyes.

'Are you in need of a dancing partner?' she asked, coming to stand next to him.

'I was taking a breather, actually,' he said.

'Me, too. Good turnout, isn't it?'

'It certainly is.'

'You should be very proud of yourself.'

'Oh, I didn't do much. It was mostly Fiona.'

'Don't put yourself down. There's no way Fiona could have managed all this on her own.'

'Molly and Jack played a big part too, and so did Reuben, and the vicar and—

'I bet it's nice to be back in Sweet Meadow after all your travelling,' Glenys interrupted, 'You can settle down properly now.'

Bill didn't know what to say to that. 'I suppose.' He had always called Sweet Meadow home, even though he hadn't lived in the town for most of his life.

'It's a pity your mum isn't here. She would have loved to have had you back for good. I often called in to see her, you know.'

Bill had known. His mum used to tell him. 'She appreciated your visits. Thank you.'

He nodded once, as though to bring an end to the conversation, but there was no stopping Glenys as she said, 'She used to tell everyone how proud she was of you.'

Bill felt a lump rise in his throat. She used to tell him the same thing. His one regret was that he hadn't visited her as often as she would have liked. He came home whenever he could, but not nearly enough, and even then it tended to be a flying visit. The problem was, he had loved his job so much that he hadn't wanted to be onshore for long. That had been part of the problem with him and Tracey, part of the reason she had called the wedding off. His mother had been so upset…

As though she had read his mind, Glenys said, 'Your mum once told me that it was her dearest wish to see you married.' She shook her head sadly, then brightened. 'It's not too late though, eh?' she added, with a wink.

To say that he was taken aback by that, was an understatement. Bill was dumbfounded. Not only was Glenys discussing things he didn't want to discuss, but she was making assumptions she had no right to make. He might be spending a lot of time in Fiona's company recently, and he might have developed a soft spot for her, but that didn't mean he was about to propose.

Fiona chose that moment to reappear, and his eyes automatically gravitated towards her. She was waylaid by Charlie from bowls, who (surprisingly) was sitting at the same table as Morris, who didn't seem to object to Patch being at the dance this afternoon, or if he did, he hadn't mentioned it.

Glenys followed his gaze.

'It's such a shame,' she said. 'Her husband dying so young. She's never looked at another man in all that time. Devastated, she was. I don't think she'll ever get over it.' Glenys patted his arm. 'It's nice she's got a friend like you. I hope she appreciates you and doesn't take you for granted.'

The possibility had never occurred to him. Fiona simply wasn't like that.

Scooting closer (too close for comfort) Glenys said, 'You'll have to pop around to mine – I won a bottle of champagne in the jumble sale raffle, remember, and I don't like drinking on my own.'

What? No! That was the last thing he wanted.

He was trying to formulate a reply when he felt a nudge on his leg. Jack had returned with Patch, and Bill was mightily relieved at the interruption as he asked, 'Did he do the necessary?'

'On every lamp post.'

'Thanks for that.'

'You're welcome.' Jack handed him Patch's lead. 'If you need me to take him out again just shout.'

Glenys put a hand on Bill's arm. He wished she would stop doing that. Using the excuse of reaching down to pat his dog, he shook it off.

She said, 'Don't forget about the champers. We'll have a chat when you're less busy.'

No, we won't, he thought. Glenys might be a kind-hearted and thoughtful woman, but she wasn't his cup of tea at all.

But he had learnt one thing from the conversation – that Fiona was as determinedly single as he.

He should have been glad, because it meant that they could continue to be friends without risk of awkwardness. So why wasn't he?

CHAPTER 13

Cripes, that hurts, Fiona thought as she eased herself out of bed on Sunday morning. She ached from her head to her toes, and every part in between. Her face hurt from smiling so much, her toes from dancing, and the rest of her from being on the go all day. She hadn't achieved that level of activity since her last day at Clover Cafe.

'You know what they say,' she grumbled aloud, as she slid her feet into a pair of slippers and reached for her dressing gown. 'If you don't use it, you lose it.' And she'd patently lost it.

Gone was the time when she could work from seven in the morning to seven at night, and beyond. Yesterday had exhausted her.

No sooner had Bill dropped her off, she'd had a long soak in a hot bath, changed into her nightie, had drunk a cup of cocoa and had put herself to bed, not caring that eight p.m. was ridiculously early.

To her relief, Molly and Jack had done the bulk of the clearing up, sending her and Bill off home with promises to return everything to Fiona this morning. Even Patch had looked shattered, and Fiona guessed that the little dog hadn't had the chance to nap, not with all the noise, the people and the dancing. She would give Bill a ring later to see whether he was feeling just as bad.

By the time she had made tea and toast and was getting dressed, she was starting to loosen up, although her feet continued to ache and her knees hadn't stopped griping. Her arms and shoulders were sore, too.

'Stop grizzling,' she told herself, forcing her spine to bend enough to enable her to put a pair of socks on. A brush of her hair and a spray of perfume had her feeling almost human again, and she went back downstairs, (trying not to wince at every step) to tackle the kitchen.

She and Bill had attempted a clean-up before they had left for the tea dance yesterday, but the standard of cleanliness in her kitchen still left a lot to be desired.

Typically, she had her arms in soapy water up to her elbows when the doorbell rang. It was Molly and Jack, and she hastened to put the kettle on as they ferried the boxes of plates, cups, sauces and other paraphernalia from the car to the house.

'Can I help you put this lot away?' Molly asked.

'If you can stack it under the stairs, that would be great. I won't bother unboxing it because most of it is destined for the cafe anyway.'

She and Molly had been ordering things online for the past week, so they would have everything to hand as soon as the decorating was finished. And with each day that passed, the cafe was a step closer to welcoming its first customers.

'How much profit did we make?' Fiona asked, knowing that several expenses such as food, crockery and cutlery needed to be deducted first, but when Molly told her, Fiona clapped her hands in delight.

Molly said, 'It's enough to pay Gavin for the plastering and the rest of the odds and sods that need doing, plus a bit extra in case something unforeseen crops up.'

'When do you think the work will be finished?'

'Two weeks, maybe three. The plaster will have to dry out before we can start painting, so that'll take a week or so, then it'll need a couple of coats of paint.'

Three weeks was no time at all – they would pass before Fiona knew it – and a feeling akin to what she used to experience as a child when the six weeks summer holidays drew to an end and she would soon have to return to school, came over her. She almost felt as though she was losing her freedom, which was ridiculous because since she had sold her business she had done very little with all the free time she'd suddenly had. Possibly the most constructive thing she had done had been to phone the council to complain about the state of the park, but her pestering them hadn't made a jot of difference. It had taken Molly's drive, determination and vision to make anything happen. Along with Bill's help, obviously. He seemed to have a knack for getting people to do things: a result of ordering crews around and being in charge of a humongous ship, she suspected.

You wouldn't believe it to look at him now, though. It was sad to think that as you grew older, people only saw the old person with the wrinkles on their face, the stooped shoulders and the shuffling gait. There were few clues left on the body to give a hint as to what they might have been in a past life. Not that Bill's shoulders were particularly stooped, of course and neither did he shuffle. Nor did she, for that matter – but it was the principal of the thing.

She was forced to admit that she wasn't a spring chicken, as this morning's aches and pains had demonstrated. She had also noticed that she wasn't as agile mentally as she had once been, and it worried her to think that she might have been stagnating.

Not anymore.

Since the day Bill had called in to tell her that the cafe in the park should reopen and that she was the best person to run it, she had felt her confidence growing. But there was one thing which continued to bother her – she couldn't run it by herself, and yesterday had hammered the reality home.

'How is the hunt for volunteers coming along?' she asked Molly.

'A couple of people have said they can help out, and Bill said he can spare a few hours. But if you hear of anyone, let me know.'

Fiona eyed her doubtfully; that didn't sound promising...

Maybe people were hanging back until it was open and they could see it in the flesh, so to speak. She didn't blame them. Anyone peering in through the windows right now wouldn't be impressed. The place looked a mess. But it wouldn't be like that for much longer.

Molly and Jack had a cup of tea with her, and after they left Fiona decided the kitchen could wait. It wasn't going anywhere and would still be here this afternoon. It was getting on for lunchtime and as she'd only had a nibble of a sandwich, one miniature lemon drizzle cake and two slices of toast since the omelette yesterday lunchtime, she was hungry. A spaghetti bolognese should do it, especially since she had a packet of mince in the fridge that needed to be used up. She would cook a batch of sauce, have one portion for her lunch and freeze the rest.

Or (and here was a thought) she could call Bill now and invite him to share it.

To her delight, he accepted!

***

Patch was incandescent with excitement when he saw Bill with his harness in his hands. 'Hold still, you daft dog,' Bill told him, trying to wrestle him into it.

Remembering his wallet, he fetched it from its usual place on the sideboard in the living room, then grabbed a lightweight jacket. He probably wouldn't need it, but it never hurt to be prepared: it could be a bit blustery where he was thinking of taking Fiona later.

Bill had no idea why Keeper's Pond had come to mind when Fiona called to invite him to share some spaghetti bolognese with her, but he thought it might do them both good to get out for a couple of hours and stretch their legs. He'd taken Patch for his walk this morning, but it had been somewhat of an effort if he was honest, and although he didn't relish sitting around on his backside all afternoon, another circuit around the park didn't hold much appeal. He wanted to go somewhere different.

So, after a delicious lunch, he said, 'Fancy a drive out?'

'I wondered why you'd brought the car. Where did you have in mind?'

'Keeper's Pond. Do you know it?'

'I've heard of it. It's supposed to be nice.'

Keeper's Pond was a bit of a drive, but not as far as Brecon, and from what Bill could remember the views were impressive. Situated on the top of the broad mountain separating the towns of Blaenavon to the south and Abergavenny to the north, the pond was a popular spot for walkers, wild swimmers, and those people who simply wanted to sit on a bench and enjoy the scenery.

The view didn't show itself until the car had crested the top of the road that traversed the mountain, but it was well worth the journey. The vista that spread out before them was one of patchwork fields, interspersed with verdant woodland and bare bracken-clad peaks. And just off to the right lay a large pond, a glittering sapphire under a clear bright sky.

The car park was full (lots of people had the same idea) but Bill managed to bag a space as someone was leaving.

'I didn't think it would be this busy,' he told Fiona as they strolled the short distance to the start of the path that ran along the pond's northern edge.

The benches dotted along it were occupied, and some people had brought folding chairs with them. Others sat on the grass. The pond itself was also busy, and he could see several swimmers in the water, and three paddle boarders at the far end. And there were dogs galore, many of them getting their paws wet at the water's edge, with the more intrepid going deeper and swimming with chuffing breaths and happy eyes.

Patch launched himself straight in, yipping happily as he swam in a circle, then he scampered back out and shook himself vigorously.

Fiona squealed as the dog showered them with droplets of water, and Bill couldn't help but laugh at the scamp's smug expression.

'Getting your own back for all the times I bathed you, eh?' He turned to his companion. 'Sorry, Fi. I hope you're not too wet, or muddy.'

'Not muddy at all, and a drop of water never hurt anyone. Look at his little face! He's having such a great time.'

Patch was now dashing around, not knowing where to sniff first, his tail wagging furiously.

'Do you fancy a sit or a stroll?' Bill asked. He was studying the path and saw that it sloped gently upwards beyond the pond's furthest point.

'Let's walk, shall we? I've got my trainers on, and it looks nice and peaceful up there. I wonder how far it goes?'

'There's one way to find out,' Bill said, taking her arm in his, and very soon they had left the pond behind and were walking along a grassy path surrounded by heather and wimberry bushes thick with tiny purple berries.

'Gosh, I haven't seen wimberries in the wild since I was a girl!' Fiona cried. 'Me and my friends used to pick them every summer, coming home with fingers stained purple by the juice. I swear we used to eat more than we picked to take home, though. You can't get them in the shops unfortunately. The nearest things are blueberries: great big dusty purple things, with zero taste. You can't beat these.' She stopped to bend down and pick a few. 'Here.'

She popped a couple in his mouth, and the tart fresh flavour exploded on his tongue.

'My mum used to make the most wonderful pies with them,' she said, eating some herself, and when Patch showed an interest, she gave him some too. 'A sprinkle of sugar on the top of the pastry and served with creamy custard. Yum.'

She had a faraway look in her eyes, and Bill gazed at her fondly. He had his own fine memories of wimberry tart and custard.

They carried on with their walk, the gradient so gradual that they only noticed it when they looked behind and saw the pond in the distance below. Bill guessed there might be a fair way to go before it levelled off, and they could be walking across this moorland for a while.

He was trying to gauge whether Fiona had had enough, when she suddenly stopped and sank down onto a grassy tump.

'Let's have a sit for a minute and enjoy the view,' she suggested, and he awkwardly sat down beside her, his knees protesting. Patch, whose tongue was lolling out of the side of his mouth, joined them, squeezing his little body between theirs, so he was sitting in the middle.

'Listen,' Fiona breathed, her head cocked to the side. 'Skylarks.'

Bill shielded his eyes from the sun, and studied the sky, immediately spotting the bird. Its trilling call was reminiscent of summers gone by, and he let the glorious sound flow over him.

'There's a red kite,' he said, pointing out a bird circling overhead. Its forked tail and the white feathers on the underside of its wings were quite distinctive. 'I've seen them in the air above the park once or twice,' he told Fiona. 'And buzzards. I saw a sparrowhawk a couple of weeks ago, as well. It's a good sign when apex predators are around, because it means the rest of the park's ecosystem is healthy.'

'You know an awful lot about wildlife.'

'Mainly thanks to Reuben. He's rather passionate about the subject.'

Fiona laughed. 'I had noticed.' She lay back and closed her eyes, her face lifted to the sun. 'I can understand why. I used to do this in the meadow when I was a child. Even then, I used to love the peace and quiet. Until the boys appeared, with their boasting and their footballs.' She was smiling as she said it, and Bill guessed that she hadn't minded having her peace disturbed.

'Good times, eh?' he said, remembering his own boyhood in the park.

He had played in it for hours on end, building dens in the woodland, kicking a ball on the field, dangling upside down from the bars of the swings. And if he had a few pence, he'd buy an ice lolly from the cafe. Those were the days. The park had been well-used and well-loved by adults and kids alike, and Bill shared Molly's dream that it would be so again.

'It'll be wonderful to have the cafe open,' he said. 'Just like the old days.'

And although he didn't say it aloud, he was looking forward to being a part of it. He could just imagine him taking the orders and serving people with drinks and snacks, whilst Fiona prepared the food. What a good team they would make!

He was inordinately excited – more than he would have thought possible. And for the rest of the day he tried to figure out why. The answer only came to him when he was in bed on the cusp of sleep. The reason he was looking forward to the cafe reopening wasn't because it was something to occupy him, or because it reminded him of his childhood. It was because he would be working alongside *Fiona*.

Now that was a turn-up for the books...

CHAPTER 14

How could somebody go from not having enough hours in the day one minute, to having so many that it was a job to find something to fill them with, Fiona thought, as she gazed at her living room window. She had a lint-free cloth in one hand and a spray bottle of glass cleaner in the other, in preparation for giving it a wipe over, when she remembered that she had cleaned the window only two days ago and it hadn't needed cleaning then. It certainly didn't need another right now. And neither did anything else. The house had been cleaned to within an inch of its life this week, and there simply wasn't anything left to be polished, scrubbed or mopped.

Putting the cloth and spray bottle away, Fiona wandered into the living room and dropped onto the sofa with a sigh. She reached for one of the library books off a pile on the side table that she had been trying to read for the past three days, but hadn't been able to get into. Cross, she closed it and went in search of her mobile, wondering whether to phone Bill. She hadn't seen him since Sunday and it was now Wednesday, so it wouldn't hurt to give him a call to see how he was.

On the other hand, she didn't want to hassle him or make him think she was angling after another trip out. The visit to Keeper's Pond on the weekend had been lovely, though…

Restlessly, Fiona paced around the room and was wondering what to do with herself when her eyes alighted on the stack of books once more and she decided she would go to the library and get some new ones out. Not only would the walk do her good and get her out of the house for an hour or so, she would also have fresh reading material, something that would hopefully capture her interest.

On her walk into town, she went via the park, but she didn't see anyone she knew and the cafe was locked up. Slowing down as she neared it, it occurred to her that she couldn't face a return to her old way of life. If these past few weeks had taught her anything, it was that she needed this cafe. When Molly had told her that she planned on re-opening it and had suggested that Fiona might like to run it, Fiona hadn't realised just how much she'd missed preparing food and serving it to hungry customers. She missed being busy, and she missed chatting and gossiping with people. Without Clover Cafe in her life, she had become bored, lonely and miserable. The reopening of the cafe in Sweet Meadow Park would keep her occupied, and hopefully she would be more sociable and much happier.

The library was busy, and she nodded and smiled at the people she recognised. A group of three middle-aged gents were gathered around a table, the books on it telling her that they probably belonged to the local history group. A huge tub of Lego was on another table, and a mother and her toddler son were sorting the blocks into colours, and several computers in a side room were in use.

Fiona went to the automated system to check her books back in, then wandered over to the nearest shelf to see what was on display. The staff picked a different theme each week, and books that reflected the theme were showcased there.

Fiona grinned when she saw what this week's theme was – baking. There were a couple of cookbooks on display (as she would expect) but there were also other goodies such as a hardback on the history of windmills, plus several novels with baking involved in one way or another. One was a lighthearted romance set in a tea shop with a patisserie chef as the heroine, which sounded right up her street, and there was also a cosy mystery set in a bakery, so she decided to give that a go as well. Now for something a bit darker – a thriller, maybe? She always enjoyed a Felix Francis. She liked historical novels, too. There weren't many genres she didn't read, and if she took a wide selection home with her, she stood a greater chance of something capturing her attention.

Another shelf caught her eye. It was full of jigsaw puzzles and although she hadn't borrowed jigsaws previously, she debated whether to take a chance. She used to love doing them as a child, but hadn't had time as an adult. She certainly had plenty of time now. And the dining table would be a perfect place for it. All she had to do was choose one and pray that all the pieces were there!

She was trying to decide between a river scene (the memory of the canal and Bill floated into her head) or a cottage garden, when she caught sight of Glenys out of the corner of her eye.

'Yoo-hoo!' Glenys called, making a beeline for her.

Fiona winced. It grated on her that libraries were no longer the silent places of her childhood, and she still expected to be shushed if she made a noise.

'Gosh, you do like to read, don't you!' Glenys exclaimed, eyeing the books under her arm. 'I envy you. I wish I had the time, but I don't have a moment to myself. I'm only here today because Mrs Griffiths on Oak Place needs me to swap her Mills and Boons for new ones. I swear she must have read all of them by now. Do you know how I can tell which ones she hasn't?'

Numbly Fiona shook her head.

Glenys glanced around and lowered her voice. 'She puts a little line under the number on page seventeen. That's her birthday. So if a book has got a mark on page seventeen, I know she's read it. With all the reading you do, you ought to try it; when you get older it's easy to forget things.'

Fiona glared at her in disbelief. The damned woman was only a couple of years younger than her! The way she was talking, anyone would think it was a couple of decades!

Glenys carried on with her inane chatter, oblivious to Fiona's ire. 'How will you get that lot home? It's a bit of a trek up your hill, isn't it? Would you like a lift? I've got my car.'

'No thank you, I like to walk.'

'Of course you do. It's good for the elderly to keep active.'

Fiona gritted her teeth and held in a retort. No matter how much Glenys irritated her, the woman was a potential customer and Fiona had no intention of alienating her.

'Take Bill, for example,' Glenys continued. 'All that walking has done wonders for him. I always see him out with his dog. I'm hoping to bump into him later. Did you know I won a bottle of shampoo in the jumble sale raffle?'

Fiona gazed at her blankly. Had shampoo been one of the raffle prizes? And if so, who had decided on that and why? It was hardly a suitable prize, was it?

'I'm hoping to persuade him to help me drink it,' Glenys was saying.

'Pardon?'

'I simply adore champagne, but I don't want to drink it on my own.'

So that's what she meant! Fiona vaguely remembered Glenys crowing that she had won a bottle.

Glenys was saying, 'I'm sure Bill will give me a hand. I bet he used to drink champagne all the time when he was abroad.'

Fiona couldn't think of a single thing to say in response to that.

'I'll pop in to see him after I've dropped Mrs Griffiths's books off. I'll invite him over to mine for a bite to eat and a few drinkie-poos. Does he like oysters, do you know?'

Fiona had no idea whether he did or didn't.

Glenys simpered. 'Never mind, I don't expect he'll need them. Candles and a bit of smoochie music should do the trick.'

Do the trick? The woman was incorrigible. Fancy being so blatant about making a play for him! It made Fiona's blood boil. Poor Bill wouldn't know what had hit him.

Or would he?

She recalled seeing him and Glenys together on the day they were giving the posters out. He hadn't seemed to mind her flirting. And hadn't he been speaking to Glenys on the afternoon of the tea dance, when Fiona had returned from 'powdering her nose'? She hadn't taken much notice at the time because she'd been intercepted by one of the members of the bowls club, but looking back they had seemed rather cosy.

Jealousy, hot and sharp, stabbed her in the chest. Did Bill have other fish to fry – more vivacious, younger (albeit only marginally), more interesting fish?

Hmph! *She* could be interesting if she wanted to be. But not Glenys's kind of interesting – Fiona didn't do simpering smiles and fluttering eyelashes. Her 'interesting' was more of the intellectual variety. At least, she hoped it was.

Glenys broke into her thoughts. 'Ooh, look at the time! I must dash – things to do, people to see. Good luck with the cafe, by the way.' She tilted her head and gave Fiona a smile, the sort of sad, pitying smile you give to a person when you want to convey sympathy for a recent bereavement. 'A word of advice: make sure you don't overdo it and that it doesn't get too much for you. You don't want to run yourself into the ground and make yourself ill, otherwise I'll be adding *you* to my list of people who need a bit of help.'

'Over my dead body,' Fiona muttered under her breath as Glenys toddled off. She'd show her! She would make a success of this cafe if it was the last thing she did!

***

'White is clean and fresh, but it's a bit clinical, don't you think?' Fiona mused, as she scanned the interior of the recently plastered but yet to be painted cafe. It was Saturday morning, and she had been on her way into town for something to do, when she had spied activity around the cafe and had headed towards it to find out what was going on.

Molly had asked for her thoughts on painting it white, and when Fiona gave it, Molly nibbled at her bottom lip. 'What did you have in mind, if not white?'

'A nice pastel shade.'

'Not magnolia?' The horrified expression on Molly's face made Fiona chuckle.

'No, not magnolia. A pale pink maybe, or turquoise?'

'Like you see on *The Great British Bake Off*?'

'Bingo! Exactly like that.'

'Will that style fit in with the old-fashioned vibe of the place? You know, the marble counter and tabletops, and the wrought-iron chairs.'

'I think it will. As I recall, the interior used to be cream – more vanilla ice cream than magnolia, to be fair – but I think we can do better than that. I'm envisioning people having an olde-worlde experience, as though they've been transported back to the 1950s.'

'How about a pale blue, with cream, pink and aqua accents?'

Fiona beamed. 'That sounds lovely.'

'And a deeper blue for the exterior?'

'Perfect.'

'Would you like to come with me to buy the paint? I don't trust myself to choose the right shades.'

Fiona knew that Molly was perfectly capable of choosing paint on her own, but she was pleased to be included, nevertheless.

'I would.' Her reply was heartfelt. Despite her best efforts, she was finding it increasingly difficult to keep herself occupied.

'We could go now,' Molly suggested. 'Unless you're busy?'

Fiona wasn't. 'Now is good.'

'I'll just tell Jack where we're going, and go grab my bag.'

Jack was outside, halfway up a step ladder, sanding down a window frame. Standing next to him was Bill, Patch at his feet.

Fiona faltered, warmth spreading through her at the sight of him, then she caught herself and greeted him cheerily. 'Hello, Bill. How are you?'

'I'm good,' he replied, smiling widely.

'Have you come to help?' she teased.

'He's supervising,' Jack said as he climbed down the ladder. He headed for Molly, so Fiona took the opportunity to chat to Bill for a minute.

'I haven't seen you since the weekend. How have you been keeping?'

'Mustn't grumble. You?'

'Tickety-boo, thanks,' she replied. She wanted to ask him whether he had helped Glenys drink her champagne yet, but she didn't want to appear to be prying, although she still felt cross whenever she thought about it. And she felt even crosser when she remembered how patronising Glenys had been when she'd bumped into her in the library the other day, and how her comments had ignited a fire in her chest.

Fiona kept telling herself that she shouldn't want to make a success of the cafe because of that woman, that she should be doing it for Molly and for the people who frequented the park. And for herself, because without it, what else did she have? There was David, his wife and the grandchildren of course, but they were busy and had their own lives to lead. She couldn't expect them to entertain her all the time. And it wasn't fair on Bill; she couldn't rely on his friendship, especially if Glenys had got her claws into him. Therefore, it was down to her to keep herself busy and occupy her time. The cafe would certainly do that.

Fiona was still thinking about Bill and the very real possibility that he might cast her aside for a more interesting, more fun prospect, when she and Molly arrived at the DIY store.

Molly grabbed a trolley and Fiona fell into step beside her.

As they headed inside, she said, 'I think Glenys has got a thing for Bill.'

Molly turned to look at her. 'Really?' She sounded surprised. 'I never would have guessed. If I'm honest, I thought he seemed quite sweet on *you*.' She bumped Fiona with her hip.

'You're imagining things.'

'Seriously, he likes you.'

Fiona shrugged, pretending indifference. 'And I like him.'

When Molly arched her brow, Fiona scowled at her and added, 'Not like that. We're just two lonely old people who enjoy each other's company.'

'If you say so.'

'I do. Now, which one is the paint aisle?' She'd had enough of this discussion. Molly didn't know what she was talking about.

***

'It'll take three coats,' Molly's dad Duncan said on Sunday morning, as he examined the large pots of paint which sat on a dust sheet in the middle of the cafe. 'The first has to be a mist coat, followed by two normal coats a couple of days apart, because you have to give them time to dry.'

Fiona and Bill eyed each other in confusion; however, it was Reuben who asked the question.

Duncan explained. 'A mist coat is a paint and water mix. If you paint straight onto new plaster, the paint can bubble or peel off. The mist coat seals it.'

Fiona made a face, glad that she wasn't the one to be applying it. Neither would Bill, on account of his knees. It occurred to her that Bill's knees were a convenient excuse to get out of doing something he didn't want to do, but she couldn't fault him. An excuse like that could come in rather handy.

For this activity it was her age that gave her a pass and considering she'd volunteered her and Bill's services for refreshment duty, everyone was more than happy. Being fed and watered at regular intervals was equally as important as painting.

As Molly, Jack, Molly's parents and Reuben divvied up the DIY tasks, Bill and Fiona fired up the barbeque, whilst keeping a watchful eye on Patch and Jet.

It was reminiscent of the day that Bill had organised the townsfolk to clean up the park, except this time there were far fewer people. No one had felt the need to round up volunteers today, aware they'd already tapped into that particular well several times already.

With the electricity now on, and the antique coffee machine serviced (the chap who had come to service it had raised his eyebrows and tutted quite a lot, but he'd managed to get it working and declared it safe), Fiona was able to offer a variety of coffees, as well as tea. The cafe hadn't got a fridge yet, so cold drinks were currently housed in two coolboxes. She was hopeful that the cold storage situation would shortly improve, if the promised donation of a second-hand chiller and freezer came to pass.

People's generosity continued to amaze her, and even the council had chipped in by arranging to have the water heaters (there was one behind the counter, and one in the tiny loo) checked over and replaced if necessary, although Fiona suspected Jack might have had a hand in that.

It didn't take long before the aroma of sausages and burgers drew people towards its source, and they soon attracted a crowd.

'I didn't realise the cafe was open already,' one chap said.

Fiona replied, 'It isn't, but it will be shortly.'

'Shame. Me and the boy could do with a hot dog.' He gazed at her hopefully.

Fiona looked at Bill, who shrugged. '£1.50 each?' Bill suggested.

'Perfect! And do you have any cold cans?'

'I can spare a couple,' she said, making a mental note to keep some back for the workers. She would also have to be frugal with the number of hotdogs and burgers she sold, as she hadn't anticipated random people wanting to purchase them. She should have done, she supposed, because few people could resist the smell of a barbeque. Teenagers were no exception.

'Give us an 'otdog,' Liam said, fishing in his pocket and bringing out a mobile phone. He flourished it at her.

'Pay for mine, Li,' Connor pleaded. 'My mum didn't give me any pocket money this week 'cause I forgot to put the bins out. I'm skint.'

Liam shrugged. 'I dunno if I've got enough, and I haven't got any cash on me.' He turned his attention to Bill, who was expertly flipping the burgers. 'How much are they?'

'Three quid for two,' Bill replied. 'But we don't take cards.'

'It's not a card. I'm paying with my phone, ain't I?'

'We don't take phones, either.'

'*What?* That's stupid.'

Fiona stepped in. 'We're not officially open yet. This—' she gestured to the barbecue and the table set up next to it which held rolls, a couple of onions, tomato sauce (plus brown for the weirdos) and a pile of paper napkins '—is supposed to be for the workers.'

'What workers?' Liam asked.

'The people who are decorating the cafe.'

The boys peered through the open door, glanced at each other, then Liam said, 'We'll paint a wall if you give us a hotdog each.'

Fiona grinned and held out a hand. 'Done.'

Liam looked at it, then wiped his palm on his joggers. But before he shook her hand, he said, 'Hot dogs first?'

'Hot dogs first,' Fiona confirmed.

'Sweet.' He put his phone away and stared expectantly at Bill.

Fiona lifted the lid of the nearest coolbox. 'Help yourself to a cold can.'

'Got any cider?' was Liam's cheeky response.

When Molly and the others stopped for a break, Fiona was surprised to see the two lads carry on working.

'They're good lads,' Duncan said, squirting a generous dollop of tomato sauce onto his burger and taking a bite. 'Mmm.'

Fiona took pity on them and called Liam and Connor to come outside. 'Here.' She handed them a burger each.

Connor said, 'Does this mean we've got to stay all day?'

'No, it doesn't. You can leave now if you want, and we'll call it quits.'

The boys exchanged glances once again. 'Nah, we'll do a bit more,' Liam said. 'Thanks, missus.'

'It's Fiona.'

Liam's response was a diffident shrug.

As soon as everyone had eaten, they went back to work whilst Fiona and Bill cleared up, pottering around quite harmoniously, as though they had been working together for years.

Fiona found herself humming. Surprised, she stopped, having not hummed for ages. The contentment she was experiencing was a surprise too, and she put it down to feeling useful once more.

But after the remnants of the lunch had been cleared away and afternoon cake had been produced and enthused over, the reality of what she was about to do reared its ugly head. In no time at all, the cafe would be officially open and *she* would be in charge.

The prospect worried her more than she used to worry about her own business. Which was odd. Had she lost her mojo? She could still bake with the best of them (she had no qualms on that score), but being responsible for the takings, the ordering, and so on, filled her with dismay.

She *had* lost her mojo. At some point between handing over the keys to Clover Cafe to Pamela, and Molly asking her how she felt about reopening the cafe in Sweet Meadow Park, Fiona's confidence had deserted her. The brave words she had told herself after her most recent encounter with Glenys, had been just that – words. And, as everyone knew, words and actions were often miles apart.

'They've done a grand job,' Bill said, standing next to her.

Fiona gave herself a mental shake and peered into the cafe's interior.

She had to admit that it did look wonderful. The walls were a pale turquoise, with a slightly deeper shade on the woodwork, The ceiling was white, which bounced light around the room, and now that the tiled floor had been given a thorough scrub, the place looked fresh and clean.

Everything needed another coat of paint, which would be tackled next weekend, then the tables and chairs had to be fetched from Molly's parents' garage, curtains needed to be hung at the windows, and all the crockery and other bits and pieces had to be brought from her house, but then the cafe would be good to go. It would need to be stocked of course, and Fiona already had a list of foodstuffs as long as her arm which had to be purchased, and she only hoped there was enough money left in the kitty.

'You're quiet,' Bill said. 'Is something wrong?'

What could she say to that? After all the hard work, both with the fundraising and getting the cafe ready, she could hardly admit to not feeling up to the job of running it. She didn't need the money (she would be the only paid person – the rest would be volunteers), so it wasn't as though she had to do it, but neither could she back out at this late stage.

There was also something else to consider – her pride.

There was no way on God's earth she was going to give Glenys Sidwall the opportunity to say *I told you so*. The woman had put her down enough already, and Fiona would be damned if she'd give her any further reason to.

CHAPTER 15

'It's not so nice this morning, Patch,' Bill observed as he peered out of the bedroom window. After the glorious day yesterday, painting and barbequing, he had been hoping that today would be equally as nice, because he had been contemplating suggesting to Fiona that they had another day out.

However, a fine drizzle put the kibosh on that, so perhaps he could suggest going out for lunch instead. He'd heard of a pub that did decent food (if his neighbour could be believed), which also allowed dogs. It was rather early and Fiona mightn't be up yet, so he would take Patch for a walk first, then give her a bell when he got back.

At this time on a murky Monday morning, the only people in the park were those hurrying through it on their way to work and he didn't encounter a single dog walker as he made his way past the kiddies' play area, and on towards Molly and Jack's cottage.

Patch stopped to sniff every blade of grass, despite having sniffed those same plants yesterday, and he also watered a fair few of them, announcing to the park's canine fraternity that 'Patch woz 'ere'.

Bill didn't mind the constant stop-start. He wasn't in any hurry. And neither did he mind the drizzle. A spot of rain would do his garden good, and it would go some way to refilling the water butt. It would also save him from having to water his veggie plot this evening. Anyway, he'd witnessed much worse weather than a drop of rain – much worse indeed.

Patch's high-pitched yip broke into his thoughts, and he glanced around to see his dog tearing after a squirrel. Chuckling, Bill watched the squirrel scoot up the nearest tree trunk, ascending into the upper branches with remarkable agility, leaving the terrier to stare in every direction other than the right one. The ability of those pesky squirrels to disappear into thin air was a constant source of amazement to the dog, and not once did Patch think to look up, not even when the squirrels chattered abuse at him from the safety of the canopy.

Bill often wondered what the dog would do if one of the little critters were to stand its ground. He had a feeling Patch would turn tail and run away – exactly like he did with those cats who refused to be chased: a gimlet eye, an arched back and hissing that a cobra would be proud of, was always enough to see Patch screech to a halt, then flee with his tail between his legs.

A cursory glance at the cottage, as Bill strolled past, showed an empty driveway, and he guessed that both Molly and Jack had left for work. Jack had a ten-minute drive to the council offices, which had been very inconveniently built three miles out of town and as far from a bus route as it was possible to get. Molly, on the other hand, worked at an estate agent in Sweet Meadow itself, but because she often flitted here, there and everywhere looking at properties, or showing prospective buyers around them, she usually drove into town as well.

Calling Patch to him, Bill strolled around the gentle bend in the path that led to the cafe and the bandstand. It wasn't possible to see the cafe from Molly's house, but he knew she could see the bandstand on the other side of the green, as well as the playground, which was in the opposite direction. Both were in a state, and Bill wondered which of them would be next in line for a Molly makeover.

If he was a betting man, which he wasn't, he might have been tempted to put his money on the playground. But that would entail a serious chunk of fundraising. But then again, that's what Molly intended to use the cafe's profits for – park restoration – so how soon the work on either project could begin would depend on how well the cafe was doing. Bill had a feeling it would do very well with Fiona at the helm. Having owned Clover Cafe for years, the cafe in the park should be a doddle for her. Although he hadn't tasted Pamela's baking, rumour had it that she wasn't half the baker Fiona was, and neither did she have Fiona's warm and friendly personality. If it came to a shootout between the two cafes (the one in the park and the one in town) he knew who would win.

He was aware that Fiona had the occasional crisis of confidence, but she needn't worry, she was—

'*Bloody hell!*'

The sight that met Bill's incredulous gaze stopped him dead in his tracks. Someone had sprayed swirls and loops of garish red paint all over the front of the cafe. The windows and the door were covered in it, and some of the brickwork hadn't escaped the assault.

He could hardly see the lovely blue of the window frames and the door, for the hideous graffiti.

Bill tried to make sense of the marks, hoping to see a name (whoever was stupid enough to do something like this, might also be stupid enough to graffiti their own name) but as far as he could tell it was nothing but a random mess.

They could have made more of an effort, he thought. This wasn't street art, this was mindless vandalism. If he got his hands on those responsible, he would give them what for! Imprisonment would be too good for them. Why did they have to do it now, after everyone's hard work yesterday? Some people were nothing but mindless thugs, with no respect for anybody or anything.

Bill's indignation abruptly gave way to dismay when he realised he would have to be the one to tell Fiona. And he couldn't delay it in case she happened to hear about the vandalism from someone else.

With a heavy heart and a ball of anger in his chest, Bill made his way to the far gate.

He wasn't looking forward to this at all.

***

'Why? What's the point of it?' Molly cried, and Fiona realised that the young woman was holding her temper with difficulty.

But whereas Molly was thoroughly outraged, Fiona was thoroughly upset.

The three of them were standing in front of the cafe and surveying the damage.

Bill said. 'It's pointless, and senseless.' He was annoyed too.

Fiona wished she felt the same, rather than teary. It would be better than being so distressed. She guessed it was probably kids who were responsible, but she couldn't help feeling that the vandalism was a personal attack, and she felt vulnerable. Silly, she knew…

Wringing her hands together, she wailed, 'Who would do such a thing?'

'Mindless idiots.' Bill's voice was gruff. 'They don't deserve anything nice.'

'Don't you dare suggest throwing in the towel, Bill Greaves,' Molly warned. 'They don't, I agree, and if we find out who is responsible I'll make it my mission to ensure they never have anything nice ever again.'

'Please be careful,' Fiona begged. 'You don't want to get into trouble.'

Molly put an arm around her, and Fiona leant into her as Molly said, 'Don't worry, I won't take the law into my own hands.'

'What *will* you do?' Fiona fretted.

'Ignore me, I'm blowing off steam, that's all.' Molly shook her head and sighed loudly. 'I'll tackle this later. I'd better go to work before I get the sack.'

Fiona couldn't bear the sight of the graffiti for one minute longer. 'Can you leave the keys with me? I'd like to make a start, if you don't mind.'

'I'll help,' Bill offered.

'Don't break your backs trying to remove it,' Molly warned, passing the keys to Fiona. 'Keep these. You should have a set of your own, anyway.'

Fiona waited until Molly left, then she unlocked the cafe door and stepped inside. Tea first, she decided as she switched the hot water on. She hadn't had a cup yet, Bill having woken her up with the news. Whilst she'd hurried to get dressed (she had felt rather embarrassed answering the door in her dressing gown) Bill had phoned Molly, who had informed them she was on her way.

It was only now that Fiona was able to catch her breath. And it was only now that her nerves were beginning to settle and the nausea was fading.

'Will hot water and washing up liquid get it off?' she asked as they waited for the tea to brew.

Bill said, 'Probably not. I reckon the paint on the glass will need to be scraped off, but scraping won't work on the stone.'

'Oh dear. What will?'

Bill took out his phone. 'Let me see… I think a pressure washer might be the best bet, but we'll have to be careful that it doesn't damage it.'

Fiona pressed her lips together. 'I don't own a pressure washer. Do you?'

He shook his head. 'No, but Duncan might. He strikes me as the sort of man who would have one.'

'He does, doesn't he. Oh, but he'll be at work.'

'We can get started on the windows. It says here that a razor blade should scrape it off.'

'What about the scraper that I clean my ceramic hob with?' Fiona suggested. 'I've used it on my bathroom mirror when I got nail varnish on it, and it got it off.'

'There's no harm in giving it a go,' Bill told her.

Leaving him and Patch to make a start on seeing whether hot soapy water would make any headway, Fiona hurried home to fetch the tool she used on her hob, plus a couple of pairs of rubber gloves and a spray bottle of glass cleaner along with her lint-free cloth. Feeling more positive (not much, but a little) Fiona was still shocked when she saw the outside of the cafe for the second time that morning, and once again she wondered at the mentality of those responsible. What had possessed them to do such a thing? It was sad to think that was how they got their kicks – by defacing the hard work of others.

And the cafe had looked so lovely, too…

***

At least the worst of it was off, Bill thought later, as he gave the window a final wipe over, being careful to avoid the newly reapplied paint on the frame. It had proved to be easier and quicker to give both the window frames and the door a fresh coat, rather than try to remove the red graffiti. All it had taken was a light sanding and a rinse down, followed by a lick of paint on the damaged areas.

The walls were a different matter though, and he feared they might be trickier. Having done more research, and with the input of several members of the public who had stopped to commiserate and give advice, it was decided that using a pressure washer might be too much of a scatter-gun approach. And after learning that the DIY store stocked a suitable liquid which should do the trick, Bill and Fiona were now on their way to purchase some.

Having worked flat out all morning, they also planned on having a bite to eat on the way.

'I'm not dressed for a visit to the pub,' Fiona had informed him when he'd suggested it. Bill thought she looked fine, but she was adamant that she didn't, and as Best Bites didn't allow dogs, that was also out of the question, so he volunteered to pop into the bakery for a pasty which they would eat in the DIY store's car park, along with a takeaway coffee.

As they sat there, admiring the trays of plants outside the store (three for two), Fiona licked the grease off her fingers and said, 'Have you given any thought as to who might be responsible?'

'I've thought about nothing else.'

'Any ideas?'

Bill put his half-eaten corned beef pasty on the dashboard and took a sip of coffee. He hated to say this… 'A couple of people come to mind, but I wish they didn't.'

Fiona didn't need him to spell it out. 'Surely you don't mean Liam and Connor?'

'They've got a track record,' he pointed out. 'It was them and their friends who trashed the flower beds near the gate. And don't forget the pond incident.'

'I thought they'd learnt their lesson?'

'So did I.' Bill had been convinced that the youffs had turned over a new leaf since Jack had saved Connor from drowning, but did leopards truly change their spots?

'They were such a help yesterday,' she lamented. 'I can't believe it was them.'

Bill didn't want to, but who else *could* it be? Liam and his gang had caused havoc in the park previously, and they still had a habit of dropping litter (illicit cigarette stubs, in particular) as well as the occasional can of lager, or a bottle of beer and sometimes the harder stuff. He could well imagine them getting pie-eyed and egging each other on. It was entirely feasible that Liam and Connor had boasted about helping with the painting, and for them to make some 'embellishments'.

Or – and this scenario was also within the realms of possibility – one of the others might have decided to have a go at decorating it themselves. A third option was sheer jealousy or vindictiveness. Who knew what went on in the minds of teenagers?

Bill snorted to himself: he had no idea what went on in his own mind half the time, so he didn't stand a hope in hell of working out anyone else's thoughts or intentions. He knew one thing, though – he would have to have a little chat with the youffs who hung around the park.

Pasties eaten and coffee consumed, Bill, Fiona and Patch (the dog had received his fair share of pasty offerings) entered the store in search of the recommended product. They located it easily, but it took Bill a while to persuade Fiona to leave because she became excited by the array of plants on sale, and the receptacles to put them in.

'Strictly Come Planting,' she announced as they returned to the car. 'I'd forgotten all about it. I don't suppose there's time to do it now because the cafe is due to open a week Saturday.'

'It won't take long to slap another coat of paint on next weekend, so I don't see why we can't have a Strictly Come Planting event in the afternoon.'

Fiona had a faraway look on her face. 'Imagine how nice the cafe would look with a planter or two outside. It would pretty it up no end.'

'It would.'

'They're not cheap though.'

'So I noticed.' The larger pots were wincingly expensive. 'Could we ask people whether they've got any old pots they might like to part with?'

Fiona's expression brightened, but quickly fell again. 'It would be very kind if they did, but we could end up with a right mishmash, and they would need to be a decent size otherwise they'll have to be watered every five minutes.'

'Yeah, you're right. Not only that, but they would probably be nicked.' If people could daub red paint all over the outside of the cafe, Bill doubted that they'd hesitate when it came to stealing nicely planted pots.

'Raised beds!' he yelled, making Fiona jump and Patch whine.

Fiona, after she'd recovered from the shock, nodded. 'That's a brilliant idea.'

'We could paint them the same colour as the door.'

She clapped her hands. 'Perfect!'

Bill continued to think about the raised beds as they began work on removing the graffiti from the sandstone, working out in his head where to place them for the best effect and how much wood was required. He would measure-up later when he took Patch for his evening walk.

So, after a tea of leek and ham pie, new potatoes and peas, he armed himself with a piece of paper, a pencil and a retractable tape measure, and ventured into the park once more.

Thankfully the drizzle of this morning had gone, and when Bill placed a forefinger lightly on the cafe door, he was pleased to discover that the fresh paint was completely dry.

The sun had already set and the light was fading fast. He needed to get his skates on if he wanted to take those measurements, so he wasted no time in retrieving the items from his jacket pocket.

Busily engrossed in drawing a quick outline of a second raised bed, his concentration was interrupted by the sound of voices, and he looked up to see Liam and four other teenagers approaching.

'Wotcha,' Liam said. He had his hood up, his jeans slung ridiculously low on his hips, and a swagger to his walk. But it was the smirk that got Bill's goat.

'What are you smirking about?' he demanded.

'Nuffink. Being friendly, that's all.' Liam pulled a face as he glanced at his mates.

One of them made a twirling motion with a finger against their temple. Bill was not amused.

'What do you know about this?' He pointed to the cafe behind him.

Another smirk. 'It's a cafe, innit?'

'Don't be cheeky.'

'What do you want me to say?'

'I want you to be honest.'

'Are you all right?'

'Of course I'm not. I'm bloody furious.' Bill could feel his anger building.

'What about?'

'*The cafe.*'

'You're not making any sense, bro.'

'I'm not your bro.'

'Whatever.'

He decided to come right out with it. 'Did you have anything to do with the red paint sprayed all over the cafe last night?'

Liam stared at him, a frown creasing his brow. 'I don't think red would go with blue.'

'It didn't. It was a bloody mess, I can tell you. It took Fiona and me all day to remove it.'

'Sprayed on? Like street art?'

'Sprayed on like graffiti.'

'Who did it?'

'That's what I want to know.' Bill glared at him.

'Whose tag was on it?'

'Tag?'

'You know, the geezer's name.'

'There wasn't a name.'

'Sometimes they're not obvious. What did they spray?'

As if you didn't know, Bill thought. Nevertheless, he got out his phone and showed Liam the photo he'd taken.

Liam studied it, then said, 'That ain't no street art.'

'I know. Do you have any idea who might be responsible?'

Liam began to shake his head, but something in Bill's expression must have made him realise that Bill was inferring that Liam himself might have done it.

'No, man.' Liam held up his hands and backed away. 'You're not laying that one on me. I never did it.'

Bill wasn't convinced. 'Do you know who did?' he pushed. 'You lot are usually in the park in the evenings. You must have seen something.'

'Get lost, old man. We didn't see nuffink, did we?'

Liam's friends scowled. One of them raised his middle finger and another folded his arms across his chest and glowered.

Bill wasn't intimidated. He had faced down far worse than this in his time. However, there was a shadow in Liam's eyes that gave him pause. The lad looked... Disappointed? Resigned?

'You *didn't* do it,' Bill blurted, certain that he was speaking the truth.

Liam shrugged and scuffed a loose stone with a trainer-clad foot.

Bill took a deep breath and drew himself to his full height. 'My apologies.'

Another shrug.

'I mean it. I'm sorry. I shouldn't have jumped to conclusions.'

'No, you shouldn't.'

'Can you blame me, though?'

Liam stared at the ground. 'We wouldn't do anything like that, bro. We like Fiona. She's nice.' Bill heard the sub-text – *nicer than you*. 'She's not gonna chuck us out of this cafe, not like that woman in Best Bites.'

There were nods of agreement from Liam's friends. Someone said, 'Pamela's a cow. She looks down her nose at us.'

Liam declared, 'Fiona's all right.'

For the first time since he had set eyes on the teenager this evening, Bill smiled. 'Yes, she is.'

Liam shot him a look. 'Dunno what she sees in you.'

And with that they were gone, leaving Bill to wonder what on earth Liam had been on about, and if he and his mates hadn't vandalised the cafe, *who had?*

CHAPTER 16

Fiona had no clue about plants. All she knew was that she liked some, but wasn't keen on others. Molly's mum Teresa, on the other hand, was a veritable font of gardening knowledge, so Fiona was more than happy to let her take charge of planting up the raised beds. And while she was doing that (with Bill's help) her husband and Jack were putting the final coat of paint on the cafe's interior.

Duncan, Molly's dad, had set up a camping stove (albeit a fancy one) and Fiona was outside the cottage (located there so she didn't get in the way) and making wraps by frying a chicken and vegetable mixture in a wok, to feed to those people who had turned up to take part in Strictly Come Planting.

Molly had somehow managed to persuade several local companies to sponsor a flower bed, and she was busy organising teams of people to take responsibility for each of the beds.

Fiona was still in the dark about where the wood for the raised beds had come from (it had appeared outside the cafe on Tuesday, having been delivered by the DIY store), but she wasn't about to look a gift horse in the mouth. Anyway, she had her suspicions, because Bill hadn't seemed in the least bit surprised to see it and had set about transforming the planks of treated wood into the raised beds that now bordered both sides of the cafe's outdoor seating area.

He had only needed a bit of help, which had mostly entailed Fiona holding something whilst Bill drilled or hammered it. Once or twice she'd been asked to steady a length of wood as Bill sawed it, but her input had been minimal. So she'd taken it upon herself to keep him supplied with coffee and food.

It had taken three days to construct the raised beds, and Fiona could tell that by the end of it, he was tuckered out, although he wouldn't admit it. She had enjoyed watching him work, noting how meticulous he was, how organised and methodical, and as he'd measured and sawed, nailed and sanded, he had regaled her with stories of his adventures at sea.

For her part, she had shared her own stories of running the cafe, and she'd also told him all about David and her grandchildren. David had called in to see her a couple of times since he'd helped her drop her unwanted items at the church hall ahead of the jumble sale, and she was going to his house for Sunday lunch tomorrow, which she was looking forward to.

She wondered what Bill would be doing tomorrow, and it briefly crossed her mind to ask David whether she could bring Bill with her, but she decided against it. It had too many 'meeting the family' vibes about it, and as she and Bill had spent almost every day together so far this week, a break would do her good. Why that was, Fiona wasn't prepared to examine too closely for fear of what she might discover; because she already suspected that her soft spot for Bill had grown considerably bigger over the past few weeks.

Her gaze lingered on him as she expertly tossed the wok and its mouth-wateringly aromatic contents, her attention on him, rather than what she was doing.

'Penny for them?' Madeleine asked, making her jump.

'Gosh, you scared me. I didn't see you.'

'You looked miles away,' the woman said. 'I've come to see if you need a hand. The kids are with their grandma arguing over the best place to put our cotoneaster. It's looking a bit sorry for itself, but I'm sure it'll soon perk up.'

Fiona thought it probably would. The garden centre on the outskirts of Sweet Meadow had very kindly donated quite a few plants, as had several of the locals, and they'd brought many plants with them today. Molly and her mum had bought the rest with the sponsorship money, and Reuben had made plaques to go in the respective beds with the patrons' names on.

Madeleine was saying, 'It's been stuck in a pot for years, the poor thing. It'll grow too big to put in our garden, so I was wondering what to do with it. I'm so pleased to be able to bring it here today.'

'It should have a nice life in the park.' Fiona glanced at a nearby bed. 'I think quite a few people had the same idea.'

Madeleine's attention was on the cafe. 'It's not long before it's open. It's looking good.'

Fiona was bursting with pride. 'It is, isn't it? We're so pleased. It's a bit nerve-wracking, if I'm honest, but I'm sure I'll get into the swing of things again.'

She took the wok off the heat and used a thermometer to check that the chicken was cooked. Perfect.

'Do you want to give everyone a shout?' she asked Madeleine. 'And if you could help with the drinks that would be great. No coffee machine today though, because I didn't want to get in the painters' way. I'm sure people can do without a latte or an Americano just this once.' She lowered her voice when she saw who was approaching. 'Maybe not her, though.'

Madeleine grinned. 'Glenys? Probably not. She can be a bit particular.'

Downright annoying, Fiona thought. The woman did have a heart of gold though, despite her overbearing ways. If ever you were in need, Glenys would be there for you. All Fiona prayed was that she would never be in a position where she needed Glenys's help.

Wincing, she hoped it didn't make her a bad person to think so negatively about someone who spent her days helping others.

Glenys cried, 'It's nice to see such a good turn-out.' Her eyes flickered towards Bill. 'Still working poor Bill to the bone, I see!'

Bill's hands were buried in soil up to his wrists.

'He's his own man,' Fiona retorted. 'If he didn't want to do it, he wouldn't.'

'The problem is, Bill is like me; he can't bring himself to say no.'

Fiona blinked. She wouldn't have described Bill in that way. He very much kept himself to himself, or he had until recently. As far as Fiona could tell, Bill had always been a bit of a loner. Since he'd returned to Sweet Meadow, he had never placed himself in a position where saying no was an option, and if she were a betting person she would bet her last penny that he had no problem speaking his mind and refusing to do something he didn't want to do.

'Anyway, I must dash,' Glenys said.

Glenys was always dashing somewhere, Fiona grumbled to herself, as the woman continued, 'I only popped into the park to see what all the fuss was about. Oh, and to have a quick word with Bill.' She began to walk away, then paused. 'When does this cafe of yours open?'

'Next Saturday.'

'Ah, yes, I remember. There's going to be an official opening ceremony, isn't there?'

'There is. The mayor is cutting the ribbon.' Although in her opinion, it should be Molly doing the honours.

Glenys nodded once then turned on her heel and tottered off towards Bill, Fiona following her progress with narrowed eyes. She wished she could hear what they were saying, but they were too far away; besides, news that the chicken wraps were ready had got out, so Fiona very quickly had a queue of hungry gardeners.

She didn't have an opportunity to speak to Bill until much later, when everyone was walking through the meadow towards the pond.

'The raised beds look fantastic,' she said. 'You must be thrilled.'

'I am. Teresa's got green fingers. She knows which plants look good together. I'm only good with vegetables. There are herbs mixed in with the cosmos and the geums. You'll be able to pick fresh parsley and put it straight into the sandwiches. After giving it a wash first,' he added with a laugh. 'And I've planted some spinach as well.'

'You'll be glad to have more time to yourself once the cafe is up and running. Your garden must be missing you.'

'My garden is fine. Anyway, I'm supposed to be one of the volunteers; you can't get rid of me that easily.' He gave her a gentle nudge with his elbow. 'That reminds me, Glenys is going to volunteer a couple of afternoons a week. Isn't that kind of her?'

'I'm surprised she can find the time.'

'You know what they say – if you want something done, ask a busy person.'

Fiona let out an exasperated sigh. Trust Glenys to want to get in on the act. However, Fiona wasn't in any position to object. She was fully aware that the cafe would need all the help it could get, and that volunteers didn't grow on trees.

Bill hadn't finished extolling Glenys's virtues. 'She's even offered to draw up the rota, but I told her to speak to Molly about that.'

Fiona clenched her jaw. No doubt Glenys intended to put herself on the same shift as Bill. 'That's nice of her,' she forced out through stiff lips.

'She also suggested doing some of the baking, to give you a break.'

'I don't need a break. Anyway, I didn't know she could bake.'

'She says she's pretty good. Not in your league of course, but she claims to make a mean Welsh cake. I'll let you know after I've tasted one.'

When would that be, she wondered. Was that what Glenys had wanted to speak to him about – tasting her Welsh cakes? Fiona snorted. She'd not heard it called that before.

As they neared the pond, Bill began to say, 'She asked me to lunch tomorr—' but Fiona cut him off.

'Have a nice time,' Fiona snapped. 'I'm going to my son's.'

'Oh. Right. You'll enjoy that. I was going to—'

'There's Reuben.' She interrupted him for a second time, not wanting to hear details of his lunch with Glenys.

Reuben was standing on a rock at the far end of the pond, and he was holding a piece of wood with a plaque on it. At his feet lay a wooden stake and a mallet. Liam was standing next to him, shifting uncomfortably from foot to foot as though moving to music which only he could hear. The boy was obviously embarrassed.

Reuben cleared his throat loudly to shush the assembled crowd. 'Hi guys, thanks for coming to our pond naming ceremony. The pond is being named after the newt who saved it from being filled in—'

'I'll fill you in, if you don't hurry up,' Liam interjected, earning himself a laugh. The shuffling increased.

Looking at him, swaying from side to side, was making Fiona feel seasick.

Reuben took the hint. 'Without further ado, I name this pond Tiny's Pond! May it be home to loads of little Tinys.' He handed Liam the plaque.

Liam tried to tug it out of Reuben's hand, but Reuben refused to let go, insisting on posing for a photo of the two of them together with the plaque. That was followed by another awkward moment when Reuben gave Liam the stake and the mallet, and Liam was left holding all three items until Reuben relieved him of the plaque, in order for the boy to ceremoniously hammer the stake into the ground.

Two hammer strikes later, and the lad was bored. 'You finish it off,' he said to Reuben, thrusting the hammer at him and snatching the plaque back.

Thankfully, Reuben made short work of erecting the stake, and he swiftly screwed the wooden plaque into place. Liam stayed long enough for a photo of him standing next to it, then he was gone, Connor with him, leaving the rest of the gardening squad to return to the cafe at a more sedate pace, because Fiona had a final offering of refreshments and cake to serve before everyone was done for the day.

She and Bill were halfway across the meadow when Glenys caught up with them.

'That was a champagne moment if ever I saw one,' Glenys said. 'Pity I've only got the one bottle.' She threaded her arm through Bill's.

He caught Fiona's eye, opened his mouth to say something, then closed it again as Glenys leant into him and lowered her voice. 'We'll have to have our own private pond naming ceremony, don't you think?'

Fiona didn't wait to hear what Bill thought. She stalked off as fast as her sensible-shoe-clad feet would allow, quickly outpacing Glenys who was wearing platform sandals and who was hanging onto Bill for dear life as she tottered through the long grass.

If Bill was silly enough to fall for Glenys's simpering ways, then Glenys was welcome to him!

***

It was getting to the point where Bill was seriously considering giving the park a miss for a couple of days.

Lately, every time he ventured into it, whether it was to take Patch for a walk or to do something in the cafe, he happened to bump into Glenys. He had gone from hardly seeing anyone on his twice – occasionally thrice – daily constitutionals, to the place becoming a veritable highway, and this Sunday morning was no exception.

Sometimes there were more people inside its gates than on the high street, he grumbled to himself, as he spied Glenys leaving through the main gate, and making sure to hang back until she was out of sight.

And the situation was only going to get worse as the park became a nicer place to visit.

Bill knew he shouldn't grumble. He had complained for years that the park needed upgrading and a large shot of TLC, but in some ways he missed the peace and quiet.

During the day, that is; the park at night used to be noisier than a pop concert.

In some respects, it still was as it continued to be a magnet for teenagers in the evening, but although they carried on consuming alcohol (and goodness knows what else) at least they had stopped flinging their rubbish everywhere.

Aside from them, people tended to linger in the park now, and it was no longer the realm of dog walkers and those who wanted to take a shortcut to the top end of town. It was common to see runners jogging along its paths, mums with young children out for a stroll, and older people too, as well as youngers kicking a ball around on the field.

And Glenys. He didn't mind Glenys – he rather admired her – but she was a bit too in-your-face for his liking. He thought her willingness to help anyone and everyone was exemplary, but he found that being in her company was hard work. When she'd accosted him yesterday (accosted was the right word) he'd had hell's job persuading her that he didn't want to go to hers for lunch today. He very much appreciated the offer (it was extremely generous of her) but he had rather been hoping to spend the day with Fiona. Unfortunately, Fiona had other plans.

To Bill's surprise, the door to the cafe was wide open and a white van was parked outside. Curious, he drew closer, hoping it wasn't anything to worry about, and breathed a sigh of relief when Jet dashed out to greet him and Patch, because the dog's presence meant that Molly or Jack wasn't far away.

When he stuck his head inside the door, he saw the pair of them, together with another chap around Jack's age, arranging the wrought-iron chairs and matching tables.

Molly beamed when she saw him. 'I thought we'd bring the furniture back. Fiona will probably rearrange it, though.'

'No doubt.' Bill chuckled. To him, they looked good where they were, but he wasn't the cafe expert.

Molly said, 'We've got the donated freezer and fridge too, so they're plugged in and ready to go. All we need now are the boxes of china and stuff from Fiona's house, and to hang the curtains. We could pop round there now.' Molly glanced at Jack and his mate, who nodded.

'She's not in,' Bill said. 'She's gone to her son's for lunch.'

'Never mind, we'll catch her later today or one evening in the week. It won't take long to get the rest of it sorted.'

Now that the tables and chairs were in situ, the place was beginning to look like a proper cafe. He knew Fiona would be delighted to see it coming together, and he couldn't wait to see her face.

***

Laura, David's wife, always cooked a lovely Sunday lunch, and today was no exception. Sometimes Fiona wondered whether her daughter-in-law felt the need to impress her whenever she was invited to lunch (or any other meal, for that matter), because she always pulled out all the stops.

Laura and their eldest, Ben, were vegetarians, so Fiona hadn't been expecting a traditional Sunday roast, but the roast beef that Laura served was absolutely delicious. There were honeyed parsnips to accompany it, and the most gorgeous cauliflower cheese. But despite enjoying the meal immensely and revelling in the company of her son and his family (the grandchildren, especially) a part of Fiona's mind was on Bill and what he was having for lunch. She hoped it wasn't Glenys.

Chiding herself for such catty thoughts, Fiona tried to put Bill to the back of her mind for the rest of the day, and she might have succeeded if he hadn't turned up on her doorstep a mere half-an-hour after David had dropped her off.

'Bill, hello.' He was the last person she expected to see this evening.

'Did you have a nice lunch?' he asked.

'Yes, thanks. You?'

'Bloody lovely, even if I do say so myself. I had—'

'Sorry to interrupt, Bill, but I've only just got home.'

'Oh, right, I see. I won't keep you, then. I just wanted to tell you that Molly and Jack have put the tables and chairs in, and the curtains are up. I thought you might like to take a look, but it'll keep until tomorrow. Come on, Patch.'

'Wait a sec. You mean take a look *now?*'

'Well… yes. You do have a set of keys, don't you?'

'I do. Wait there.' She nipped into the kitchen to fetch her coat from the cupboard under the stairs, and stuffed her feet into a pair of slip-on shoes. 'Let's go,' she announced, locking her front door.

It was pointless being cross with Bill, she decided, and she also wanted a gander at the cafe now that the furniture was in it.

'Are you sure? I mean, if you're too tired—'

'I *am not* too tired.' Had Glenys been filling his head with rubbish about her not being able to cope, and that the cafe might be too much for her?

'Of course you're not. I just meant that you can see it tomorrow, or the next day. Or whenever.'

'Has Glenys seen it?'

Bill faltered. 'No. Why would she?'

'I thought she might have been with you, but I expect you probably popped in on your way to or from her house.'

'I haven't been to Glenys's house.'

'Oh?' Fiona's heart skipped a beat. 'You had lunch out, did you?'

'I ate at mine.'

'You cooked lunch for *Glenys?*' Fiona failed to keep the incredulity out of her voice.

Bill's expression was one of bewilderment. 'Why would I do that?'

It was Fiona's turn to be confused. 'I thought you and Glenys were having lunch together?'

His face cleared. 'She asked, but I politely declined.'

'Oh, I see.' Fiona pulled herself together and changed the subject by saying, 'I can't wait to take a look at the cafe now that it has its tables and chairs back.'

But the lightness in her heart and the relief she felt on knowing that he hadn't spent the day with Glenys, lingered well into the evening.

CHAPTER 17

Bill hadn't been to the seaside for ages because although he had been to the coast several times since he'd retired from the Merchant Navy, none of those trips had been particularly memorable.

Today, he felt, would be different because Fiona was accompanying him.

Porthcawl was where they were headed, and Bill was looking forward to it immensely. Even the one-and-a-half-hour drive to get to it (mostly along the busy motorway) proved to be enjoyable. With the windows down (not too far because of the wind drag) and music from the 70s on the radio, which they sang along to (mostly out of tune but with great enthusiasm) the journey was over in a flash.

'I can see the sea!' Fiona squealed as the car crested a hill.

Sure enough there was a sliver of blue in the distance; and a state of excitement akin to that which he used to feel when he was a child, hit Bill in the chest. All that was lacking was a bucket and spade, and some pocket money to spend on the slot machines in the arcade.

Bill didn't head for the town centre or popular Sandy Bay Beach, but instead drove to Rest Bay, where it was quieter and dogs were allowed on the sand all year round.

Fiona stayed by the car with Patch as Bill went to the machine to buy a ticket, but when he got there he happened to glance back, and the sight of her made him pause.

She was standing by the car, her face turned up to the sky, the sun highlighting the silver in her hair and making her skin glow. It struck him yet again that she was a fine-looking woman. Not that her physical appearance made any difference, because she was equally as lovely on the inside as out. More, actually.

Returning to the car with his ticket, Bill thought how lucky he was to have such a friend.

'How long have we got?' she asked, as he placed the ticket on the dashboard.

'All day. We don't have anything to get back for, do we?' Yesterday had been very hands-on, with the pair of them ferrying umpteen boxes from Fiona's house to the cafe, and then having to find homes for the various plates, cups, saucers, cutlery, pots, pans and numerous other pieces of equipment that were needed. Now that everything was in place (Fiona was expecting a delivery of dry and non-perishable goods tomorrow afternoon, and fresh stuff on Friday), today seemed an ideal day to take a break.

'Not that I know of,' she replied.

'Excellent!' He offered her his arm. 'I thought we could go down to the beach, then have a walk along the front.'

Fiona took it, threading her arm through his, and the three of them made their way out of the car park and down a little path which led past the lifeguard station and onto the sand. Once they were on the beach, the dog scampered away, running exuberantly in this direction and that, overwhelmed by all the unfamiliar sights, sounds and smells.

Bill felt a bit like Patch himself, as he breathed in a deep lungful of brine-scented air. God, he'd missed the smell of the sea! The sight of it, too.

The tide was going out, the breakers small, exposing more rippled sand with each retreating wave. Holidaymakers had staked their spots on the damp sand, and several were paddling in the shallows. Children (and some adults) wielded buckets, spades and nets, and there was a lively game of volleyball going on.

Patch danced about, running up to other dogs and saying hello before racing off again. There was simply too much going on for him to settle on one thing.

Fiona slipped off her sandals and wiggled her painted toes. 'Ooh, that feels so good. Can we walk down to the sea?'

'I don't see why not.'

'Are you going to take your socks and shoes off?'

'I wasn't planning on it.'

'How will you paddle?'

'I wasn't planning on that, either.'

'Go on, I dare you. Or have you got ogre feet and you don't want anyone to see?'

Bill barked out a laugh. 'I do not have ogre feet.'

'Prove it.'

He did, taking his shoes off and shoving his socks into them. 'There. Satisfied?'

'That wasn't so hard, was it? Go on, admit it – you like the feel of sand between your toes.'

'I do, but not when I put my socks back on.'

'I saw a standpipe by the lifeboat station. We can wash our feet there.'

'They'll still be wet,' Bill pointed out, before realising that he sounded incredibly wimpy. He felt the need to explain that he'd had more than his fair share of wet feet over the years, but before he could say anything Fiona produced a small towel from the bag she carried over her shoulder.

'Ta-dah!'

'You've brought a towel?' He was incredulous.

'And sun cream, and wet wipes, hand gel, plasters, paracetamol, hankies, sunglasses…'

'Good grief! Why?'

'You never know when something will come in handy.'

'But… *a towel?*'

'I don't normally carry one,' she admitted. 'I popped it in my bag this morning, in case it was needed.'

Bill shook his head in disbelief as she folded it up and put it away. This woman never ceased to amaze him!

After Bill rolled his trousers up to his knees, he and Fiona strolled down the beach arm-in-arm, and he marvelled at what a lovely time he was having already. If he had been on his own with Patch, he had no doubt he would have had a perfectly pleasant time but being able to share it with someone made it even nicer.

'It's cold!' Fiona squealed when the first wave trickled over her feet.

'You'll soon get used to it.' Bill took a couple more steps, halting when the water lapped around his ankles. Shading his eyes, he gazed out to sea.

A cargo ship was on the horizon, heading towards one of the docks near Bristol, presumably. Then his attention was caught by Patch chasing through the wavelets after a seagull. The dog's alarmed expression when he suddenly realised he was out of his depth, made Bill laugh.

After a bit more splashing about, they decided it was time to retrace their steps up the beach and walk along the coastal path instead.

After Bill had rinsed his sandy toes under the tap, Fiona handed him the towel, a smirk on her face. He took it with feigned bad grace, and she wrinkled her nose at him.

'Told you so,' she crowed. 'Sun cream?' She held out a bottle of Factor 15.

The day was getting warmer, so he thought he better had. Smearing it over his face, he asked, 'Has it soaked in?'

'Nowhere near. Here, let me.'

He held his head still as her soft fingers rubbed the cream into his cheek. It was strangely intimate, and it left him feeling all at sea for a minute or two. Luckily, he was able to compose himself while she put her sandals back on, and although he wondered what had caused him to feel that way, he pushed it to the back of his mind.

Between the sea and the road leading from Rest Bay to Porthcawl town, was a strip of grassland lined with sandy paths winding through wildflowers and low-lying gorse bushes. It was the perfect place to walk a dog, and Patch couldn't contain himself. He was almost frantic with joy, and when Bill spied evidence of rabbits, he realised why the dog was in such a state of hyper-excitement. By the time they had reached the end of the grassland and had stepped onto the promenade, the terrier's tongue was almost dragging on the floor.

Nearby was a kiosk selling ice cream, tea, coffee and so on, so Bill bought a bottle of water, then produced a flattened bowl out of his back pocket which he promptly popped open into the required bowl-shape with his thumbs.

'That's clever,' Fiona said. 'I wondered whether I should put a little ramekin in my bag for Patch, but I assumed – rightly, as it turns out – that you would have it covered.'

'What's a ramekin?'

'A small dish for baking individual portions.'

You learn something new every day, he mused.

She said, 'How about a big metal dog bowl for outside the cafe? When people stop to give the dogs a drink, they'll be able to see inside, and it might encourage them to come in.'

'Good thinking.' Now that Patch's thirst was quenched, Bill said, 'Do you want a coffee before lunch?'

Fiona checked the time. 'It's twelve-thirty already. Maybe afterwards?' She gave him a stern look. 'If I remember rightly, I was promised fish and chips.'

'And fish and chips are what you shall have! Not far from Sandy Beach is, what I've been reliably informed, the best chippie in the area. They even have a sit-in service, but I'm afraid they don't allow dogs.'

'It always tastes better eaten outside,' Fiona said. 'I'm sure we can find a nice bench somewhere.'

'There used to be a park opposite. I wonder if it's still there?'

Fiona caught his eye and beamed at him. 'A park would be perfect.'

Two portions of fish and chips, a small sausage (for Patch) and two cans of fizzy lemonade later, saw Bill and Fiona polishing off the final scraps of vinegar-drenched chips, and licking their salty fingers. They were sitting in the park opposite to eat their lunch under the shade of one of the many trees, and Bill's tummy was now full to bursting.

Fiona groaned. 'You weren't joking when you said it was the best fish and chip shop around. That was yummy.'

'Room for an ice cream?'

Another groan. 'Not yet. I think I need to walk this off first.' She indicated the empty wrapper on the picnic table in front of her.

'Tell you what, how about if we carry on around the headland? We can let Patch off the lead again and have a sit in the sun. Then on the way back we'll have a coffee and an ice cream on the esplanade. It's a bit of a trek, though.'

'I don't mind. All the exercise I've been doing lately has done wonders – I haven't slept this well in years.'

Bill knew what she meant. Being busy most days had done wonders for him, too.

But little did he know that tonight he would have one of the worst night's sleep in years.

***

Fiona gazed enviously at the grand houses facing the promenade. Many of them, she noticed, had been made into flats, and as they strolled along the front, back to Rest Bay and the car, she imagined what it would be like to live in one. It would have to have windows which faced the sea, and a terrace or a balcony would be even better.

'I'm surprised you haven't bought yourself a little place on the coast,' she said. 'One of these would be lovely.'

'I did consider it, but Sweet Meadow called me back. I also thought about selling up and buying somewhere smaller, but I moved into my mother's house when I retired and I've stayed there ever since.'

'Because of the memories?' That was the main reason she hadn't moved out of the house she'd lived in with Bradley. Plus, it was David's childhood home. Also, where would she have moved to? It would have had to have been somewhere in Sweet Meadow, because it seemed senseless moving to another area, then having to commute to Clover Cafe every day, so in the end she decided that moving was pointless. After she'd sold the cafe, she had briefly considered buying one of the retirement flats in the new complex on the other side of town, but she couldn't face the hassle. Besides, she was perfectly comfortable where she was, and she didn't feel the need for a retirement place just yet. Maybe when she became less mobile she would revisit the idea. But not now, especially with Sweet Meadow Cafe just around the corner. She could almost fall out of bed and roll into it.

'Because of laziness,' Bill said, in answer to her question. 'Inertia, mainly. I couldn't be bothered to sell up and buy somewhere else. It was easier to stay put.' His pace slowed even more, as he turned to look at her. 'I'm glad I didn't.' His voice was soft, and it sent tingles down her back.

Unable to help herself, she leant into him, her shoulder resting against his. 'Me, too.' Her voice was equally as gentle. If it wasn't for Bill, she wouldn't be about to take on Sweet Meadow Cafe.

If she was honest, she still wasn't entirely sure she was up to it, but with Bill's encouragement, support and help she was sure she would manage.

Fiona wasn't under any illusion that it would be easy – she knew she would find it tough – but she hoped she would enjoy it as well. No matter what happened, she would give it her best shot, she was determined about that.

But strangely, she had the feeling that what she was going to enjoy most of all was seeing Bill on a regular basis. She had grown accustomed to his presence. More than accustomed, if she was honest, but that was something to think about at another time. Not right now. She had the rest of the day to enjoy first. And even when she gratefully sank into the passenger seat of Bill's car, with her feet aching and her face glowing from the sun, she wasn't ready for this lovely day to end.

'I know we've had a big lunch,' she said, after Bill had strapped an exhausted but very happy Patch into his harness on the back seat and got behind the wheel. 'But would you like to pop back to mine for a spot of supper? By the time we get home it'll be gone seven and I, for one, will need a little something before bedtime.'

'As will I, so yes, please.'

The homeward journey was less lively than the outward one, but the car was filled with quiet contentment, and Fiona guessed that Bill must be as tired as she, so she refrained from talking in order to allow him to concentrate on the road.

Patch, the exhausted little pup, slept all the way back to Sweet Meadow, while Fiona spent the journey watching the scenery and debating what to make for supper. Sandwiches were out of the question because she had a feeling that she would be sick of the sight of them by this time next week. Neither did she fancy anything with eggs, so she wouldn't be making an omelette. Pasta was probably too heavy after the lunch they'd had, although she did have ham and cheese she could add to it.

Her mind drifted to the contents of her freezer, and she remembered there were at least three portions of homemade tomato soup in the middle drawer. Today mightn't be soup weather, but she had eaten soup in forty-degree heat in Turkey one year, so perhaps the temperature outside didn't matter. And as for Patch, she had begun keeping a tin or two of dog food on hand in case it was needed, so the terrier wouldn't go without.

Whilst Fiona warmed the soup, Bill fed a sleepy Patch, then when the soup was ready she served it up with rustic bread and salted Welsh butter.

It was a perfect end to a perfect day.

'My goodness, this is delicious!' Bill exclaimed after his first mouthful.

Fiona had to admit that it wasn't bad, even if she did say so herself. Not only was it tasty, it was also healthy and nutritious, packed full of roasted ripe tomatoes and with absolutely no additives or preservatives whatsoever. She had made the bread herself as well, although most of the hard work had been undertaken by the breadmaker.

After a cup of tea and a slice of rich chocolate cake, both she and Bill were replete.

'I suppose I should make a move,' he said.

Twilight was descending and it would be dark soon, and Fiona was almost ready for her bed. It had been an exciting day, and she was pleasantly tired. With the prospect of another busy day ahead tomorrow in the cafe, she needed her rest. As did Bill, especially since he'd had the added strain of driving to Porthcawl and back. He must be absolutely shattered, the poor man. She got to her feet to show him to the door.

'See you tomorrow for the delivery,' he said, pausing on the step. 'Thank you for today.'

'What do you mean? *I* should be thanking *you*. It's been wonderful.'

'It has. We must do it again.'

'I certainly hope we will.' Impulsively, she stepped towards him. Her intention was to give him a hug, but somehow when his arms came around her waist to hug her back, her mouth accidentally brushed against his, and suddenly their lips met and he was kissing her. Or she, him. She didn't know which.

All she knew was that her heart seemed to stop, at the same time that her pulse throbbed in her ears. A trembling started in her knees and worked its way up her body until she felt so weak she thought she might keel over if it wasn't for Bill's solid embrace.

Lost in the kiss, the world beyond ceased to exist, as unfamiliar sensations swept through her.

But suddenly she was abruptly brought back to earth by Glenys's voice saying, 'I'll pop by in the morning after I've fetched your shopping, Mrs Pemberton,' and her neighbour's answer, 'You're a love. Drive safely.'

Tearing her lips away, Fiona released Bill and leapt back, dismay coursing through her as she heard Glenys walk to her car.

What had she done? What had she been thinking? Without doubt, she hadn't been thinking at all. Oh God!

Then Fiona's horrified gaze met Bill's and she saw her own shock and chagrin reflected in his face, and all she was capable of was a muttered, 'Goodnight,' as she closed the door.

***

Patch didn't want another walk, he was too tuckered out. But Bill couldn't settle, and there was no way Patch would let Bill go out without him, so the dog reluctantly scrambled to his feet and allowed his master to attach the lead to his collar.

'Sorry, boy, but I can't— I have to— Oh, dear.' He had only just got in, having managed to find a parking space right outside his house (a miracle in these narrow, terraced streets), but the short journey from Fiona's house to his had been undertaken on autopilot. He couldn't for the life of him remember a single thing about it. His thoughts had been too full of Fiona and the kiss they had just shared.

A walk around the park might clear his head a little. But even if it didn't, it was better than staring mindlessly at the TV, or tossing and turning in bed. He would only get cross and he'd learnt long ago that physical activity was better for him than doing nothing when he was upset, so he left the house and made his way to the park.

Night had fallen and for once the park was silent. No teenage high jinks from the bandstand, no lingering smell of cigarette smoke. Not even a rustle in the undergrowth from a mouse or a hedgehog, although at one point he thought he heard footsteps as he neared the cafe, and Patch also barked once, so someone might have been hanging around, but when the cafe came into view there wasn't a soul in sight and the night was calm once more.

However, the tranquillity failed to soothe him or make him forget the feeling of his lips on Fiona's, or the softness of her as he had held her in his arms. And it did absolutely nothing to quell the longing he felt to kiss her again.

His heart gave an irregular beat as he recalled the panicked look in her eyes, and he was filled with dismay at the thought that he might have destroyed their friendship. He wished he could remember which of them had made the first move. He didn't know for sure, but he thought it may have been Fiona.

Surely *he* hadn't? He'd had his heart broken once and he was adamant it wouldn't happen again.

Which was one of the reasons he was in such a quandary now. As much as he loved being with her, he didn't want Fiona to get the wrong idea.

Bill froze. What if she already *had*?

He was mortified. Oh heck, he should never have allowed this to happen. It was his own fault.

No more, he vowed. He would be friendly and polite, but reserved. He had let his guard down but it wasn't too late to put it back up. And none too soon, either – because he realised that it wasn't just Fiona's feelings he needed to worry about. It was his own.

His feelings for her were bordering on *serious*.

And that would never do.

CHAPTER 18

Fiona hadn't had such a poor night's sleep in a long time. But then again, she supposed it was to be expected: she hadn't been kissed by a man in a long time. Not since her husband had been taken from her.

Oh, Bradley, she lamented. What would he think if he could see her now?

She knew the answer to that question even as she thought it – he'd be cheering her on. As everyone had told her over the years, Bradley wouldn't have wanted her to mourn him forever. He would have been dismayed to think that she had been without companionship and love all this time. She could picture him remonstrating with her, telling her to enjoy the rest of her life, and if that meant letting Bill into her heart, then so be it.

Bill was a good man, Fiona felt. Underneath the gruff and grouchy exterior, lay a warm and considerate person. Which was probably why he had looked as shocked and horrified as she'd felt.

She knew *her* reason for her distress at that kiss, but what was his? Was he worried that he might have upset her? Or was he concerned that the kind of intimacy they had shared on her doorstep last night would signal the end of their friendship.

That it could signal the start of something new instead, if only she would let it, wasn't something she wanted to think about.

What she wanted to think about was *Bradley*, and the uneasy feeling of guilt that was running through her. Bradley was her husband and always would be, and she didn't know how to be with anyone else. She wasn't ready. She would *never* be ready – because no one could replace the man she had vowed to love and cherish for the rest of her life.

Abruptly she remembered that she had taken his watch into the jewellers weeks ago and hadn't yet collected it, and her stomach twisted. How could she have forgotten?

She had been too busy with the cafe, and Bill, and enjoying herself, to remember that she needed to pick up Bradley's watch. David hadn't mentioned it either, which made her feel even worse. It was as though she and her son were gradually erasing him from their lives, their thoughts, and their memories; which she knew was daft, but she couldn't help how she felt.

She would fetch it right now, she decided. The delivery for the cafe wasn't due until this afternoon so she had plenty of time to nip into town.

The jewellers had been there for years, and she knew the chap who owned it. He was old-school, able to do many of the repairs himself, and she trusted him to do a good job.

'I had to send away for a new crystal,' he told her. 'And while I was waiting for that to arrive, I gave the mechanism a good clean and replaced the broken strap. It's as good as new.'

He laid the watch reverently on the counter and Fiona picked it up. It *did* look like new. It looked the same as it had when she'd bought it from this very jewellery shop all those years ago. It had cost her an arm and a leg, and she'd saved up for months, but she'd wanted something special to mark Bradley's fortieth birthday.

He had been killed not long afterwards, but she still recalled how delighted he had been with his present and how he had worn it every single day until the day he'd died. She had given it to David on his eighteenth birthday, and although he hadn't worn it much at first (preferring a sports watch which told him his heart rate and whether he was getting quality sleep), she had noticed that as he'd grown older, he had begun wearing it more often. It always warmed her heart when she saw it on his wrist.

With tears in her eyes, she paid for the repairs then hurriedly left the shop, dabbing them away with a tissue and trying not to bawl.

'Good heavens, whatever is the matter?' Fiona heard someone say. She felt a tap on her arm and looked around to see Evelyn Brown peering at her, squinting through thick-rimmed glasses.

'Hello, Evelyn how are you?' she asked the old lady, her voice hoarse with emotion.

'I'm good, or as well as can be expected at my age. But you clearly aren't.'

'I'm fine.'

'Pull the other one. Has someone upset you?' Evelyn glared at the shop's door. 'Do you want me to have a word?'

Fiona smiled blearily at her through her tears. 'Not at all. I've just had Bradely's watch repaired and I got a bit upset. Silly, really.'

'It's not silly. We are all entitled to a little weep when we think of those we've loved and lost. But best not to do it in the middle of the high street, eh? You'll get people talking. Come on, let's have a nice cup of tea and you can tell me all about it.'

'There's nothing to tell.'

'Get away with you! I'm sure you've got lots of news. Molly says that you're going to be in charge of the cafe in the park.'

'I am, yes.' Fiona nodded, falling into step beside the old lady as they made their way slowly along the pavement towards the square.

Fiona didn't want to have a cuppa in Best Bites, but it seemed churlish to refuse just because she had once owned the place. Besides, there was nothing to go home for, just four walls and an empty house, so she may as well keep Evelyn company for a while.

Evelyn said, 'Molly tried to get me to do a couple of hours a week, but I'm too old for that malarkey. She forgets I'm eighty-seven. Anyway, you've got Bill Greaves to help you out. I used to be friendly with his mother. Lovely woman. Connie was a few years older than me, but when you get to my age it doesn't make much difference.'

They reached the cafe and Fiona held the door open for her. 'Shall we sit over there?' They had their choice of tables as the place was less than half full.

Evelyn pulled out a chair and eased herself onto it with a wince. 'Old age doesn't come by itself,' she grunted. 'I can't stand for long, these days. I'm all right if I keep moving, but as soon as I stop I need to sit down.'

Fiona hung her bag on a chair and went to take a seat, but changed her mind when Evelyn told her that orders had to be made at the counter now, because there was no longer any table service.

Fiona tried not to tut. It had always been table service in her day, and she intended Sweet Meadow Cafe to be the same. But things move on, and Pamela Edwards evidently had a different way of doing things. Her place, her rules, Fiona thought, as she approached the counter.

Pamela did a double-take when she caught sight of her. Her eyes widened, then just as quickly turned into a suspicious glare. 'Come to check out the competition, have you?'

'Not at all. I'm having a quiet cup of tea with Evelyn Brown, if that's all right with you?'

'You've not stepped foot in this place since you left.'

'I have, but only once, and I'm sorry for that.' She wasn't, but there was no point in making waves and the little white lie wouldn't hurt.

'Yeah, I bet.' Pamela drew herself up. 'What do you want?'

Charming, Fiona thought. If this was the way she spoke to her customers, no wonder the place was half empty.

'Two cups of tea, please, and a Danish pastry.' A Danish was what Evelyn used to have whenever she came into Clover Cafe. Fiona didn't have much of an appetite. She supposed she should eat something, but she hadn't been able to force anything more than a cup of tea down her throat this morning because she had been too upset.

She was still upset – she was simply hiding it better now, that's all.

Pamela set about making the tea, slapping the teapot down on the tray and slopping milk into a stainless-steel jug. Fiona felt sad when she thought about the lovely patterned milk jugs that used to be here when she'd owned it. None of them had matched, but that had been part of the charm. These soulless stainless-steel monstrosities were an abomination to good taste, and in her experience none of them ever poured properly.

Fiona paid and took the tray to the table.

Evelyn reached for a cup. 'She was ninety-one when she passed, so she had a good innings,' she said, picking up the teapot and beginning to pour.

'Who are we talking about?'

'Bill's mother.'

'Ah, right.' Fiona had hoped chatting with Evelyn might take her mind off Bill, but that wasn't to be, and her heart squeezed when she heard his name.

Suddenly, Evelyn leant forward and clutched Fiona's arm just above the wrist. 'I hope you don't mind me asking, but are you and Bill courting?'

Fiona froze. 'Courting?'

Evelyn frowned. 'Silly me, it's not called that these days. What do the youngsters say…? Dating? Seeing each other? Going steady?'

'Er, no we're not.'

'Shame. You made a lovely couple at the tea dance. I said as much to Molly. After what poor Bill has been through, a good woman in his life wouldn't go amiss.'

'I don't follow.'

'You *know*… that dreadful business with that American woman he was engaged to.'

Fiona didn't know anything about it. 'What American woman?'

'Hasn't he told you? I thought he would, seeing as the pair of you are so close.'

'We're not that close,' Fiona replied, pushing the memory of just how close they had been last night, to the back of her mind.

Evelyn ploughed on. 'He probably wants to forget all about it, and I don't blame him. Being jilted at the altar isn't something you shout from the rooftops.'

'That's awful! She left him on their *wedding day*?'

'Not quite. She ditched him three days before, but that was bad enough.'

Poor Bill. Fiona's heart went out to him. 'Do you know why? What went wrong?'

'Dunno, Connie never said.' Evelyn sounded aggrieved. 'It near broke her heart. She was upset enough about not being able to go to the wedding, and then for that to happen… As you can imagine, she wanted to be there for her son – even grown men like Bill need their mothers when things go wrong – but he went straight back to sea and stayed there.'

'Why wasn't she invited to the wedding?' Fiona was aghast. It seemed so callous and not at all like the Bill she knew.

'It's not that she wasn't invited, because she was. She refused to go. She was scared of flying and hated boats. And with Bill only having his mother on his side, it didn't make sense to cart his fiancée's family over to Wales. It would have been expensive, too.'

'So Bill was getting married without his mother there?'

'That's right. Connie put a brave face on it, but I could tell she was upset. Still, Bill promised her that they would come to stay with her for a week or so when they came back from their honeymoon, so at least she would have got to see them, but I doubt whether that would have been any consolation, and goodness knows how she would have coped if Bill had given her grandchildren, but that would have been another story.'

'When was this?'

'Oh, now, let's see... thirty-five, thirty-six years ago.'

'And he never married?' Fiona asked, despite knowing the answer.

'Never. His mum would have given her right arm to see him settle down, but as far as I know there's not been a whiff of another woman since. Seeing you and him together, I thought—' Evelyn sighed. 'Never mind. It looks like he's still a confirmed bachelor. Glenys Sidwall will be disappointed. She's got her sights set on him.'

Fiona wasn't surprised to discover that Evelyn had come to the same conclusion as her regarding Glenys. Mind you, Glenys had set her sights on quite a few men over the years, so it wasn't unreasonable to make that assumption.

'He's a good catch, is Bill,' Evelyn was saying. 'He's got his own house, his own teeth, and his own hair. I dare say he's got a decent pension, and it's common knowledge that Connie left him a few bob as well as the house. And not only is he quite well off, but he keeps that house spotless, so he's housetrained. I know he's a bit of a misery guts, but you can't have everything, can you?'

Thankfully, the conversation moved away from Bill as Evelyn gossiped about what the people in her street were getting up to, and Fiona was able to forget about him for the time being. There would be time enough to think about him when he came to help with the delivery later.

And if she was honest, she was dreading it.

***

Fiona put the last bag of flour on the shelf, then dusted her hands off on her pinny. There, that was everything put away. All that was needed was the delivery of fresh stuff on Friday morning, and she would begin baking in the afternoon. With the opening ceremony on Saturday, she had a lot to do but there was little point in starting too early as she wanted everything to be made fresh, which meant leaving it as late as possible.

Once again, she glanced out of the window and her gaze roamed around the park. And once again Bill was nowhere in sight. She had told him the time the delivery would be arriving, but he hadn't shown up.

Maybe he had forgotten?

Or maybe he was avoiding her.

The latter was entirely possible, given the expression on his face last night, but he couldn't avoid her forever. He was supposed to be helping in the cafe for one thing, and for another she would be in the park on a regular basis, so they were bound to bump into each other all the time.

While she had been sorting out the delivery, Fiona hadn't been able to stop thinking about what Evelyn had told her. Fancy Bill being jilted three days before his wedding! The poor, poor man. He must have been devastated. Had it put him off marriage for good, or hadn't he found another woman to compare to the one he'd lost? Fiona guessed she would never know. It wasn't the kind of thing she could ask, was it?

It was now getting towards five o'clock and as he hadn't put in an appearance, she decided to take a stroll along his street and knock on his door. Part of her didn't want to because she was scared of her reception, but if he *was* avoiding her then the sooner they got this first post-kiss encounter out of the way the better, and they could go back to the way they had been before.

Could they though? a voice in her head asked.

Ignoring it, she rinsed her hands, slung her cardi around her shoulders, made sure the cafe door was firmly locked, and set off. She knew Bill usually walked Patch early in the morning and late afternoon (and sometimes at night too, if he couldn't sleep – Bill that is, not Patch), but as she had yet to see him in the park this afternoon, she hoped he would be in.

Although she knew she was playing with fire by visiting him and that it would be better for her state of mind (and her heart) if she didn't, she firmly believed they needed to clear the air. Or to at least pretend last night had never happened.

Fiona asked herself what she would have done today if the kiss hadn't taken place and he hadn't shown up as planned, and she knew she would have gone to check on him, so that was what she was going to do.

She would make sure he was all right and leave it at that. She would be her usual friendly self and make no reference to the elephant in the room, then she would go home and try to forget that she had feelings for Bill that she wished she didn't have. And from what Evelyn had told her, Fiona guessed Bill would be more than happy to brush last night under the carpet as well.

As she neared Bill's house, she noticed his car parked outside. It being there didn't mean that Bill was in, but it shortened the odds a fraction.

Jabbing the bell with her finger, she listened for the sound of Patch's barking and her heart sank when all she could hear was silence.

Hope fading, she rang it a second time, waited a few seconds more, and was just about to leave when she heard a flurry of barks.

When the door eventually opened, Bill seemed distracted. 'Sorry, we were in the garden.'

'Er, hi. I, er, thought you were going to help with the delivery today and it's not like you not to turn up when you say you will, so I thought I'd better check that everything's OK.' Fiona reached down to stroke the dog's ears as the terrier wound himself around her legs like a cat.

'Ah, yes, the delivery. Sorry about that.'

'It's no bother, I've sorted it,' she said hurriedly, in case he thought she was remonstrating with him or trying to make him feel guilty.

'I, er, had to go out.'

'Oh, right… Anywhere nice?' Fiona could have kicked herself as soon as the words left her lips. It sounded as though she would have liked an invite.

His voice was stiff as he replied, 'I had an appointment.'

Fiona was mortified. 'Oh, I see. In that case, I won't keep you. I just wanted to make sure you were all right. After yesterday.' Oh god, she was making a right hash of it. Any second now and she'd be mentioning the very thing she didn't want to talk about – but she couldn't seem to get control of her mouth.

Bill frowned and scratched his chin. 'Yesterday, right…'

'I mean, I was worn out last night after all that walking. I had a hot bath and went straight to bed. I couldn't keep my eyes open.' She was aware she was waffling, but she couldn't seem to stop.

'Hmm.'

'My feet ached like the devil this morning.' She was still waffling and from his expression she guessed that Bill was unimpressed. She didn't blame him. There was an uncomfortable silence before she added, 'Right then, I'll be off. Glad you're OK.'

'Thanks for popping by.' His tone was stiff and formal, and it cut her to the quick.

'See you, then.'

'Yes, see you.' He ushered Patch inside and as she walked away she heard the door close firmly.

That was that, then. Not for one second did she believe his story about having an appointment. He had clearly been lying to her and he'd used it as an excuse not to help with the delivery. He'd used it as an excuse not to see *her*. And no wonder, knowing what she knew now. Fiona guessed that, like her, a romantic relationship wasn't on the cards for Bill.

But unlike her, Bill hadn't been daft enough to fall in love.

CHAPTER 19

Bill felt awful. Fiona's bewildered face hovered at the forefront of his mind as he closed the door, and he feared he had upset her. He hadn't meant to come across as gruff and unfriendly (he had been aiming for polite and friendly, yet slightly distant), but he'd taken it too far. And now he was worried that she was upset.

And he shouldn't have lied about having an appointment. He should simply have turned up at the cafe as planned this afternoon, helped her put the delivery away, and then gone home. He could easily have acted as though nothing untoward had happened last night – as long as Fiona hadn't brought the subject up. But even if she had, he could have brushed it aside with a brief apology and an excuse that the lovely day out had addled his brains. He would have assured her that nothing like that would ever happen again, and that would have been the end of it.

But, oh no, he'd made up a daft excuse and had then been offish with her.

Serve him right if he felt bad. He never should have allowed himself to develop feelings for her. If they hadn't sneaked up on him, maybe he would have been better able to deal with them, but he had been unprepared for the emotions that had overtaken him yesterday.

He'd not slept a wink, and had tossed and turned all night, much to Patch's disgust as the dog slept on his bed. Patch had eventually curled up on his blanket near the window, leaving Bill to suffer alone.

And suffer he had. His thoughts had bounced from Tracey to Fiona and back again, and he had spent hours analysing how he felt about the two very different women, and how he had managed to stir up emotions that he'd been convinced he would never experience again.

As he'd boarded the ship that was to take him away from the woman he loved, but who hadn't loved him enough to marry him, he had vowed he would never put himself in that position again. He'd had his heart broken once and he simply *would not* allow it to happen a second time.

Unfortunately, he suspected it was already too late. He was in love with Fiona, and there was nothing he could do about it.

***

If I'm not careful I'm going to turn into an owl, Bill thought as he ushered Patch out of the door. God, what a day! He would be glad when it was over, but there were still another two and a half hours of it to go, and no doubt he wouldn't get much sleep again tonight, either. Which was why he was taking Patch for another walk. It would be the dog's third, but the terrier wasn't complaining. The pooch seemed positively happy at the prospect of a stroll after dark, and appeared to be much more up for it than he had been last night.

At least one of us had got a good night's kip, Bill grumbled to himself, and he was hoping that another walk might be just enough to send him into the land of Nod when his head hit the pillow, rather than lying wide awake until dawn. He was exhausted. He hadn't fully recovered from the long walk along Porthcawl's front yesterday, or the journey, so when he added the emotional upheaval that he had been subjected to into the equation, it was no wonder he was utterly drained. However, his mind was churning faster than a washing machine on spin, and he suspected tonight might be as bad as last night.

For no other reason than to ring the changes, Bill decided to walk around the park in the opposite direction to the one he usually took. It led him over the field and through the meadow with its summer blooms.

A moth fluttered past his face, and he gently wafted it away as Patch scampered through the long grass, disturbing more of the delicate creatures. Aside from the occasional vehicle in the distance, the only sounds were Patch's enthusiastic snuffling and the tweet of a sleepy bird who had yet to realise it was nighttime.

Bill paused, drinking in air that was still pleasantly warm from the day.

The moon was gibbous, hanging above the horizon, with a gold tinge that Bill knew would fade to silver as it rose higher in the sky. A few stars twinkled, and he tilted his head back to squint at the familiar dots of light. Once, a long time ago, he had set himself the challenge of learning to navigate by their position in the sky, but he'd never dared put it into practice, not with so much at stake, the ships he had commanded having been huge and phenomenally expensive.

A watery plop caught his attention, and he dropped his gaze to the pool. Its surface rippled briefly with expanding concentric circles before fading away. A frog, he presumed. Or a fish leaping for insects.

It was so peaceful here, and he lingered for a while. A bench to sit on would have been nice, though. Maybe he would suggest it to Molly as something to buy with the profit from the cafe, or maybe he would make another donation…

Bill had been trying to keep his mind away from Fiona, but thoughts of the cafe brought her sharply back into focus. What was he going to do about her? Or, to phrase it another way, what was he going to do about the way he felt about her? It was no good pretending that he didn't love her, because he did. The fact that he didn't want to be in love with anyone, was neither here nor there.

But could he honestly work with her in the cafe, seeing her day after day, and knowing they would never be more than friends? He didn't think he could. Neither could he avoid her, unless he was to forgo his walks in the park, and even then he would probably bump into her at some point because Sweet Meadow was too small a town to avoid anyone for long.

His morose musing was interrupted by another splash, a much larger one this time, caused by Patch pawing at the water.

'Stop it, you daft dog,' Bill grumbled. 'Making your own waves won't work—'

Waves… sea… hmm… He recalled something Fiona said yesterday, and he let out a grunt. That was it! He could move, get a little retirement flat near the coast. It would solve the problem of Fiona.

A tune from The Sound of Music flitted into his head, and he hummed it sadly, substituting the name Maria for Fiona. How to solve a problem like Fiona… La, la, la…

The sea had healed him once, it would do so again. Long walks along the shore, the smell of the ocean in his nose, the sound of the waves… It would help fill the void that Fiona had unwittingly created in his heart, even though it would be a wrench to leave Sweet Meadow. But it couldn't be worse than the way he would feel knowing that Fiona was nearby but so far out of reach. Putting distance between himself and the woman he loved had worked once. He hoped it would work a second time.

Decision made (although he didn't feel any lighter for it) Bill called Patch to him and retraced his steps. It was time to go home; the walk had achieved its purpose.

As he strolled back through the meadow, he mulled over what needed to be done and how soon he could start the ball rolling. Ideally, he would like to put the house on the market tomorrow, but he dreaded telling Molly. She worked for the only estate agent in town, so it was inevitable she would find out. He would leave it until Monday. Get the cafe's opening ceremony over and done with first. Five days wasn't long to wait, but it might prove to be a long time indeed, since he would be spending a considerable amount of it in Fiona's company. He didn't see how he could get out of it honourably; he had promised he would help, so he had to keep that promise. Today had been bad enough; he had hated lying to Fiona about why he'd failed to help with the delivery, and he didn't intend to do it again.

He had almost reached the path when he heard a very annoying noise – the sound of glass breaking.

'For Pete's sake,' he growled under his breath. Those damned kids were going to be the death of him! He didn't mind them being in the park, as long as they behaved themselves. But smashing their bottles of beer and cheap vodka wasn't the way to go. They knew people walked their dogs here. Sliced-open paws weren't a laughing matter. How would they like it if they cut *their* feet on broken glass? If he had his way, he would make them take their shoes and socks off and walk over their damned broken bottles barefoot.

Gah! There goes another, and he flinched as more glass was smashed.

Eyes narrowed and jaw clenched, Bill put Patch back on the lead so the dog wouldn't run ahead and risk getting his paws cut, then he stomped towards the sound. He would give those yobs a piece of his mind, and if he recognised any of them he would have a word with their parents. It probably wouldn't do any good, but at least he'd have tried.

As he marched past Molly's cottage, he debated whether to give her and Jack a knock, but decided against it. He could hear Jet's muffled barks and guessed they'd be along soon to see what was going on, and besides, Bill didn't want to waste any time detouring from the path. He wanted to catch the little blighters in the act!

With gritted teeth, he rounded the bend and the cafe came into view. The bandstand was just beyond it, but he couldn't see anyone.

They must have realised they were making a racket and had scarpered before they got caught.

Damn.

Hang on! He could see a figure on the path hurrying out of the far gate.

'Oi! You! Stop right there!' he yelled, breaking into a shuffling run, Patch yipping excitedly as he scampered alongside him.

If he got his hands on the blighter, he'd—

His foot tangled in Patch's lead, and Bill let out a yell as he tried to step over it so he didn't tread on his dog, but his balance was all out of kilter and to his dismay he found himself falling sideways. Instinctively, he put his arm out to save himself, but as his hand connected with the ground, he heard a crack and felt an almighty pain in his shoulder.

Damn and blast, he thought – he'd only gone and broken his ruddy collarbone.

Bugger.

***

A black shape hurtled along the path, and Bill prepared for impact as Jet bounded towards him. Thankfully Patch intercepted him, and the dogs bounced around each other in a sniffy greeting.

Footsteps followed quickly behind, and Bill flinched as a bright light pierced his eyeballs. He would have put an arm up to shield his face, but the one was incapacitated and the other was trying to keep the injured one still because the slightest movement was absolute agony.

'Get that bloody light out of my eyes.'

'Bill? Is that you?' Jack called.

'Who do you think it is? Father Christmas?'

'Why are you sitting on the ground?'

Molly came into view, pushing past Jack and the dogs. Jack grabbed Jet's collar and Patch went to the man to be petted, which Bill was relieved about, because the thought of Patch clambering all over him made him feel sick.

He felt sick enough as it was. The pain was coming in waves, radiating from his shoulder and into his neck and his arm. Even breathing hurt.

Molly knelt beside him. 'What happened?'

'Kids, smashing bottles,' he rasped, trying to breathe shallowly, as the slightest movement of his upper chest was agony. 'Chased after them. Fell. Broken my collarbone.'

'Oh, dear. Does anywhere else hurt?'

'Don't think so.'

'Can you move your legs?'

Bill wriggled his toes. 'It's just my collarbone.'

'There's no *just* about it. Jack, take the dogs inside, and be careful, there might be broken glass around.'

'You can say that again,' Jack said. But he wasn't looking at the ground. He was shining the torch at the cafe.

Bill followed his gaze, moving his head cautiously, and what he saw made him forget his collarbone for a moment.

Every pane of glass was broken.

***

Bill had never ridden in an ambulance before and he hadn't wanted to do so this evening, but Molly had insisted on calling the emergency services, so he'd had no choice. To be honest, if she hadn't, he might still be sitting on the path in front of the cafe, trying to summon the courage and the energy to get to his feet. Even with the help of two paramedics and some gas and air, he'd had difficulty getting up. He hadn't realised how much he relied on his arms when getting to his feet. Not that he sat on the floor anymore, not with his knees. But even getting out of the wheelchair that they'd put him into to take him from the ambulance into A & E had proved difficult.

Jack had travelled in the ambulance with him, and Bill was very grateful for his presence. Molly had remained to look after Patch. Jet was used to being left on his own for short bursts, but Patch wasn't, and Bill had fretted, so Molly had stayed behind at the cottage to look after the dogs.

Bill was continuing to fret, but it wasn't about his dog – it was about something else. 'If I'd taken Patch on my normal route, I'd have caught the blighters in the act.'

Jack replied, 'It might be a good thing you didn't.'

'First the graffiti, now this. I thought it was youffs, drunk again, but Liam and his gang wouldn't damage the cafe. I'd stake my life on it.'

'I don't think it was them, either,' Jack said. He had pulled up a chair and was sitting beside Bill's trolley.

Bill was propped up, with his arm in a sling, waiting for the results of his X-ray. They'd already been at the hospital for several hours, and he wondered how much longer he would have to wait. All he wanted was to go home. And considering it was likely they would send him home with his arm in a sling and some painkillers, Bill didn't see the point in keeping him here. He was tired, in pain, and very, very irritable.

'Sorry for the trouble I've caused,' he said, for the third or fourth time.

'There's nothing to be sorry about. It was an accident. And you're no trouble.'

'Why don't you get off home? I'll be fine.'

'I'm not leaving you here on your own.'

'But you've got work in the morning.'

'I'm still not leaving you.'

'What about Molly? She's got work, too. She won't settle until you're back.' He was also worrying about Patch again. What if he and Jack were still here when it was time for Molly to leave for work? Who would look after Patch? 'Someone needs to sort all that glass out and board up the windows,' he added, chewing on his bottom lip.

'Stop worrying; I've taken care of it.'

'You have?'

Jack held up his mobile. 'Gavin will board up the windows until we can get new glass put in.'

'When will that be? Not in time for Saturday, surely?'

'*Absolutely* in time for Saturday, and Molly thinks it's a good idea to get wooden shutters made for the outside. Not only will they look cute – her words, not mine – they'll prevent anything like this happening again.'

'I wish I knew who was responsible.' Now that the shock was starting to wear off, Bill was getting angry again. He wished he could get his hands on them. Or him. After all, he'd only seen one person. He wished he could remember more, but all he had was a fuzzy image of a figure hurrying out of the gate.

A harried-looking chap in a white coat stopped at the foot of Bill's bed and glanced at his notes. 'Mr Greaves?'

Bill nodded with relief. Finally, he could go home.

The doctor said, 'I've had a look at your X-ray. You've got a displaced fracture of your right clavicle.'

Bill tried not to sigh. He already knew that he'd broken his collarbone. He didn't need a doctor to tell him.

The doctor, oblivious to Bill's impatience, continued, 'It will require an operation unfortunately, so as soon as we can find you a bed we'll get you admitted.'

'You *what?*' Bill's eyes shot to Jack in disbelief. 'I thought I'd be going home.'

'Not for a couple of days, I'm afraid,' the man said.

That had been the last thing Bill had expected to hear, and when Jack returned to Sweet Meadow to fetch what Bill would need for a stay in hospital, he could have cried with frustration.

The person who had smashed the cafe's windows had a lot to answer for.

CHAPTER 20

It was early for a knock on the door, but thankfully Fiona was up, even if she wasn't dressed yet. She debated whether to answer but decided she'd better. Anyway, she was curious as to who might want her at this time on a Thursday morning, and if it was someone canvassing for the local elections, she fully intended to send them away with a flea in their ear.

Oh dear, have I forgotten to do something, or should I be at the cafe this morning and it's slipped my mind, Fiona wondered when she saw Molly standing on her step.

Then she realised that Molly had Patch with her, and her heart lurched. *Oh, God, please no, not Bill. Please don't tell me something has happened to him.* She didn't think she could stand losing anyone else she loved.

With her hand clutching her dressing gown, Fiona whispered, 'Is it Bill?'

'Yes, but it's not serious. Well, it *is*, but it's not life-threatening. He's had a fall.'

The relief made her legs weak, and she sagged against the doorframe. He was still alive, that was all that mattered. Anything else she could cope with.

It took an effort but she pulled herself together and asked, 'Has he broken his hip?'

'His collarbone. A displaced fracture, apparently. They're operating this morning. Can you look after Patch today? Jack and I have got to go to work, you see.'

'Come in, come in.' Fiona ushered Molly and Patch inside and closed the door. 'Of course, I can. He's got a bowl here, and I always keep a couple of tins of the food he likes on hand. He'll be perfectly fine. How did it happen?'

'Bill was in the park last night, quite late, taking the dog for a walk, when he heard someone breaking the cafe's windows. He tried to chase after them, but fell. Jack went with him to the hospital and stayed until he was admitted.'

Fiona sank into a chair. She could feel the colour draining from her face, and her hands began to shake. She honestly didn't know where to begin to unpick this, but her overriding thought was that Bill could have fared far worse if he had managed to catch the perpetrator. The silly, silly man.

Unable to help herself, she burst into tears.

Molly said, 'I thought you might be upset, which was why I didn't phone you with the news. I wanted to tell you in person.'

'He could have been killed,' she sobbed. 'You hear about things like that happening all the time. They could have had a weapon.'

Molly put an arm around her. 'He'll be all right, you'll see. He'll be as good as new in no time.'

Fiona wasn't so sure. At their age broken bones took longer to heal, and sometimes the shock of something like this never went away. Yes, he would mend, but it would take a while, and the after-effects could linger for some considerable time.

However, crying wouldn't do him any good, she thought, dabbing at her damp cheeks with the sleeve of her dressing gown. What Bill needed was help, not tears. And right now, the best thing she could do was take care of Patch: it would be one less thing for him to worry about. And she knew he *would* worry – Patch meant everything to him, and Bill would put the dog's wellbeing before his own recovery.

After she had said goodbye to Molly, Fiona hastily got dressed and hurried out of the door, Patch at her heels. The poor little chap seemed rather bewildered. She guessed he must be wondering where his master was, and she could tell he was beginning to fret.

Patch wasn't the only one. Every time Fiona thought about Bill, her heart raced and she felt sick with worry. Having an operation wasn't to be taken lightly. Glancing at her watch, she wondered what time it was scheduled for. No doubt they would keep him in tonight, and possibly tomorrow, but a lot depended on how the operation went and whether the doctor was pleased with his recovery.

Could she visit him this evening? *Should* she? She wanted to, but was it wise?

A van was parked outside the cafe, and Fiona recognised it as belonging to the builder.

'Hi, Mrs Tedstone. It's not the best, is it?' Gavin said, on seeing her.

Fiona gazed at the shattered windowpane. The other had already been boarded up, and he was busy knocking the remaining jagged shards out.

She shook her head sadly and wished she knew who was responsible for the destruction and why they had done it. Was that how they got their kicks, by damaging things?

Fiona tied Patch up outside, well away from any risk of broken glass, filled a bowl with fresh water and laid out a blanket for him to lie on.

'The glazier has been to measure up,' Gavin informed her, 'but he's not able to fit the glass until tomorrow.'

'Can I go inside and clean up?' She was itching to put everything to rights again – or as much as she could.

'Absolutely, just let me…' He used the handle of a screwdriver to tap out the last shard. 'There, all yours.'

'Can I make you a cuppa?'

'That would be lovely, thanks. Milk and one sugar. After I've had that, I'm going to finish boarding this one up, then fit shutters to the outside. They won't be able to smash the windows a second time.'

She bloody hoped not!

Fiona was reaching into the cupboard for a dustpan and brush when she heard Glenys's voice, and she rolled her eyes. She could do without seeing her today.

'What's gone on here, then?' Glenys was asking the builder.

'Somebody smashed the window last night,' Gavin replied.

'That's a shame. It won't be able to open on Saturday now.'

'Yes, it will,' Fiona said, going outside. 'The glazier will be here tomorrow.'

'That's cutting it fine.' Glenys peered over Fiona's shoulder. 'I take it Bill's helping?'

'No, he's—' Fiona took a breath. 'He's in hospital.'

'*What?*' Glenys pressed a hand to her chest. 'What happened? Is it serious?'

'He's broken his collarbone. He had a fall last night in the park, chasing after whoever did this.' Fiona gestured to the nearest window.

Glenys looked stricken. 'Oh, dear. That's dreadful.'

'He's having it operated on this morning.'

'I take it he didn't catch them?'

'No, thank God!'

'Did he see who it was?'

'I'm not sure. I don't think so. I didn't think to ask – I was more concerned about Bill and his poor shoulder.'

Glenys's eyes filled with tears and immediately Fiona felt awful for her snarky thoughts. The women clearly cared more for him than Fiona had given her credit.

Glenys fluttered a hand in front of her face. 'Look at me, getting all upset. What must you be thinking?' There was more hand-fluttering, as she added, 'I'm sure he'll be all right. A fractured clavicle isn't pleasant and he'll need a fair bit of help, but there shouldn't be any permanent damage.' Her gaze sharpened. 'Oh, dear, he'll not be able to volunteer in your little cafe for a while though, will he?'

The same thing had crossed Fina's mind, but she honestly didn't care. Bill's return to full fitness was more important.

Glenys said, 'How will you manage now?'

'Didn't you say *you* were going to volunteer?'

'Did I? Well, I would, *of course* I would, if I had the time. Maybe when Mrs. Pemberton is back on her feet…?' Glenys collected herself. 'I can't stand here chinwagging all day. I'd better get going. Toodle-oo.'

Fiona watched her go, shaking her head slowly. She knew full well why Glenys wasn't up for volunteering anymore – because *Bill* wouldn't be able to. Typical!

She went back inside and began to sweep up. There was glass everywhere and it amazed her how far some of the pieces had travelled, but she eventually managed to gather up every last bit, along with a couple of nails, putty from around the frames, and what looked like the rubber stopper from the end of a walking stick.

By the time she had safely disposed of the broken glass, Gavin had boarded up the other window, and was now working on the shutters.

There was nothing more she could do for now, so after offering Gavin another cup of tea she decided to go home. A spot of brunch wouldn't go amiss, then she would have an easy afternoon before visiting Bill later. No matter what had taken place on her doorstep the other night, she was still his friend whether he wanted her to be or not. As soon as Molly came home from work, Fiona would drop Patch off at the cottage and be on her way.

She simply had to see for herself that he was all right. And besides, if he was up to it, she wanted to share her thoughts on who might be responsible for vandalising the cafe.

***

Tired, grumpy, hungry, and very sore were perfect words to describe how Bill was feeling this afternoon. He'd been lucky in that he had been second on the surgeon's list, so he'd had his operation early on. Then he had been taken back to the ward, had gone back to sleep for a few hours (despite being continually woken by one nurse or another) and was now firmly awake because his shoulder ached like the devil. So when one of the nurses offered him pain relief, he almost bit her hand off.

Feeling a bit more comfortable now, he began to think about his stomach. It was twenty-four hours since he'd eaten, and he was starving. A cup of tea wouldn't go amiss, either.

All of this added to his grumpiness, but what was really driving it was his worry about Patch. Before Jack had left after dropping off an overnight bag, he had assured Bill that Patch would be well taken care of and wouldn't be left on his own. But that didn't stop Bill worrying.

Who was looking after his dog right now? Had Molly or Jack taken the day off?

Oh, dear, he was such a nuisance. They must be cursing him from here to next week. He hated bothering anyone and until the unfortunate incident last night he hadn't had to. Hopefully he would be allowed to go home tomorrow, though how he was going to manage with one arm, he didn't know. Trust it to be his right one. If it had been his left, he would stand a better chance of coping.

The way he felt right now, he wouldn't trust himself to fill a kettle, let alone cook a meal. And who was going to walk Patch if he couldn't? There was no way he was going to impose on Molly or Jack any more than he had already.

He continued to brood as he tackled his meal of shepherd's pie and salad (*salad, I ask you? Surely it should have been accompanied by carrots or peas?*), with a piece of fruit and a weird pot of bright orange jelly for afters. And as he ate, he became more morose with every mouthful. Cutting up his food was impossible, and as for holding a spoon in his left hand whilst trying to keep the pot of jelly still and not have it wander all over the table… God help him. He would bloody starve to death at this rate.

His eyes widened and he dropped his spoon with a clatter as a thought occurred to him. How was he going to open the tins of dog food?

He had just decided that he would have to change to pouches and hope they would be easier to get into, when he realised he had a visitor.

Bugger – it was Glenys. What was she doing here?

'Aw, my poor love!' she cried, scurrying to his bedside and nearly knocking over one of the auxiliary nurses in her haste. 'How are you feeling?' She picked up the chart at the bottom of his bed and began reading his notes.

'That's private,' he told her crossly.

'Don't mind me, I'm a nurse, remember?'

'I thought you were retired?'

'I am. Let's see… BP slightly raised, temp normal, pulse OK.' She looked up. 'Have you been to the toilet yet?'

'None of your business.'

'Don't be shy, we all use the loo. And the nursing staff will want to know. They won't let you go home until you've had a—'

'I'll tell them when they ask,' Bill interrupted testily.

Glenys gave him an arch look, but at least she returned the chart to its holder at the foot of the bed. 'I see you've eaten. That's a good sign.'

Bill followed her gaze and shuddered. Then seriously wished he hadn't, gritting his teeth until the pain subsided. *Remind me not to do that again*, he thought wearily.

'So, do you want to tell me what happened?' she asked, giving him a stern look. 'Aren't you too old to go chasing after burglars?'

'You seem to know all there is to know.' His reply was testy. Trust Glenys to have heard about it.

'Thank God you didn't catch them.'

Bill was cross that he hadn't. He'd have given them what for.

She carried on, 'What were they after, that's what I'd like to know; it's not like there's anything in the cafe worth stealing.'

'I don't think they were out to steal anything. I reckon it was the same lot that graffitied the place.'

'I always said that those kids were a menace, hanging around the park at all hours of the night – now look what they've done. Poor Bill.'

'It wasn't them.'

Glenys tilted her head. 'How do you know? Did you see who did it?'

Bill let out a slow breath. 'No.'

She gave a satisfied nod. 'Well, then. You can't say that it *wasn't* them, can you? And who else could it be?'

That's what Bill wanted to know. But never mind what Glenys said, he was convinced that Liam and his mates weren't responsible, and he was too tired and too sore to think about it now. All he wanted was for Glenys to leave so he could go to sleep.

'I've been thinking,' she said, oblivious to his discomfort as she plumped his pillows and straightened the bedcover. 'You're going to need a bit of help for a while. Why don't I pop in and do a few bits and pieces for you?'

Bill's head sank deeper into the pillows. He suddenly felt exhausted. The ward was busy with visitors, but he knew that if he closed his eyes he'd be asleep in seconds and he fought to keep them open.

'I could do a bit of washing, make you something to eat, run the vacuum cleaner around. Things like that.'

Bill murmured something. He didn't know what, because his eyelids had drifted shut and he was out for the count.

***

Was that Fiona's voice, or was he dreaming? Bill slowly surfaced, the noises around him reminding him where he was.

'Shall we leave him to sleep?' she was saying, and he forced his eyes open.

'No, stay,' he croaked. He licked his lips, his mouth dry.

Jack was hovering behind Fiona, and Bill managed to dredge up a faint smile.

Fiona said, 'I'm not going to ask how you're feeling because it's obvious, but I am going to put your mind at rest, I hope. Patch is fine. He's missing you of course, but he's eaten some lunch, and me and him had a little nap on the sofa this afternoon. He's had two walks, and he's with Molly and Jet now. I'll pick him up and take him back to mine when I get home, and he can spend the night with me, if that's OK?'

It was more than OK. He knew Fiona would take good care of his dog. 'Thank you.' His voice was hoarse and his throat scratchy, and he licked his lips again.

'Would you like some cordial? We've brought you a bottle, and some snacks because we didn't know how long you would be in for.'

'Yes, please.'

As Fiona swilled out a jug and refilled it with fresh water, Jack gently helped ease him into a more upright position. She put the plastic beaker into his good hand, and he was grateful that she didn't try to fuss him, but let him get on with it.

Shakily, hoping neither Fiona nor Jack realised how weak he felt, Bill lifted the beaker to his lips and drank greedily. When he'd finished, she took it from him and popped it on the table. He noticed that the remnants of his lunch had been cleared away whilst he'd been asleep.

Fiona unpacked the bag she had brought with her, and Bill watched in fascination as she produced numerous wrapped parcels.

'This is a cool bag,' she said. 'Have a look at this lot, and anything you don't fancy I'll take home with me, or you can save for later. It'll be OK in here until tomorrow if you keep the zip closed.'

She showed him what was in the foil and greaseproof wrapped parcels, and Bill couldn't believe his eyes. Fiona had made him a picnic, and not just any old picnic – this was fit for a king.

'Goodness, how long do you think I'm going to be here for?' he gasped, worrying that she knew something he didn't. Had she spoken to the nurse?

'A day or so, I expect,' she replied cheerfully. 'I know what it's like after an operation; your appetite is all over the place, so I thought I'd bring you a bit of everything. I also know what hospital food is like,' she continued with a wry smile, adding, 'I had my appendix out about ten years ago. I don't believe the food has got any better.'

'It hasn't.' Bill didn't have anything to compare it with, having never been in hospital before, but the meal he'd eaten earlier had been bland, lukewarm and uninspiring. He chose a slice of gala pie, his tummy rumbling in anticipation.

She said, 'I'll put this in your locker for you to pick at when you want, assuming you don't want me to take any of it home.'

'No, I like it all,' he assured her. 'Thank you.'

She brushed aside his thanks with a wave of her hand.

He felt quite emotional and as he watched her pack the snacks away, he had a lump in his throat when he realised that everything she had brought could be eaten one-handed. There was nothing that needed opening or peeling – except for the bag, and he could always get a nurse to do that for him.

Blinking, he focused on the view from the window until he'd managed to fight off the imminent tears. If Fiona or Jack noticed, they covered it well, and as he tackled his slice of pie the conversation turned to the cafe, the clean-up operation, and who might the likeliest culprit be.

'I reckon it's Pamela,' Fiona stated.

'Pamela from Best Bites?' Bill was surprised.

'I'm not a hundred per cent certain, of course,' Fiona said, 'but she's been against the cafe from the start, and yesterday morning when I popped into Best Bites for a cup of tea with Molly's gran, Pamela was downright obnoxious. She accused me of checking out the competition.'

Jack's eyes were as wide as Bill's. 'It's a possibility. But without any evidence, we can't go accusing her.'

'I wouldn't do that,' Fiona assured him. She turned to Bill. 'Can you remember anything?'

'I've been trying. All I saw was a figure leaving the park. They weren't running, but they were walking quickly.' He searched his memory. 'They were dressed in dark clothing, but I couldn't tell whether they were male or female. Hang on, there is something… I'm not totally sure, so don't hold me to this, but I think whoever it was might have had a stick with them.'

'A branch?' Jack asked.

Bill frowned, scouring the hazy memory. 'No, I don't think so. It was thin and straight, like a walking stick.'

'Were they using it to help them walk?' Fiona asked.

Bill shook his head. 'They were carrying it, I think. Sorry, it's all a bit of a blur. I only caught a glimpse before I fell.'

'A glimpse might be enough,' Fiona said. 'Now, who do we know that uses a walking stick?'

Bill couldn't think of anyone, and he was too tired to think about it. Valiantly, he stifled a yawn.

Jack was frowning. 'If they were carrying it, then they don't need to use it all the time.'

'Good point,' Fiona said.

Despite Bill's best efforts, the yawn escaped him.

'I think it's time we left,' she said. 'Visiting hours are almost over, and you look done in.' She got to her feet and put a hand on his good arm. 'It'll be OK, Bill. You'll be home in no time, and I promise I'll take good care of Patch.'

He knew she would, but for the first time in what felt like forever, he wished he had someone who would take care of *him*. Just as long as it wasn't bloody Glenys!

***

'Are you OK?' Jack was gazing at Fiona in concern as they walked to the car park.

Fiona bit her lip to stop it from trembling and shook her head.

Jack put his arm around her shoulder and gave her a squeeze. 'He'll be all right, you know.'

'I know.' Her reply was a strangled sob. 'But he looked so frail and ill. Oh, God.' The tears came thick and fast, and she couldn't hold them back.

Jack gathered her into an embrace, and she wept into his chest until she had cried herself out.

'I'm sorry,' she sniffled, fishing in her bag for a tissue. 'I don't know what came over me.'

Actually, she did. Seeing Bill lying in his hospital bed, looking so helpless and drawn, had broken her heart. All she had wanted was to give him a big kiss and a cuddle, but he'd made it clear that he didn't want that kind of affection from her.

Seeing someone she loved in so much pain, had rocked her to her core. After vowing not to allow love into her heart again, and not to open herself up to heartbreak, she had done precisely that. And look where it had got her!

She loved Bill, and it hurt. But she realised that it would hurt even more if he wasn't in her life, so she needed to do anything and everything she could to keep him there. And if that meant being a good friend to him and nothing more, then that's what she would be.

***

As the visitors left and the ward settled down for the evening, Bill found himself slipping in and out of sleep. The abominable ache in his shoulder kept waking him up (he wasn't due another dose of painkiller yet), as did the comings and goings of the ward staff.

But along with his broken collarbone, there was another part of his body that was broken.

His heart.

Fiona was everything he could ever wish for in a woman, apart from one thing – she didn't love him.

The question was, did he want her in his life as a friend, or was it best to cut all ties and relocate to the coast as he'd been thinking of doing? Could he live without seeing her again?

He didn't believe he could.

Shifting uncomfortably, his pillows having slipped, Bill was thankful that he didn't have to make that decision right now. He would give himself time to heal, and then see how he felt.

But as he drifted off to sleep again, he cursed his own laziness. If he had sold his mum's house after she'd died, he wouldn't have returned to Sweet Meadow, and he wouldn't have had his heart broken for the second time in his life.

CHAPTER 21

'Steady.' Jack gripped Bill's good arm by the elbow, and as he guided him into the house Bill was immediately struck by how empty it was without Patch.

God, he missed his dog. Fiona would bring him back soon, and he couldn't wait to see him. He couldn't wait to see her, either…

Jack said, 'Sit down and I'll grab your bag from the car, then I'll put the kettle on. I bet you could do with a nice hot cup of tea.'

He could. The tea in hospital simply hadn't tasted right.

Jack helped Bill lower himself into the chair, and he grunted as his backside hit the seat. Shuffling awkwardly and with a great deal of wincing, he got comfy. Or as comfortable as could be expected with a shoulder intent on making his life a misery – and he wasn't just referring to the ache. Doing the simplest of things, such as brushing your teeth, was made that much more difficult when you could only use one arm. And let's not mention the getting dressed fiasco. It had taken him a full twenty minutes, and that was with the help of one of the nurses. God only knows what he'd be like when he had to do it on his own. Changing into his pyjamas this evening was going to be fun.

Jack reappeared with his bag. Unfortunately, that wasn't all – he also had Glenys with him.

She was beaming. 'I guessed they might let you out today. How are you feeling?'

'Like I've been run over by a bin lorry.'

'We'll soon have you on your feet again,' she chirped.

We? Who was *we*? Oh heck, he had become one of Glenys's projects, hadn't he? Great, that was all he needed.

Jack popped his bag on the floor. 'I was about to make Bill a cup of tea. Would you like one, Glenys?'

She flapped a hand at him. 'I'll see to Bill. You go. I'm sure you've got lots to be getting on with.'

Jack shot him a questioning look, but what could Bill do? He could hardly beg Jack to stay, so he nodded. 'Thanks, son. I appreciate everything you've done. I'm sorry to have been such a nuisance.'

'Will you please stop apologising?' Jack replied. 'You're *not* a nuisance. Molly said she'll pop by later to check on you, and see if you need anything. And I'll be back at bedtime to give you a hand if you need it.'

'Thanks, son, but Molly needn't bother. I'll be fine.'

'He'll have me, won't you, Bill?' Glenys piped up. 'Don't you worry, Jack, I'll see to him.'

'I don't need taking care of.' Bill was becoming irate.

'Now, now, don't be like that. Of course you do, and I'm going to start by making you a nice cup of tea and a spot of lunch. And while the kettle is boiling, let's empty your bag, shall we, and put everything away.'

Bill's glare followed her as she scurried into the kitchen, and he heard her fill the kettle. He sent Jack a despairing look which Jack completely misinterpreted

'Don't worry, Glenys will take good care of you.' Jack patted his uninjured shoulder.

Bill had no option but to give in, as Jack said, See you later.' Then he was gone, leaving him alone with Glenys.

'Kettle's on,' she announced, returning to the living room and picking up his bag. She placed it on the sofa and began pulling everything out. 'While it comes to the boil, what can I get you to eat? Scrambled egg? Cheese on toast? A bowl of soup? That's assuming you've got any of those. I'll just unpack this, then I'll have a rummage in your fridge and cupboards.'

Bill's irritation grew with each word she uttered. He did not want her rummaging anywhere, thank you.

'I'll do that,' he said sharply, as she removed his underwear from the bag.

Her reply was cheerful. 'It's no bother. I've seen dirty underpants before.'

You've not seen *mine*, and less of the dirty, he thought crossly. Anyone would think he wore the same pair for weeks on end, when in fact, he put a clean pair on every day.

'What's all this?'

Bill snapped his attention back to Glenys. She was holding the cool bag and peering at its contents. He had only managed to eat about a third of it – Fiona had packed far too much.

'It's full of food.' She wrinkled her nose. 'I'll throw this out, shall I?'

'Don't you dare. Fiona brought that into hospital for me.'

'When?'

'Yesterday afternoon.'

She pursed her lips. 'It'll have gone off by now.'

'The cake and biscuits won't,' he insisted.

Scowling, she set the slice of cake and the biscuits to one side and gathered up the rest, taking it into the kitchen. She was back a minute later with a cup of tea.

Bill took it from her and sipped it gratefully. 'Aah, that's better. I don't know what they do to the tea in hospital, but it tastes like dishwater.'

'I'll see about getting us some lunch,' Glenys said. 'Then I'll put a load of washing on. How about if I change your sheets? There's nothing nicer than fresh sheets.'

'I only changed them on the weekend. They're fine.'

'What about your towels? Do they need doing?'

'No, thanks.'

'Shall I just—?'

'No, Glenys, honestly. It's fine.'

She looked put out and he felt guilty, but he wasn't used to being fussed over and he found it a bit claustrophobic. Thankfully, she disappeared into the kitchen once more, giving him a chance to draw breath. It was nice of her to call in, and even nicer to offer so much help, but what he really wanted was to be left alone so he could process the last couple of days. He wanted to see Patch and Fiona too, and he hoped they—

The opening of his front door and the sound of little paws interrupted his thoughts, and Bill felt a smile stretch across his face as his dog skittered into the living room and bounded into the chair, throwing himself into his arms and smothering him with licks. Bill winced, ignoring the pain as he kissed the furry little head. Patch whimpered and squirmed, his tail going nineteen to the dozen.

'Get off!' Glenys cried, hurrying into the living room. 'Down! Down!'

'He's OK,' Bill said through gritted teeth, as he tried to hold the wriggling little body with one hand, but Patch jumped down, giving Glenys a baleful look and slinking under the chair. It seemed that Glenys wasn't his favourite person.

'Dogs shouldn't be allowed on the furniture,' Glenys continued, then added, 'If he knocks your shoulder, you could end up back in hospital. Hello, Fiona.'

Fiona was standing in the doorway, Patch's lead in her hand. Her face was expressionless. 'He's just had a walk, so he should be all right for a while,' she said, draping the lead over the arm of the sofa.

Glenys thrust the cool bag at her. 'Is this yours?'

'Er, yes.'

'I've emptied it, so you may as well have it back.'

Bill tried to meet Fiona's eye, but Patch leapt onto his lap again and by the time he had calmed the dog down, he realised that Fiona had gone.

'She's not left, has she?' he asked over the top of the terrier's head.

'She has, but don't worry, you've got me now. Which is just as well, considering she's intent on going ahead with the cafe. She'll have enough on her hands with that. Frankly, I don't know why she's bothering, not after all the trouble she's had with it. Nasty business. I think it'll be too much for her, but she won't listen to me. Sit forward and let me plump your cushions for you. There, isn't that better?'

Bill wasn't listening. His mind was on Fiona, and he wished with all his heart that *she* was the one plumping his cushions, not Glenys.

***

Fiona pulled Bill's front door closed with a gentle click, then leant against it, breathing deeply. She had heard every word Glenys had said, and it made her blood boil. Maybe the woman was right and the cafe *would* prove to be too much for her, but Fiona wouldn't know until she tried. Anyway, she wouldn't give Glenys the satisfaction of saying *I told you so*. Not just yet. She would give it her best shot, then if she had to pack it in, so be it.

But right now, all she could think about was the way Glenys had bulldozed her way into being Bill's unofficial carer. Oh, and the hundred-and-one things she had to do before the cafe's official opening tomorrow.

She had been depending on Bill's help, but that was out of the question now of course, and he would be incapacitated for several weeks, if not months, so it was down to her.

With a sigh of resignation, she straightened up and set off for the cafe. Those cakes and pastries weren't going to bake themselves.

***

A bang on the newly reglazed cafe window made Fiona jump, and she looked up from her pastry-making to see Liam and Connor peering through the glass.

Wiping her hands, she unlocked the door. 'Shouldn't you pair be in school?'

'It's half-past four.'

'Goodness, is that the time?' What with the delivery arriving early this morning, walking Patch and taking him back to Bill's house (she growled to herself when she thought about Glenys being there), then spending the rest of the day in the cafe, she didn't know where today had gone.

'School finished ages ago, but we had detention.'

'What did you do to deserve it?'

'Called Mr Fenner an old fart. He's a right saddo.'

'What does he teach?'

'Welsh. But when I swore in Welsh, he didn't know what it meant and I had to translate. I told him to—'

'That's OK, I don't need to know.'

'Whatcha doing?'

'Making stuff for tomorrow.'

'Can we have some cake?'

'No. Now go away and let me finish, otherwise I'll be here all night.'

'Aw, go on…'

'I haven't got any. I'll make it fresh in the morning.'

'A biscuit? *Please?*' Liam wheedled.

Fiona relented. 'Just one.'

'And a can of pop?'

She rolled her eyes. 'Go on, then.' She would put the money in the till later.

'We heard about Bill,' Connor said, around a mouthful of chocolate chip cookie as Fiona carried on with making her pastry. 'Is his arm in a cast?'

'No, he broke his collarbone and they can't put that in a cast. He's got a dressing on it and his arm is in a sting.'

'I bet it hurt.' Liam's eyes were wide.

'It's bound to have,' Fiona agreed. She wondered whether Glenys was still there, trying to shove her size six feet firmly under Bill's table. Huh! Glenys was going to have a shock when she realised that Bill wasn't in the market for a wife, or any kind of relationship.

'I heard he fell over chasing after the fecker who broke your windows,' Liam said. 'I heard he nearly caught 'em, too.'

'Not exactly,' Fiona said, and went on to explain what had happened. 'You weren't in the park around that time on Wednesday evening, were you?'

'I didn't do it. It weren't me.'

'I never said it was,' Fiona replied calmly. 'But you and your friends are often in the park in the evening, so I wondered if you saw anyone.' She put the pastry in the fridge. 'Someone you know, maybe?'

'Like who?' That was from Connor, who was scrutinising her intently.

Fiona knew she shouldn't say this and that it would be tantamount to an accusation, but she said it anyway. 'Pamela Edwards, the woman who owns Best Bites?'

'Her?' Liam's voice was filled with scorn. 'Nah, we didn't see her.'

Connor said, 'Everything was good when we left, nothing was smashed.'

'Except you.' Liam gave him a shove. 'He's a lightweight,' he said to Fiona. 'Can't hold his beer.'

She refrained from telling them that they shouldn't be drinking at all, but she knew they wouldn't listen to her and all she would succeed in doing was souring their fragile relationship.

Connor added, 'Wouldn't be surprised if it was her though, the way she's been mouthing off. She's a right—'

Fiona put up her hand. There was no need to call the woman names, although privately she agreed with Connor.

'She hates us, she does. Won't let us in the cafe. Don't wanna go there anyway – the food is naff. I wouldn't go there if you paid me.' He scowled and scuffed the tiled floor with his trainer-clad toe.

'That's a shame,' Fiona sighed. 'I was hoping you might have seen someone.'

'Nah, only that old woman, Glenys. She lives near my gran, that's how I know her. She can't half move for an old biddy with a stick. Fair legging it, she was.'

Fiona froze. 'Back up a sec. Did you say *Glenys?*'

'Yeah.' The boys exchanged worried glances. 'That's OK, innit?'

'And you say she had a stick. Are you sure about that?'

Another exchange of glances. 'Yeah. So?'

Fiona nodded to herself. It was all beginning to make sense. 'Would you like another cookie, lads?' she asked with a smile. Hell, after what they had just told her, they could have the whole batch!

CHAPTER 22

Wasn't this woman ever going to leave, Bill asked himself silently, as Glenys got the vacuum cleaner out. She had certainly made herself at home and had wasted no time in rooting around his house. She had already done a load of washing that hadn't needed doing, because Bill always liked to wait until he had a full load. He'd also heard her in the bathroom, banging about and running the taps, and when she'd come back downstairs she had told him that she'd given the bathroom a good scrub from top to bottom and that if he felt so inclined, he could eat his tea off the toilet seat, it was that clean.

Bill decided to give that a miss. He wished he could give Glenys a miss as well, but she didn't seem to want to go. He was very grateful, and she was doing a sterling job, but he just wanted to be left alone.

However, there was no chance of that!

She had already had a go at the kitchen after she'd made them both some lunch (steak pie and chips, and she'd had to cut his pie up for him, much to his dismay) and after cleaning the bathroom, she had whipped out a duster and a tin of polish, and now she was threatening to hoover.

She was in for a surprise if she did: Patch hated the vacuum cleaner with a passion. He would dance around it, darting forward to give it a nip then scurrying away in case it retaliated, and all the while he would be barking at the top of his voice.

'Can you not do that right now?' he asked wearily. All he wanted was a nap, but that was impossible with Mrs Fusspot here. He had twice asked her (nicely) to leave, but each time she had replied, 'I'll just do a couple more odd jobs, then I'll be off.'

Bill doubted whether he'd be able to get rid of her before bedtime.

He froze. Oh, no! She wasn't going to insist on helping him have a *bath*, was she? He drew the line at that!

She said, 'I'm not leaving until I've hoovered that carpet. It's a disgrace. There are dog hairs everywhere, and over the chairs and sofa.'

Bill squinted. There were a few, but not many. His living room was hardly a disgrace. 'If you're serious about helping, Patch could do with a walk.'

Glenys drew back like a cobra about to strike. '*Me* take Patch for a walk? I don't think so. Can't you ask Jack? Or Fiona? She's always eager to please.'

He frowned. What was that supposed to mean? 'None of them are here. You *are*,' he pointed out.

'I'm here to help *you*, not to walk your dog.' She pulled a face. 'I don't much care for dogs.'

That was obvious. Patch knew it too, and Bill wouldn't normally suggest that she walked him, but she *had* offered to help and the kind of help he needed right now was of the dog-walking variety.

'It'll take months for you to recover your strength,' she carried on, 'and you can't expect all and sundry to walk your dog for you. You'd be better off having him rehomed.'

'*Excuse me?*' Had she said what he thought she'd said? He made a face: she couldn't have. He must have misheard.

Glenys was on a roll. 'They're not hygienic, you know. They carry all sorts of diseases. And fleas.' She shuddered. 'You need to be so careful with that wound. You don't want it to become infected. Anyway, I can't keep on hoovering up dog hairs. They'll block the cleaner.'

'It's *my* cleaner to block,' Bill snapped. He'd already had his fill of Glenys and her well-meaning ways, but telling him that he should find a new home for Patch took the biscuit. 'I'd like you to leave.'

'I haven't done the hoovering yet,' she protested.

'And nor shall you. This is my dog's home, as much as mine. He's not going anywhere. *You* are.'

Glenys put her hands on her hips. 'Is that all the thanks I get? I've worked myself to the bone for you cleaning this house, and—'

'You heard the man. *Get out.*' Fiona had appeared in the living room for the second time today, but this time, instead of looking hesitant she looked livid.

Never had Bill been so happy to see her.

Glenys bared her teeth. 'You're welcome to him. See how far you get looking after him while running that cafe. I've said it before, and I'll say it again – it's too much for you at your age. Don't come running to me when you need help with it.'

Fiona's hands curled into fists, and she drew herself up. 'I wouldn't run to you if you were the last person on earth, not after what you've done.'

Bill wondered whether he should step in before the two women came to blows, but abruptly some of the fight went out of Glenys. Was it his imagination, or did she look shifty?

'I don't know what you mean,' she said.

'I think you do.' Fiona took a step forward.

Glenys took a step back, but then she seemed to rally. 'What is it that I'm supposed to have done?'

'I spoke to Mrs Pemberton. She's lost the rubber end off her walking stick.'

When Glenys said, 'So?' Bill had to agree with her. He had no clue where Fiona was going with this.

Fiona continued, 'Guess where it was?'

Bill watched in fascination as the colour drained from Glenys's face. What the hell was going on?

Fiona's eyes were flinty as she said, 'I found it in the cafe.'

'So?' Glenys repeated, though with far less belligerence.

'Do you know how it got there, Glenys?'

Glenys shook her head, but there was fear in her eyes. Bill wished Fiona would hurry up and explain – he was dying of curiosity here. His weariness of earlier had fled, and he couldn't wait to find out what was going on. Even Patch, who was sitting on his knee, was watching and listening intently.

Fiona took another step closer to Glenys. Glenys shifted to the right, edging nearer to the door, and Bill wondered whether she was about to make a dash for it.

Fiona smiled. 'It came off when you broke the windows.'

Bill's astounded gasp made him wince, as the sharp intake of breath caused an even sharper pain in his poor shoulder.

Glenys glanced at him, then back to Fiona. Her expression was sour. 'I saw you and Bill kissing on the doorstep. Very cosy you looked.'

'Is that why you did it?' Fiona asked.

'*I* didn't do anything, and you can't prove I did. That rubber end could have come from anywhere. Just because Mrs Pemberton lost one off the end of her walking stick, doesn't mean that the one you found belongs to her. Anyone could have smashed those windows.' She clapped a hand to her mouth and gasped, somewhat theatrically Bill thought. 'Perhaps Pamela Edwards did it? Have you thought of that, eh? She hates your guts.'

Fiona said softly, 'You were seen.'

Glenys froze, her mouth open. After a too-long pause, she said, 'I don't believe you.'

'I don't care whether you believe me or not, it's true.'

The two women eyed each other up and neither appeared to want to back down, so Bill decided to throw his hat into the ring.

Quietly he said, 'Fiona, I believe you. Glenys, I want you to leave. And if I see you anywhere near the cafe in the park again, I'll be having a word with the police.

Let them sort it out. Maybe they'll discover who was behind the vandalism and maybe they won't, but do you honestly want to be investigated?'

Mutely, she shook her head.

'I thought not. Now, please go. I won't ask you again.' Speech over, he slumped back into the cushions with a groan. He was spent, physically and mentally.

Fiona followed Glenys into the hall, to make sure she left, he presumed, but she was soon back.

She said, 'You look done in. I'm going to take Patch for a long walk, and while I'm out I suggest you have a nap. You look like you need one. Can I get you anything before I go?'

Maybe it was the exhaustion, or maybe the ache in his shoulder was affecting his thinking, but what he said next slipped out of his mouth before he could rein it in. 'You.'

He hadn't even realised he'd said it until he noticed her eyes widen as she said, 'Pardon?'

Telling her that she had misheard was an option, but he didn't take it. He was sick of trying to hide his feelings, sick of denying them to himself, and he was heartily sick of running away from love. He'd had decades of avoiding a relationship for fear of having his heart broken again, but it was too late for that now. If Fiona didn't feel the same way, he would simply have to deal with the pain.

'You,' he repeated. 'Fi, you probably don't want to hear this, but I love you. You're a remarkable woman – brave, beautiful, warm-hearted, kind – and I've lost my heart to you.' He dropped his gaze, concentrating on Patch, who was curled up in his lap.

'You don't mean that.' Her voice was flat.

'I do,' he insisted, his heart hurting worse than his collarbone ever could. She was going to reject him because she was still in love with her husband, and the pain of it was tearing him apart.

'What about Tracey?'

His eyes shot to hers. 'You *know* about her?'

She nodded. 'Evelyn told me. She was friends with your mother.'

He took a deep breath. 'Tracey is my past. She should have stayed there, but I stupidly allowed her and what she did, to affect the present. I'm not prepared to let her affect my future. Can you…? Do you think…you could ever feel anything for me?'

Fiona hadn't moved. He wished he could read her expression, and when she swallowed, Bill prepared himself for the worst.

'Yes, I can. I mean, I do. Feel something for you, that is.' She gave a nervous laugh.

He stared at her, willing her to continue, and she cleared her throat.

'I didn't believe I would ever get over Bradley's death, and I'm right, I never will. I will always love him. But he's not here and I don't want to spend however many years I have left on my own.' She paused. 'I never set out to fall in love. It was the furthest thing from my mind. But it crept up on me. *You* crept up on me. I love you too, Bill.'

He let his breath out in a whoosh. 'Thank God for that! I thought… Glenys told me that you would never look at another man.'

'She was right. I wouldn't have, but I got to know you first, as a friend, and by the time I realised I had fallen in love with you, it was too late.'

'Snap!' Bill smiled at her, and she beamed back, and they stayed that way for a few seconds, grinning like a pair of idiots.

Bill was the first to speak. 'Can I kiss you?'

'I'll be cross if you don't.'

'You'll have to come to me. I don't think I can get up.'

He watched her as she moved closer and knelt by his chair on the side of his good arm. Then she tilted her head, and the only thing Bill was aware of was the softness of her lips and the way she gently held him.

'Is this OK?' she asked. 'I'm not hurting your shoulder, am I?'

'What shoulder?'

Poor Patch had to wait a while for his walk, but Bill didn't think the dog minded. After all, Patch thought the world of his new mistress.

CHAPTER 23

Fiona had been up since the crack of dawn and had started work in the cafe not long afterwards. It was only a quarter past eight and she was already shattered, but she still had loads left to do.

As she surveyed the array of savoury snacks, cakes and cookies, she belatedly wondered whether she had been too ambitious – this cafe was hardly The Ritz, was it? But pride and the desire to do her best had made her push the boat out. That, and the knowledge that she only had one chance to make a good impression. If she pulled out all the stops today, hopefully people would be impressed and would want to come back.

Molly burst in through the door, making her jump, crying, 'Good grief! Have you done all this today?'

'Not all of it, no. I did some of it yesterday. I hope you're here to give me a hand?'

'I most certainly am. I would have been here earlier, but Jack and I popped in to check on Bill to see if he needed anything, and to walk Patch. For someone who's broken his collarbone, he's very chirpy.'

Fiona smiled softly to herself. He had been rather chirpy yesterday evening, too. And just as chirpy when she'd spoken to him on the phone before bedtime (Jack, bless him, had helped Bill get ready for bed and had made sure he'd had a cup of cocoa and some painkillers before he'd left). Bill had still been chirpy when he'd phoned her this morning.

Fiona felt the same. Heck, she was positively bubbling with happiness – when she wasn't fretting about the cafe, that is.

Molly was staring at her. 'You look different.'

'Different how?'

'I'm not sure.' Molly's stare turned into a squint. 'I can't put my finger on it. Has something happened?'

You could say that, Fiona thought, hugging the knowledge that Bill loved her and she loved him, tight to her chest. However, today was not the day for that kind of declaration. Today she needed to focus. But how could she, when she was so darned happy!

Bill loved her!

She still couldn't believe it! When he'd told her how he felt, it had taken a second or two for it to sink in, and then she had experienced such a surge of joy it had taken her breath away. She'd never thought she could feel this way again. It was both terrifying and wonderful.

'Fiona, are you all right?'

She abruptly realised that Molly was still staring, but her expression was now one of concern.

'I'm fine. Just busy.'

Molly's expression cleared. 'Of course you are. What can I do to help?'

'Could you put the outside tables and chairs on the terrace?' They were stacked inside the door.

Molly nodded and patted the bag she was holding. 'And I've got bunting to put up, and a ribbon for cutting.'

'I still say it should be you cutting that ribbon. You're the one who has made this happen.'

'I thought the event would have more gravitas if someone important did it.'

Fiona slapped the spatula she was holding down onto the counter. 'Don't you dare infer that you're not important! What has the mayor ever done for this park? Or the council, for that matter – Jack excepted.'

Molly was laughing. 'Not a lot.'

'Exactly!'

'To be fair, *you've* done more than me – look at this lot.' Molly gestured to the display cabinet with its selection of tasty goodies. 'You deserve a medal. I'm so pleased you decided to come on board.'

'Ah, about that...' Fiona had spent a restless night thinking about the unexpected turn her life had taken over the past few weeks, and especially yesterday. And she had come to a decision. 'I'm very flattered that you asked me to run the cafe,' she began, feeling awful as she watched Molly's face fall as she guessed what was coming. But Molly needn't worry – Fiona had a solution. 'And I'll happily help out when I can, but I don't think I can take it on.' She paused, telling herself to stop beating around the bush and just come out with it. 'I *know* I can't take it on. I'm frazzled already, and let's be honest, the reason I sold the cafe in Clover Square was because I couldn't cope any longer. And I can't cope with this cafe, either.'

Molly looked stricken. 'But it's due to open in a couple of hours. We can't let everyone down!'

'We're not going to. The cafe will open today, it'll open the next day, and every day after that, if that's what you want – just not with me at the helm.' The boat analogy made her smile, and she thought Bill would approve.

'But, if you're not—?'

'Hi Fiona, hi Molly,' a voice said from the doorway, and Fiona grinned.

'Molly, I think you know Madeleine. Madeleine, you and Molly need to have a chat. But you'd better make it quick – we've got a cafe to open!'

***

Fiona was feeling considerably less flustered now than she had felt earlier this morning, despite the official opening being only thirty minutes away. People were already beginning to congregate, and all the tables outside were taken.

Molly was mingling, and it was great to see her so chatty and upbeat. For a moment, Fiona had feared Molly was going to cry when she'd told her that managing the cafe wasn't for her, but Madeleine appeared to have done a good job of convincing Molly that the cafe would be safe in her hands, and Fiona had taken Molly to one side afterwards and had assured her of the woman's capabilities. Running the cafe was a perfect job for Madeleine, and Madeleine was in sore need of a job. It was a win for both of them. And not only was Madeleine a good baker, she was thirty years younger than Fiona, which meant she had bags more energy and stamina.

Fiona would help out during busy periods and when Madeleine had a day off, but the cafe wouldn't be her responsibility. She felt revitalised, as though a weight had been lifted, and she found that instead of being worried about the ceremony, she was looking forward to it. If only Bill could be here; but when she'd spoken to him on the phone earlier this morning, she could tell that he was still in a great deal of discomfort.

'Where do you want these?' Madeleine asked. She was holding a plate of custard slices.

Fiona smiled at her. 'It's your cafe, dear, you decide.'

'Yes, but you've—'

'Just think of what I've done as laying the groundwork. It's up to you how you build on it.'

Madeleine's eyes filled with tears. 'Thank you.'

'*I* should be thanking *you*. I was kidding myself thinking I could take it on. You've done me a favour; I would have felt awful letting Molly down.'

Madeleine found a place for the custard slices, then stood next to Fiona as she gazed out of the window. Glenys hadn't put in an appearance so far, and for that Fiona was thankful. She was praying the woman wouldn't turn up. And she was also hoping that Pamela would be too busy with her own cafe to be able to pay this one a visit.

It did irk her that both Glenys and Pamela's predictions that the cafe in Sweet Meadow Park would prove too much for her were true, but she'd get over it, especially now that she would have something else to keep her occupied – *Bill*.

A flurry of activity outside alerted her to the mayor's arrival and she shooed Madeleine with her hand. 'The mayor is here. Get ready because as soon as she cuts the ribbon, everyone will be in here like a shot and—' She stopped talking, a broad smile spreading across her face as she spied her son.

He'd come! What a lovely surprise! She'd mentioned it the last time they spoke on the phone, but she hadn't expected him to turn up. And he had brought Laura and the children! And there was Liam and Connor, plus a couple of their friends, and Teresa and Duncan. Reuben was here, of course, and... ooh, look, Gavin the builder, and Harper the electrician had come along, and—

'*Bill,*' she whispered, her heart soaring and her tummy fluttering at the sight of him.

He was standing off to the side, his arm in a sling and a jacket draped around his shoulders. Jack was with him, the two dogs safely leashed beside him.

Fiona's eyes filled with tears and she blinked them away furiously. She had cried enough last night when she'd got home from Bill's house. She had cried for Bradley and for herself, and for all the years they should have had together, but hadn't. Then she'd dried her eyes and tucked him away in her heart where he belonged. She would never forget him (how could she when he was part of her?), but Bradley was gone and

Bill was very much here. He was her focus from now on and he was the main reason she had wanted to give up the management of the cafe in Sweet Meadow Park. She had been given a second chance at happiness, and she didn't intend to waste a single minute of it. There were so many more places to explore and beaches to walk along, and always with Bill by her side.

Oh lord, whilst she had been daydreaming the mayor had given her speech and was now about to cut the ribbon, which she did, to enthusiastic applause and cheering. Then Molly opened the door to the cafe and escorted the mayor inside to sample the treats on offer.

As Fiona predicted, a stampede followed, and for the next half an hour she didn't have time to draw breath.

When the rush finally died down and Fiona was able to leave Madeleine alone for a few minutes, she popped a pot of tea on a tray, together with a selection of sweet and savoury bites, dropped the money for them in the till, then went in search of her family.

She found Bill first. He was sitting at one of the tables, an empty cup in front of him, looking pensive. Fiona put the tray down. 'Penny for them?'

'Eh? Oh, hello, my lovely. I was miles away, remembering what the park looked like before Molly bought the cottage. Who'd have thought it would undergo such a transformation! And as for the cafe, you should be proud of yourself.'

Fiona poured him a fresh cuppa and put the plate of food within easy reach of his good arm. 'I am,' she said. 'I'm proud of both of us. We're a team, remember? We did this together.' She captured his gaze. 'And I hope we'll continue to do things together for many more years to come.'

Bill nodded. 'Just as soon as my collarbone is healed. But I fear I'm not going to be much use in the cafe until it does.'

'The cafe will manage just fine without you,' she said, then added, 'It'll manage without the both of us. *I'm* not going to run it – Madeleine is. I'm too old for this. I want to spend my remaining years with you, having fun and going places.' She was suddenly hesitant, fearful that she'd jumped the gun and presumed too much. 'If that's what you want.' Her voice was small.

Bill reached across the table and took her hand. 'I want that more than anything. I love you, Fi, with all my heart.'

Fiona didn't think she would ever get used to him saying that. 'And I love *you*, Bill.'

A shadow fell across the table and Fiona glanced up.

'Hi, Mum. Great turn-out. Everyone's saying how good the food is, and the interior of the cafe is a designer's dream.'

'Hello, David.' She lifted her cheek for a kiss. 'I'm so pleased you're here.'

'I wouldn't have missed it for the world. You've outdone yourself. This cafe is going to be a brilliant success.'

'It will,' she agreed. 'But it'll be a success without me. David, there's someone I'd like you to meet. Remember me telling you about Bill?'

'I certainly do.' David held out his hand, then the sling on Bill's shoulder registered and he shook his head wryly. 'Sorry, wasn't thinking. Nice to meet you at last. I've heard a lot about you.' He glanced at Fiona. 'All good, I hasten to add.'

Bill chuckled. 'That's a relief.'

He was still holding her hand across the table, and Fiona was conscious of David's curious look. Oh, dear, she'd wanted to tell him in her own time, but it was too late now; from the look on her son's face he had already guessed that something was going on.

She said, 'David, I... we... I mean, Bill and I—'

'It's OK, Mum. In fact, it's more than OK, it's about time.' He leant to kiss her cheek again, then turned to Bill. 'Take care of her, won't you?'

'I will, you have my word on it.'

Fiona leapt in. 'Hang on, you pair! One, I can take care of myself, and two, I think you'll find that it's Bill who needs to be taken care of right now, not me.'

Bill beamed at her. 'How about we agree to take care of each other? Will that do?'

It certainly would, but secretly she was looking forward to having someone to fuss over. After all, without the cafe, she had to have something to keep her occupied.

Sighing contentedly, Fiona gazed at the cafe, which was alive once more with chatter, and laughter, and the rich aroma of freshly ground coffee. She had a lot to thank it for, and she knew that the cafe in Sweet Meadow Park would always hold a special place in her heart.

After all, it had brought *her* back to life, too…

Other books in the series

The Cottage in Sweet Meadow Park
Christmas in Sweet Meadow Park

ACKNOWLEDGEMENTS

A book is a bit like a fashion show - all the audience sees are the models prancing down the runway looking beautiful, whereas behind the scenes it's all frantic costume changes and the fear of falling flat on one's face! Writing a book (ie, getting the story from your head onto paper) is only half the battle. In fact, it's just the start of the process, because there is so much more that the reader doesn't see, and this usually involves a host of other people.

One of those is Catherine Mills, the bestest of Besties, who not only laughs at my blurb writing skills (which are abysmal), she notices when a character previously called Kevin suddenly becomes Keith! Then there's Valerie Brown, proofreader extraordinaire, who gives the finished product the once-over and finds yet more things that need tweaking. Thank you both; I don't know what I'd do without you.

My friends in the Romantic Novelists Association (my fellow Cariads) also deserve a mention for plenty of reasons, but the one that springs to mind is that meeting with this lovely group of writers on a monthly basis gives me an excuse to visit the big city and wear something other than leggings and walking boots.

And I can't sign off without thanking my hubby for listening to me witter on about Bill and Fiona as I tried to get their story straight in my head. I think he got to know my characters almost as well as I did by the end of it! And thanks for all those cups of tea, but could I have a custard cream with the next one, please? Or a Garibaldi?

But there is one person above everyone else, who needs to be thanked the most - and that's you. Because you chose to read this book, out of all the others you could have chosen, and that means the world to me. Thank you xxx

ABOUT THE AUTHOR

Liz Davies writes feel-good, light-hearted stories with a hefty dose of romance, a smattering of humour, and a great deal of love.

She's married to her best friend, has one grown-up daughter, and when she isn't scribbling away in the notepad she carries with her everywhere (just in case inspiration strikes), you'll find her searching for that perfect pair of shoes. She loves to cook but isn't very good at it, and loves to eat - she's much better at that! Liz also enjoys walking (preferably on the flat), cycling (also on the flat), and lots of sitting around in the garden on warm, sunny days.

She currently lives with her family in Wales, but would ideally love to buy a camper van and travel the world in it.

Printed in Great Britain
by Amazon